DWELLER

JEFF STRAND

ISBN: 9798606262281

PROLOGUE

1946

"We should've brought more ammo," Thomas said, wiping the blood out of his mustache. He brushed his wet fingers along the oak tree he leaned against, then picked up his empty rifle by the barrel, holding it like a baseball bat. Phil was surprised the metal didn't burn his hands. "Why the hell didn't we bring more ammo?"

Phil didn't answer. They all knew why: because they weren't fighting Nazis this weekend, they were camping by the lake. The only reason they'd brought the rifle in the first place was because Christine was paranoid about bears. Phil had humored her—there was no reason not to—but he'd never expected to need any weapon more powerful than a fishing hook. The war was over. One fully loaded rifle should have been more than enough to protect them from nature for a couple of days.

It hadn't protected Christine, though. She'd been the first to die.

The creatures had gotten Darla, too, but instead of ripping her apart they'd dragged her away. Thomas, Phil, Mikey, and Nancy had

1

chased after her, racing through the woods and screaming her name. When they found her half an hour later, she looked worse than Christine. They probably wouldn't have recognized her at all if it weren't for those elegant shoes she insisted upon wearing, even on a camping trip. They sure wouldn't have recognized her once-white blouse. Or her face.

Mikey had screamed and vowed revenge. And he'd fought like a brave soldier after those things ambushed them. Had they known how many creatures were out there, though, Thomas probably wouldn't have wasted the mercy bullet he put in Mikey's forehead before they fled.

At least their enemies had fared worse. Three dead humans, five dead creatures. Unfortunately, that left at least five more of the creatures—that they'd *seen*—and Thomas wasn't going to be doing any more running on that leg, maybe ever. Phil's vision was still fuzzy from bashing his head against the ground when a creature pounced on him. Nancy was the only one of them not in terrible shape.

"Do you think they can climb trees?" Thomas asked.

"I don't know. They've got two arms and two legs—I don't see why they couldn't."

"Maybe they can't, though." Thomas coughed, and a rope of red spittle dangled from his lower lip. "Let's not kid ourselves. I'm not going anywhere. Unless you want to carry me on your back, you need to hide me somewhere and leave me behind."

Phil nodded. "You and Nancy hide in the tree. I'll go get help."

"No," said Nancy. "I'm going. You're hurt too bad."

"I'm fine."

"Your head is bleeding and your words are slurred. I'm going."

"I'll go with you."

"Honey, you'll slow me down." She reached for Thomas' rifle. "Give me that so I can beat them to death if I need to."

Thomas hesitated for a moment, then handed it to her. Nancy

gave him a quick kiss on the lips. "I'll bring back help. I swear." She looked at Phil. "Don't let anything get him."

"I won't," he promised.

Nancy ran off.

Getting Thomas up the tree wasn't easy, but when they heard a rustling in the nearby bushes it encouraged Thomas to move more quickly, ruined leg or not. They climbed to about thirty feet high and waited.

They saw the first creature about three minutes before it saw them. It immediately shouted out in the guttural sounds of an ape, and was soon joined by two more. Then another three. Then another six.

But though it sounded like an ape, it couldn't climb like one. The creatures punched at the tree, kicked at it, and tried to shake it, yet didn't seem able to actually ascend the branches. *We're safe for now*, Phil thought.

Thomas bled to death before dark, so Phil had nobody to talk to.

By the end of the second day he was talking to himself.

THE YOUNGEST ONE, the runt, was hungry. He was also getting impatient waiting for the food to fall out of the tree, so he searched for bugs. Caterpillars were his favorite. He let a bright green one crawl along his talon, then popped it into his mouth and chewed slowly.

He cried out as his mother's head burst open.

Loud noises everywhere. His father moved toward him, arms outstretched, but several red holes popped in his chest, all at once, and his father fell to the ground. The youngest one screamed and scurried away, just like his mother and father had taught him.

He hid in the bushes for a while, sad and scared.

When he finally went back, food was helping other food out of the tree. Some more food was poking at his brothers and sisters with the same kind of stick that had made his oldest brother's eye explode two days ago. All of them were dead, even Beka.

The youngest one turned and ran.

He ran and ran, as fast as he could, so that the food wouldn't kill him, too.

When he stopped running, he wept.

1

1953. Age 8.

Toby Floren was ready for the Martian invasion. More than
ready. If those green killers from outer space dared show
up at his house, he'd lop their tentacles off with his
pocketknife, steal their laser guns, and then disintegrate them. If
nobody was watching, he might disintegrate Mrs. Faulkner, too,
and blame the aliens. He'd only taken two or three blackberries
from her yard—not even the biggest ones—and she'd screamed at
him as if he were a masked bank robber stealing bars of gold.

Toby thought his pocketknife might work even better against a
bank robber than an alien, so if bank robbers attacked, he'd be
ready for them, too.

He stabbed at the air. His mom had made Toby promise, hand
on his heart, that he wouldn't take the blade out when she or Dad
weren't around, so he just lunged with the handle. "*Yahh*!" he said,
imagining his knife plunging right into one of those sucker-filled
alien tentacles.

What if they were invaded by Martian bank robbers? It would be the greatest day ever.

Any Martians, bank robbers or not, were doomed if they caused any problems in *his* town. As soon as he saw their leader, he'd fling the knife. The alien leader would duck, but Toby would have anticipated the move and thrown the knife at the wall, where it ricocheted off and struck the alien's exposed brain. With their leader gone, the other aliens would be quick to worship Toby, and he'd use their foolhardy vow of allegiance against them, destroying their entire army with a well-placed explosive device in their spacecraft.

Perfect.

He stabbed at the air again. He almost snapped out the blade, but if he accidentally cut himself, his parents would know that he'd broken their rules, and they'd take away the pocketknife. By his next birthday, he was certain that they'd let him open the blade unsupervised, and also that they'd let him go out into the woods further than...

Toby looked around. He'd been so engrossed in his fantasies that he wasn't paying attention to where he was going. He hadn't been paying attention for quite some time. None of his surroundings looked familiar.

As Dad liked to say: "This ain't good!"

What should he do? If he kept wandering, he might continue to go deeper and deeper into the woods. If he called out for help, his parents would know that he'd gotten lost and they'd restrict him to the backyard. There was nothing wrong with the backyard—it had a swing set and a sandbox and a few decent anthills, but it was nowhere near as wonderful as the forest.

Fortunately, he hadn't been walking long enough to get out of earshot of his parents. So he'd simply stay here, wait for Mom and Dad to call him in for dinner, and then run toward the sound of their voice. They'd never know that he went out further than he was supposed to.

Toby grinned. It was a great plan.

He was *mostly* sure he wasn't out of earshot. You had to be really deep in the woods not to hear his mother yelling.

Toby sat on the ground, leaned against a tree, pursed his lips, and began to whistle. He was starting to get pretty good. Not quite to the point where he could whistle an actual "tune," but he could now whistle notes that sounded different from each other. Previously, he'd been limited to squeaking and blowing soundless air. Any day now he'd be able to whistle the *Lone Ranger* theme.

He sat there for a while, whistling and playing with his unopened pocketknife.

He sure hoped he wasn't lost. It was too nice of a day to be ruined with a lecture.

What if the woods were haunted? No matter how sharp or long it was, a knife blade wouldn't save you from a ghost. Toby wasn't exactly sure what a ghost could do to you—

they couldn't vaporize you like aliens or drink your blood like Dracula—but they had to be able to do *something* bad, right? Maybe they dragged you off to meet the devil.

He really should have paid attention to where he was walking. He'd do that from now on.

Some bushes shook.

That wasn't anything unusual. The bushes in this forest were always shaking. But this sounded like it was caused by something *big*.

He stood up. The sound wasn't that far away. So many ghastly things it could be...but Toby quickly decided that he wasn't scared of any of them. Nobody was going to ever call Toby Floren a coward. He was going to march right over to those bushes, find out what was shaking them, and let that intruder know that he wasn't going to put up with any funny business in his forest.

The bushes rustled again. Toby's bravery faltered for a moment, then returned in full force and he walked forward, prepared to deal with the menace.

He froze. The large cluster of bushes was about ten feet away, and there was definitely something hiding in them. Not an alien or something boring like a deer, but a...person?

"Hello?" he said.

Toby screamed as it emerged from the leaves.

It wasn't huge—maybe the size of his dad. Covered with brown hair. Sunken yellow eyes. Claws. Teeth.

Toby wasn't sure if it reached for him, or if he just *thought* it did, but he turned and ran, not caring which direction. His knife slipped out of his hand but it didn't matter, he just left it behind; it wouldn't do any good against that beast anyway.

He fled for his life.

It didn't sound like the monster was following him. He didn't look back to be sure.

He didn't stop running until his foot struck a root or a rock and he fell to the ground, throwing out his arms just in time to avoid bashing his nose against the dirt. So much pain shot through him from his palms to his shoulders that for a split second he thought his arms had snapped right off. But they hadn't, thank goodness, and he scrambled back to his feet and continued running. He still didn't dare to look behind him, for fear of seeing a pair of giant wet jaws coming toward his face.

After a couple of minutes, he forced himself to stop.

He finally looked back. Nothing was chasing him.

It was real. Toby was absolutely positive of that. There might not actually be ghosts, or alien spaceships headed toward earth, or vampires in coffins, but there *was* a monster in these woods, with long, sharp claws and scary fangs. He knew the difference between the imaginary monsters he liked and the real ones he didn't like.

And now he was completely lost.

He didn't care anymore about getting in trouble—he just didn't want to die in these woods, either by wandering around until he starved to death or by getting eaten. He called out as loudly as he could: "Mom! Dad!"

Nothing.

He cried out again: "Mom! Dad! I'm lost!"

What if the monster were drawn by the sound of his voice? What if it found him first?

He had to risk it. He shouted for his parents once more, screaming so loud that it hurt his throat, crying now.

Off in the distance, his mother's voice: "Toby?"

He ran toward her.

Now THAT HE was home safe and facing punishment, Toby wished that he'd made more of an effort to find his way out of the forest without calling for help. He sat in the living room, across from his mother and father, staring at the floor and squirming uncomfortably.

"Didn't we tell you to stay within sight of the house?" his father asked, in a very stern tone that Toby had heard many times before.

"Yes, sir."

"Look at me."

Toby looked into his eyes. Fifteen minutes ago, he wouldn't have thought there was anything scarier than his father when he was angry. Even now, he wasn't so sure.

"Why did you disobey us?"

Toby shrugged.

If he'd had time to think about things, he probably could have made up a story that would have gotten him in a lot less trouble. Unfortunately, he'd rushed right into his mother's arms and sobbed about having seen a monster, which had earned him a few minutes of sympathy and comfort but was now very much working against him. Even though he knew he was telling the absolute truth, he also knew that it was a tough story to swallow, and that he'd have been much better off lying about what happened and easing his parents into the whole "monster in the woods" part.

"Where's your pocketknife?"

"I dropped it when I was running."

"From the deer?"

"It wasn't a deer."

"Well, whatever it was, you shouldn't have been out that far to see it. And now you don't have a pocketknife. What do you think I should do about this?"

There was only one correct answer to this question. "Make me go get your belt," Toby said, quietly.

His father nodded. "Go get it."

Toby didn't think that the belt had ever been used to hold up his father's pants. It was strictly a tool of punishment, and it did that often and well. Toby had tried various tricks to get out of the spankings, including pretending that he couldn't find the belt or that he thought his father meant a different, thinner belt. None of these had worked out in his favor.

This particular spanking wasn't that bad—three quick smacks and it was over. His mother's lecture on responsibility took quite a bit longer. When it was over, Toby was sentenced to a week without dessert (a fate worse than a thousand spankings with a steel electrified belt) and forbidden to go into the woods by himself, at all, until further notice.

But his dad never stayed mad for long, and before it started to get dark they hiked out into the woods together to try to find his pocketknife. Toby tried to remember where he might have dropped it, but really, he'd been fleeing in pure terror at the time and didn't have the slightest clue how to get back there. He wasn't scared of the monster, though, not with Dad around.

"You need to be able to recognize landmarks," his dad said. He pointed straight ahead. "What do you see?"

"Oak trees."

"Yes, but look exactly where I'm pointing. Even if it's just a bunch of trees, you should be able to find things to help you find your way. What do you see?"

"Three of those trees kind of look like a W."

"Exactly." Toby's father took him by the hand. "Watch for that kind of thing and you won't get lost."

They weren't able to find the pocketknife. His father frowned when Toby described the monster yet again, but Toby couldn't help himself. He wasn't making it up and he hadn't imagined it and now that he was already in trouble he wasn't going to pretend he hadn't seen it. As they looked for the knife, he watched for traces of the monster—footprints, hair, a fang, anything—with no success.

Dessert was apple pie. Not one of his favorites, so Mom and Dad weren't *that* mad at him.

The restriction on going into the forest by himself was lifted a week later. It was three more days before Toby summoned the courage to actually do it. He stayed well within sight of the house, and encountered no sign of the monster.

Summer ended. Toby returned to school and thoughts of the monster faded.

By the time summer returned, he occasionally laughed to himself about the silly time when he'd imagined seeing a hairy, clawed, fanged beast in the forest.

2

1960. Age 15.

When Toby next met the monster, his hair still had traces of Nick Wyler's urine. Nick hadn't actually peed on Toby, thank God, but he'd seasoned the toilet bowl before Toby's head plunged into the murky depths.

"C'mon, hurry up!" urged Larry Gaige, moments before the dunking. Larry was far and away the biggest creep at Orange Leaf High. His physical build would've made him football team material, if he had any interest in fighting other kids his size. He held Toby against the wall of the bathroom stall, with Toby's head pressed next to a detailed but inaccurate drawing of a vagina.

"I'm trying!" Nick insisted. He stood next to the toilet, trying to relieve himself but suffering from performance anxiety. Toby personally had always had a real issue with the lack of doors in the bathrooms, so he could understand why it might be difficult for Nick to pee with two other guys in the stall.

Toby struggled some more, mostly for show. He was short, thin, and outnumbered, and knew he wasn't getting out of this bathroom undunked unless a teacher happened to walk in, searching for smokers. Calling for help was not an option. Larry got his thrills by causing humiliation, not pain, but he *would* hurt you if he had to.

"Let's go, let's go!" said Larry, kicking Nick on the back of the leg. Toby heard a few drops hit the water and a few more hit the seat.

"Why don't you do it? I haven't had enough to drink today."

"Are you kidding me?" Larry gave his friend a look of absolute disbelief. "Just yank the stopper out of your dick and take a piss!"

"Maybe if you left the stall for a minute...?"

For a moment, Toby thought that Larry was actually going to let him go so that he could focus his attention on beating the crap out of Nick. His optimism was quickly extinguished as Larry slammed him against the wall hard enough to make him bite his tongue. He winced and tasted blood.

The sound of a healthy stream of urine hitting the toilet water filled the stall. Nick was cured.

"Okay, that's enough," said Larry. "We've gotta hurry up."

"I can't stop once I've started!"

"*Jesus Christ!*"

"Just let me finish!"

Larry stood there, visibly fuming, as Nick continued the challenging process of relieving himself. Toby kept praying that a teacher or some other adult visitor would walk in and question the presence of three teenage boys sharing a restroom stall, but as the stream slowed to a trickle and then to a spatter, Toby knew his moment of extreme indignity had almost arrived.

Larry shoved Nick out of the way before he was completely done. Nick punched him in the arm. "I bought these pants with my own money!"

Ignoring his friend, Larry pushed Toby to his knees in front of the toilet bowl and then quickly pushed his face toward the aromatic liquid. Toby squeezed his eyes shut and held his breath as his face dipped into the warm water. He gagged and desperately tried not to inhale as the toilet flushed and the water swirled around his head.

Once the water had completely exited the bowl, Larry let go of his neck. He and Nick walked out of the stall, laughing. Another scrawny twerp successfully humiliated.

Could've been worse. *Had* been worse, several times. Still, Toby's cheeks burned from shame and he felt like he was going to throw up as he coughed and gagged and gasped for breath.

Toby left the stall, turned on one of the faucets, and tried to rinse the piss out of his hair. He could tattle on those jerks and get them suspended, but suspensions were temporary, and there wasn't much the school board could do if the bullies decided to lie in wait for him next to his front porch with tire irons and broken bottles.

Okay, he didn't actually believe that Larry and Nick would kill him, or even hospitalize him. The most violence they'd inflict was a hard punch to the stomach, maybe some light bruises elsewhere. But there was a code of honor at Orange Leaf High: you didn't rat out your peers. Not even awful, reprehensible, deserve-to-die peers. Nobody liked a rat fink. If Toby went to his parents or a teacher, he'd be scorned by every kid in school.

He was already the Weird Kid in a school that was severely lacking in other weird kids. If he became the Weird Kid Who Was Also A Rat Fink, he might as well kiss any glimpse of hope for making friends—real friends, maybe even a girlfriend—goodbye. He didn't have many friends in elementary school or junior high, but at least the kids there talked to him, sometimes. But most of his half-friends had gone to West End High, and his out-of-the-way address put him in the Orange Leaf High district, so he was starting over.

Anyway, someday he'd get Larry and Nick back. He was doing chin-ups every day. He could do eleven or twelve of them now. By the end of the year, who knew how big his muscles might be?

"Time for a dunking!" Larry might say, pulling Toby into the stall. Toby would drop to his knees, and Nick would laugh and laugh at how easy it was to overpower him. But, oh, how his laughter would stop when Toby suddenly used his brute strength to rip the toilet right out of the floor!

"Holy cow!" Nick would scream. "How many chin-ups has he *done?*"

Toby would smash the toilet into Larry's face, shattering the porcelain and splashing its abhorrent contents all over him. As Larry dropped to the tile floor, unconscious, Nick would stand there, paralyzed with fear.

"Please don't kill me," Nick would whimper.

Toby would shake his head and chuckle. "I'm no killer," he would say. But then he would give Nick a stern glare, a glare that chilled Nick's blood. "Dunk yourself."

"But I'll be shamed and ridiculed!"

"Don't make me tell you twice."

Nick would thrust his own head into the toilet, sobbing like a baby. Toby would watch him flush and flush and flush, inwardly amused but far too mature to point and laugh. Perhaps he'd allow the other students to file through the restroom to witness the defeat and learn from it, or perhaps he'd keep it to himself and merely raise an eyebrow at Larry and Nick when they started to get out of line. Either way, Toby Floren would be the victor.

But that would be later. For now, he had to go back to class with wet hair and embarrassment scorching his cheeks.

A FEW OF the other kids snickered as Toby returned to history class, but Mr. Hastings didn't say anything about his appearance or tardiness.

During lunch, kids continued to snicker when they looked at him, even though his hair was dry. Clearly, Larry and Nick had shared the uproarious news of their latest conquest. Toby hoped for a sympathetic glance from somebody, anybody, but didn't receive one. At least a couple of the kids who smiled in his direction had been dunkees themselves.

He sat in his usual spot at the corner table, doodling in his notebook while he ate a roast beef sandwich. There weren't enough tables in the lunchroom for him to sit by himself, so he sat with his standard group, but an empty seat separated him from the others.

At least his sandwich was good. Mom had made an outstanding dinner last night, and the leftovers were even better in sandwich form.

"What're you drawing?" asked J.D. Jerick, through a mouthful of potato chips.

"Nothing."

"Let me see it."

Toby shook his head. He'd fallen for this before. J.D. had expressed an interest in his art, and Toby had proudly explained exactly how the robot's jet pack functioned in zero gravity. Then J.D. had let out a donkey-like laugh, grabbed Toby's notebook, and showed it to everybody at the table. Robots weren't cool at Orange Leaf High.

"C'mon, I just want to see what you're drawing."

"No way."

"I'm not gonna do anything."

Toby closed his notebook. There wasn't much he could do when he was overpowered by physically imposing bullies like Larry and Nick, but J.D. was a different kind of bully, and Toby wasn't threatened by him at all.

J.D. made a lunge for the notebook, but Toby slid it out of the way. "Just let me see it, Zit Farm. What is it, naked pictures of the teachers?" He raised his voice. "You really shouldn't be drawing naked pictures of teachers, Toby Floren!"

Toby gave him the finger.

"By the way, you reek. What have you been doing, swimming in the toilet?"

Toby gave him the finger with both hands.

"Loser," said J.D.

Toby returned his attention to his notebook and his sandwich while the other kids at the table laughed. Why were they on J.D.'s side? Couldn't they see that he was a complete cretin?

He sketched for a few more minutes, knowing that J.D. was watching him and wasn't going to let the matter drop.

"What're you drawing?" J.D. finally repeated.

Toby held up the picture: a hand giving the finger.

J.D. frowned, obviously not thinking that the drawing was very funny. Toby grinned, but stopped grinning when he saw Mr. Hastings staring right at the drawing from across the lunchroom. The teacher made a beeline toward him, and Toby knew that his day was about to get even worse.

TOBY WANTED to take a shower when he got home, but he wasn't up to explaining the need for the shower to Mom. He also didn't want her to think that he had a different, much more private reason for taking a shower at an unusual time. Though he supposed he could just make something up, he'd probably get caught in the lie—he had an active fantasy life, but his skills at deceit were almost non-existent.

"I'm home!" he shouted out, hurrying up the stairs to his room and hoping that Mom wouldn't ask him to sit with her in the living room and talk about his day.

"Do you have any homework?" Mom called up to him.

"Lots!" he called back. He dumped his backpack on his bed, then pulled out the unnecessary books. He had to do about twenty math problems, a 250-word essay on chapters six and seven of *Robinson Crusoe*, and study for a history quiz. No problem. He picked up the backpack, slung it over his shoulder, and headed back downstairs.

"Where are you going?" Mom asked. She was seated on the

living room couch, half-watching television while writing a letter. She wrote to Grandma once a week, every week, and had ever since she married Dad, even though she hadn't mailed the letters for a couple of years.

"Woods."

"I thought you said you had homework?"

He lifted his shoulder, bouncing the backpack. "It's in here."

"Oh, okay. Good."

Toby grinned. "See how easy your life is, having a son who's so diligent about his homework?"

"It is. It's very relaxing."

"Because, you know, there are a lot of dumb and lazy kids out there."

"I know."

"I'll be back before Dad gets home."

Toby walked about half a mile into the woods, to his favorite spot. Two trees had grown together at the base, forming a surprisingly comfortable seat where the trunks split apart. He set his backpack on the ground, sat on the trees, and began to work through some math problems. Math was his least favorite subject outside of physical education, but he liked Mr. Hesser's nerdy sense of humor, and paid enough attention to ace every test. His report card was always straight A's except for music. He enjoyed playing the trumpet but was very, very bad at it.

He completed the math problems, then started on his essay. He'd already finished the entire book—he didn't like reading books a chapter at a time, and even if the book wasn't anything spectacular he usually found himself reading through to the end. This one he loved.

He finished up the essay, then spent a few minutes studying for his history quiz. The forest was a wonderful place to study, free of distractions, and it didn't take much time for the material to sink in. He put his books aside, ran through a list of mental questions and answers to test his knowledge, then stood up, satisfied. Now he could enjoy the rest of his evening.

Then he remembered the sensation of his face splashing into the contaminated water, and his mood soured.

Jerks.

What was wrong with them? Why was humiliating a fellow student their idea of a good time? What pleasure could they get from doing something like that?

Well, admittedly, Toby would get a *lot* of pleasure from dunking Larry and Nick's heads in a toilet, preferably the same toilet at the same time, but that was purely revenge based. He hadn't done anything to them to deserve this.

Jerks. Creeps. Idiots.

Forget about them, he thought. Why let a pair of bullies ruin his evening? His homework was done, he didn't have to work at the grocery store tonight, it wasn't raining, the weather hadn't turned cold yet, and he had the entire forest at his disposal. Screw 'em. He was going to enjoy himself.

He walked for a while, but it didn't make him feel any better, so he picked up his pace to a jog. He kept his eyes on the ground so that he wouldn't trip—the forest wasn't exactly the safest jogging environment, and Toby had extreme tendencies toward being a klutz.

He was only able to jog for a few minutes before he got a stitch in his side, so he rested for a moment until the pain faded, then resumed his jog. Boy, was he in terrible shape. This was embarrassing. He hoped the woodland creatures weren't laughing at him.

There had to be a way to get back at the bullies without risking a broken nose. What if he bought them each a "Thank You" card for the toilet incident? That would really mess with their minds. It could be a really colorful card, maybe with a piece of chocolate inside, presented to them with no trace of irony. Something like that might really fuel their sense of paranoia.

They'd wonder exactly what he had planned for them. Their stomachs would hurt whenever they saw him. It would be glorious!

"What does this mean?" Larry would ask, reading the card for the 73rd time. "Has he gone deranged? Or does he have a ghastly fate in store for us?"

"I do not know!" Nick would answer. "But the suspense may drive me mad!"

Toby felt a little better as he ran.

His dad always got home at 7:15 sharp, which gave him another two hours to goof around in the woods. Maybe he'd see how far he could get in an hour. He spent a lot of time in the woods and knew the few square miles behind his house well, but it was a vast forest that offered new discoveries all the time. Mostly just different trees, but still...

He moved through the woods for about half an hour, alternating between jogging, walking fast, and a couple of brief bursts of sprinting. He should probably join track at school. Might make him some friends. Or one friend.

He stopped running.

Something was lying on the ground in front of a small clearing. Toby walked over to investigate. It was a wooden sign, lying on its side, mostly covered by bushes. The red lettering had faded to almost the same grey color as the wood, but the words were still legible: *Danger. Keep Out.*

Wow.

A couple of years ago, Toby had discovered an old rusted car, right there amidst the trees. It had looked like something from the 1930's. He'd spent long nights wondering how it got there. Rationally, he knew that the answer was straightforward, that there had probably just been a path at one time that had since been abandoned and overgrown. But there were dozens of much more interesting scenarios, and they'd captured his imagination until a few weeks later when he found the deer carcass. He'd searched the vehicle thoroughly, but alas, there was no hidden stash of mobster cash.

Danger. Keep Out promised something even more exciting.

What could it be? An abandoned mine? An old bunker filled with explosives?

Toby slowly stepped through the clearing, which was a circle about fifty feet in diameter, watching his feet to make sure he didn't walk in a bear trap or something like that. The clearing itself seemed to be devoid of anything interesting. He walked around the perimeter, then walked across it several times, but didn't see anything that looked even remotely worthy of the sign.

They wouldn't put out a sign like that for no reason. There had to be *something*. Maybe it was the former site of a horrible plague.

No, even in ancient times, people probably took stronger precautions against the spread of a plague than simply putting out a wooden sign.

He kept searching the area, but there was nothing. What a rip-off.

What if the sign had been moved? He just needed to keep searching. He continued to walk around the area, not going quite so far as to crawl around on his hands and knees, but making sure he was searching thoroughly. If there was something great out here, he was going to find it.

About five minutes beyond the sign, he found a path. A narrow uphill path that looked recently used.

Well, maybe not. There weren't any distinct footprints or broken branches or anything specific to indicate that somebody might have recently taken a stroll around here. Still, Toby had a weird feeling, something he couldn't quite pinpoint, that he wasn't the only person to have used this path today.

This meant that, as a rational, intelligent human being, his best bet was to get the hell out of there as soon as possible.

Instead, he stepped onto the path and followed it.

3

The path ended at the entrance to a cave. A cave! Toby knew there were caves out in this forest somewhere, but there weren't supposed to be any within walking distance of his house. How could something like this have eluded him all this time? He could've been hanging out in a cave for years!

There were some rusted metal hinges—almost worn down to dust—on the left side of the cave entrance, but the door itself was long gone. There was, however, a large pile of brush in front of it. Had the wind blown it there, or had somebody put it there? It wasn't a very good camouflage. Must've been put there by Mother Nature. The cave door wasn't a perfect rectangle, but it was obviously man-made, or at least an enhancement of a natural entrance.

Toby pushed the brush out of the way and peered inside. Totally dark.

He removed his backpack, reached inside, and dug around until he found the small penlight he used for reading. He turned it on and shone it inside the entrance. It didn't help much, but at least it might keep him from walking into an open pit and plummeting eight hundred feet to his death.

He replaced his backpack and stepped through the entrance. He immediately recoiled—it smelled *awful* in here. Not like something had died, but like something had failed to empty about six months' worth of garbage. Noxious. He took one more step forward and shone the light around.

The rock ceiling was low enough that he could scrape against it with the tips of his fingers if he reached up. The cave was extremely narrow, not quite claustrophobic, but he wouldn't be able to lie sideways on the floor. He couldn't see the far end, so he continued walking forward, very slowly and carefully.

He bet that Larry, Nick, and Frank wouldn't have the courage to walk into an unexplored cave like this. Those babies would be standing at the entrance, whining "There might be bats inside! There might be bats inside!" Losers.

A few more steps in, his light washed against the far wall. More rock. Nothing particularly interesting about it. Toby ran the beam of his flashlight around the perimeter, and there was...nothing.

So this was it? One small room?

Toby turned in a slow circle, shining his flashlight all over the cave, and it really did seem to be a single room, maybe twice the length of one of his classrooms. Not that impressive. Still, he wondered what its purpose was. Obviously, somebody had used it for something, or there wouldn't be hinges and the sign. It could have been the start of a mine. Maybe the owner was a bumbling incompetent and after bringing all of the equipment out here and digging for a couple of days he'd realized that there were no minerals to mine. He'd sheepishly sent everybody home, put up the sign, and declared bankruptcy.

Or, the workers had been attacked by rats. Giant rats. Well, not *giant* rats—not fifty-footers, but rats twice the size of normal ones, with glistening greasy fur and glowing red eyes and pus leaking from their ears. As the workers drilled, a section of the wall collapsed and thousands of them swarmed out. The three closest men were consumed immediately, their shrieking forms reduced to skeletons within seconds, like a cow falling into piranha-infested water. The others had panicked and opened fire, killing one rat for every fifty that latched onto their flesh. The owner made it to his automobile just in time and sped off, running over his assistant in his haste to drive out of the area. He'd abandoned the mine idea and concocted an elaborate story to keep himself out of prison.

Yeah.

Toby did another circle with the flashlight. Kind of disappointing, but still, he'd found a cave! There might be other caves nearby. An entire system of caves. He could get a girlfriend for sure if he knew his way around a local cave. They were dark, slightly spooky, romantic...

Something bellowed.

The sound, which came from inside the cave, startled Toby so badly that he dropped the flashlight.

Another bellow. It sounded like God himself was shouting from the cave walls.

Toby raced for the exit—or tried to. His foot came down on the flashlight, slipped out from under him and twisted with a painful *crack*, and he fell to the ground.

He scrambled on his hands and knees toward the exit, hurting his foot even worse but not caring, terrified that the entire cave was going to collapse and splatter him under tons of rock and dirt.

Toby made it outside without the cave ceiling splattering him. Now the only noise was his own frantic breathing. What on earth had it been? What made a noise like that? It wasn't his imagination, and it was unlikely to have actually been God, so what was it?

The question was answered quite satisfactorily when the monster emerged from the cave.

Toby hadn't believed that there was such a thing as truly paralyzing fear. Sure, you could be held immobile by bullies, and you could be frozen in place when your father came at you with his belt just because you knew that running away would result in worse punishment, but Toby had never imagined being literally too frightened to move. His muscles ached with the effort to move them, yet he couldn't budge. He just knelt on the ground, staring at the horrific sight before him.

He remembered it. Very well.

It was covered with thick brown hair, except for some bare patches on its arms and legs. It stood upright, like a human, though its arms and legs were slightly twisted, as if they'd been broken and not healed quite properly. Its claws—good God, its claws were huge, curved white razors at least three inches long on each finger. Its yellow eyes were set deep inside of its face.

Its jaws were a complete horror show, with teeth that were almost cartoonishly large and sharp.

He'd remembered the monster as being bigger, although of course back then he'd been smaller. It was still an imposing, terrifying creature. One that clearly had every intention of devouring Toby, chewing his face off while he lay paralyzed on the ground. Not even chewing—biting it clean off in one chomp.

The monster regarded him closely. It narrowed its sunken eyes as if studying him. Wondering which body part to bite into first.

It walked forward. Toby noted that its toes also had talons, though not nearly as lengthy or sharp as those on its fingers. It still looked like it could rip off a few big strips of flesh just by stepping on him.

Though Toby's body remained frozen, suddenly his voice worked, and he let out a long, loud scream.

The monster flinched as if he'd struck it.

Toby screamed again.

The monster stood there, motionless, staring at him.

Toby could feel perspiration pouring down his forehead, his arms, and the back of his neck. He still couldn't get up, but his hands were quivering. He just waited, knowing that at any moment the monster was going to let out another bellow—a war cry—and lunge at him like a cougar.

He desperately wished he had a weapon.

There was a rock near his right hand, but he couldn't move to grab it.

The monster continued to stare at him. It seemed alert, as if waiting for Toby to make a sudden move.

Do something! Toby willed himself. *Don't just lie here. Get up and run!*

Getting eaten by a forest monster was, admittedly, a pretty cool way to die...but not if he just lay there and let it happen!

Grab the rock! Grab the rock! It's right here, you idiot!

His body clearly wasn't going to help him out of this situation.

The monster crouched down. It was less than five feet away.

Toby wanted to scream again until his lungs were shredded, but instead he heard himself say: "Hi."

Hi? What the hell?

The monster didn't react. Which made sense—wild carnivorous animals typically did not respond to friendly greetings.

Then it tilted its head a bit, as if intrigued.

"Hi," Toby repeated. "I'm Toby Floren and I'm sorry I went into your cave. I didn't know you were in there. You must have a secret passage or something."

Why was he talking to it? What did he expect it to say back?

Of course, you'd talk to an angry dog to soothe it, so...

"What's your name?" he asked.

The monster, of course, did not answer.

"My name's Toby Floren." Yeah, he'd already said that, but his actual words didn't matter as long as he kept up the calming tone. "I live about four miles from here. It's that white house with the blue shutters. I'm not sure if you've seen it. I hope you haven't. The last book I read was *Robinson Crusoe*."

He hadn't been eaten yet, so this seemed to be working.

The monster ran its thick, black tongue over its teeth.

Toby stopped talking.

This was it. Death at age fifteen. Dying a virgin. His greatest accomplishment in life was providing entertainment for bullies.

But at least he wasn't crying.

Not that anybody was around to see if he was crying or not. He might as well cry.

Then the monster slowly stood up, not taking its eyes off him. Toby would have expected his body to run out of perspiration by now, but his clothes were completely drenched and sweat continued to flow.

Toby wasn't sure if his muscles were working now or not. He didn't dare to move.

The monster clenched and unclenched its fists, then cocked its head sharply to the left. The message seemed clear: *Get out of here.*

It was a message that Toby was more than happy to obey. He got up, careful not to make any sudden moves, and backed away. There was a jolt of pain as he stepped with his injured foot—he'd probably sprained his ankle—but he could still walk and he continued to back away, step by step, following the path. The monster stood there, watching him until he went around a curve and the trees blocked their view of each other.

He wanted to run after that, but he couldn't risk screwing up his foot even more, especially if he took a downhill tumble. He'd just stick to a quick but safe pace, and hope that the monster didn't change its mind about its dinner plans and chase after him. It might just be toying with him, letting him get far enough ahead that he thought he'd escaped, at which point it would pounce upon him and gobble his ass up. He would be very happy for that not to be the case.

What was that thing? Why would it even need teeth like that, except to scare the hell out of people? How could it even close its mouth around them?

Was it the same one he'd seen all those years ago? It couldn't be, could it? How had it lived out here this long without being discovered?

He looked back. Nothing seemed to be coming after him.

As Toby walked home, he decided not to tell his parents about what happened. They might believe him, or they might search his room for pot. Either way, they wouldn't allow him to go back out there, and Toby had every intention of returning. Unless he'd missed a *really* important day of science class, this was some sort of undiscovered creature, and Toby was going to get credit for the finding. He couldn't go back after dark, but if his foot wasn't in too bad of shape he'd go back this weekend, this time with a camera.

And Dad's shotgun.

4

Toby spent most of his evening in the waiting area of the emergency room. His ankle was indeed sprained, though just mildly, and he kept an ice pack against it, which was more uncomfortable than the pain from the injury.

"How'd you hurt it?" Mom had asked.

Toby had tried to come up with an excuse that was credible yet masculine. "Jumping hurdles."

"How'd you really hurt it?"

How did she always know he was lying? "Tripped."

"You should be more careful."

"I'm considering that. I've heard good things about that lifestyle."

Dad was watching *Wagon Train* on television when they got home. "What'd you do?" he asked, looking away from the set.

"Tripped."

"You should be more careful."

"You guys must stay up all night thinking up this amazing advice."

"Nobody likes a smart-ass."

"I'm sure *somebody* has to."

"Not in this house." Dad gave him a glare that made it clear that he wasn't in a joking mood, which was the case about eighty percent of the time. They had a late dinner of pork roast and mashed potatoes, and then went to bed.

Toby thought that his injured foot might cause the bullies at school to find another target for a while. It was, admittedly, not the most intelligent thought that had ever passed through his brain. He tried to hold his head high, even when his hair got hit with half-sucked sour balls and droplets of snot, but it was probably the most hellish week he'd ever spent at that goddamn school.

He lay in bed, frustrated beyond belief. School took up all of his day and his job at the grocery store took up Tuesday, Wednesday, and Thursday evening. He could have snuck out of the house after his parents were asleep, but seeking proof of the monster in the thick, deep woods after dark crossed the line from "glorious bravery" to "suicidal stupidity." Really, he should wait for his ankle to be completely healed before venturing out there again, but he knew he didn't have the patience.

He hoped the monster hadn't moved on. It was probably nomadic (Toby didn't actually have any evidence of this, but it sounded right) and would eventually move to warmer climates as the Ohio winter began. But if it had that nice little cave to live in, it might stick around for a while longer. It wouldn't know that Toby was planning to come back with a big gun, would it? It was smarter than, say, Mrs. Faulkner's poodle, but still a dumb animal, right?

Saturday morning, he woke up at 6:58, two minutes before the alarm. He got up and dressed as quietly as possible to avoid waking his parents, then took his camera out of his desk drawer. It wasn't a very good camera, and he also wasn't a very good photographer, but it would be sufficient as long as he could get close enough.

Then he retrieved the shotgun from the hallway closet, where it had moved on his thirteenth birthday, when Dad decided that Toby had demonstrated enough responsibility that he didn't need to keep the shotgun locked away in his bedroom. The unspoken understanding was that Toby still wouldn't touch the weapon, which was reserved for hunting trips and protection against intruders. Toby had never been expressly forbidden from sneaking it out of the house and taking it into the woods to hunt monsters, so this morning he was going to obey the letter of the law and not the spirit. When his picture made it onto the cover of a scientific magazine and bought Dad a new gold-plated shotgun with his newfound wealth, he was sure he'd be forgiven.

He put a bag of trail mix, a Thermos of cold water, and a small first aid kit into his backpack, then strapped it onto his back. He hung the camera around his neck with its cord, then picked up the shotgun and quietly exited through the back door. Yeah, they probably weren't going to approve of the whole shotgun thing. Still, it wasn't as if his plan was to march into the kitchen, holding the monster's severed head. The shotgun was only an emergency precaution. A find like this would be worth far more alive than dead. He'd be more popular with the kids at school if he blew the fucker away, but Toby Floren wasn't the kind of guy who would put meaningless social status over scientific progress.

He walked through the forest, moving at a careful pace. Though he was in a hurry to get to the cave, he didn't want to take a misstep and hurt his ankle even worse. Being carried out of the woods on a stretcher would not improve his social life.

After the first mile or so, Toby's foot really started to ache and he questioned the wisdom of this expedition, even without the whole "deadly monster" part. Wise or not, he wasn't going to turn back. He couldn't think of any famous people who would say "One should always allow sprained ankles to keep you from your accomplishments, because they kind of hurt, and the path to success should be as comfortable as possible!"

He forged onward. If he made it all the way out to the cave and the monster had abandoned it, Toby intended to be in a pretty lousy mood for the rest of the weekend. For now he'd remain optimistic. It would still be there.

As he approached the clearing, he took the shotgun off his shoulder and held it ready to fire—keeping the safety on but his finger on the trigger. He cautiously walked through the clearing toward the path, staying alert. The monster wasn't going to take him by surprise. No way.

The fear started to return as he walked along the path. He forced it out of his mind. No room for fear. This was a day of bravery, dammit.

He stared at the entrance to the cave for a long time. The pile of brush that he'd moved the last time hadn't been replaced.

Even at his bravest, he knew he couldn't just go strolling through the entrance. The cave might not have a secret passage, exactly, but there was definitely someplace for the monster to hide that wasn't immediately visible with a penlight sweep. If it was in there, he'd either have to wait for it to come out, or draw it out.

He decided to wait. For now.

He waited for about an hour, watching the cave entrance closely (but safely, about fifty feet away with a couple of trees for cover) and listening for any signs of footsteps, animals moving through bushes, or gnashing fangs. Nothing.

It could be asleep in there. It could be out on the prowl. It could be in Indiana.

Next step: Draw it out.

Toby picked up a rock, one about the size of his fist. Then he decided that in the unlikely chance that he actually struck the monster, it might be better to have a smaller rock that didn't send the beast into a bloodthirsty rage, so he dropped that and picked up another rock about the size of a silver dollar. He leaned the shotgun against the tree, swung his arm back, and then hurled the rock at the cave entrance.

The rock missed by a good ten feet, which was kind of embarrassing. Toby selected another rock, took careful aim, and threw again. Another miss.

Jesus. No wonder the bullies picked on him.

He thought about walking closer, then decided that it was better to waste time with a few failed attempts to accurately throw the rock than to risk being too close when the monster emerged. He picked up a third rock, licked his index finger and held it up to test the wind resistance, concluded that there was no wind, and flung the rock as hard as he could.

It went directly into the center of the cave entrance and disappeared from sight.

Toby listened closely but didn't hear a grunt or an "*oomph*" or anything to indicate that he'd hit the monster. He waited for about a minute, then picked up another rock and threw it. Not as impressive as his last throw, but this one also went into the cave.

Still nothing.

Okay, the big decision. Did he dare venture into the cave, or should he keep throwing rocks?

Rocks. You couldn't really go wrong with rocks.

He threw another rock, which also went into the cave. He was getting pretty good at this.

"C'mon, you toothy freak, let's see your grotesque face," he said as he threw the next rock. "Get out here, you big dumb ape!"

The monster walked out of the cave.

Toby's stomach dropped as he watched it step out into the light, moving at an almost sluggish pace, like an annoyed neighbor coming outside to investigate what woke him up at four in the morning. It looked to each side, and then directly at Toby.

They locked eyes.

The monster began to walk toward him.

Shit!

Though it wasn't running, there was definite menace in its gait, like a predator who knows its prey can't escape and is in no rush to deliver the killing blow. Toby immediately forgot about the idea of photographing the monster and quickly grabbed the shotgun, uttering a string of rapid obscenities under his breath.

You weren't supposed to be able to attribute human emotions to animals, but this thing looked *pissed*.

I'm gonna die! Toby thought as he fumbled with the shotgun, nearly dropping it onto the ground. *Oh my God, I'm gonna die!*

The monster wasn't even ten feet away. Toby wanted to scream in an effort to gain its pity again, but he couldn't find his voice. Nothing in his body ever worked when he needed it to!

But then he had the shotgun pointed at the monster's chest. He squeezed the trigger.

For a split second Toby frantically wondered why the weapon hadn't fired. He realized that the safety was still on. However, the monster took a big step back and let out a pitiful whimper. It held its clawed hands up in front of its face.

Toby flipped off the safety but didn't shoot. He backed up a few paces, putting enough space between himself and the monster that he didn't feel that his bloody death was seconds away. The monster kept its hands over its face, almost sounding like a puppy as it whimpered in fear.

Toby felt a bit of his courage return. "That's right, asshole!" he shouted, waving the barrel of the gun at the monster. "I'm a lot scarier than you, aren't I?"

Picture. He needed the picture. Unfortunately, he wasn't sure how to snap the picture while still keeping the shotgun safely pointed at the thing that wanted to devour him. He backed up a couple more steps, and then tried to balance the shotgun with one arm while grabbing the camera with his free hand. The instant the barrel wavered, he changed his mind. Maybe he'd skip the photograph.

No. That's why he was out here, risking a great big bite mark in his throat. If he didn't get proof, he'd have wasted the effort. He needed *some* kind of reward for all of the forthcoming foot pain and nightmares.

He let out a snort of laughter. The answer was obvious. He rested the barrel of the shotgun on one of the tree branches, keeping it pointed at the monster. After a moment of hesitation to make sure the branch didn't snap under the shotgun's weight, he picked up the camera with his left hand and peered through the viewfinder.

Say cheese...

He snapped a quick photograph. It might not have been a very good one, but he didn't want to get greedy. He let go of the camera and clutched the shotgun in both hands again.

Now what?

He could shoot the monster. Blow open its chest, get photographs of its corpse from every possible angle, then bring the authorities back here. He'd be world famous. The coolest kid in Orange Leaf. Maybe the coolest kid in Ohio.

The monster lowered its hands from its face.

No, he wasn't going to kill it. You didn't kill something like this. It could be the last of its kind.

Or it could be one of thousands, which were circling him at this very moment. That was a new spin on the situation that Toby hadn't considered. He nervously glanced around at the trees around him, but there didn't seem to be any reinforcements.

The monster was no longer whimpering, though it still looked frightened. And sad.

He couldn't kill this thing, even if it weren't a scientific discovery. He'd been the one to invade its territory. And it had let him go when it had the chance to kill him.

Toby lowered the shotgun. One act of mercy for another.

Of course, he kept his arm tense, ready to bring the shotgun right the hell back up if the monster rushed at him. But it didn't. It just looked at him.

"Uh, sorry about that," said Toby.

The monster did not acknowledge his apology. Toby felt kind of silly for having said it. He couldn't exactly gauge the monster's facial expression, especially not with all those teeth, but it almost seemed to look grateful.

Did it live out here all by itself?

How old was it?

It was far from cute, but Toby couldn't help feeling sorry for it...not that he would hesitate to blow its head off if necessary.

They stared at each other for a long moment.

"Do you...talk?" Toby asked. "Do you speak English?" Toby was 99.9% sure that the monster didn't talk and that he was asking a very stupid question, but if the monster *did* talk, it would be much stupider for them to stand here staring at each other when they could be communicating through spoken language.

The monster didn't respond. It just kept looking at him.

"I'm not going to hurt you," Toby promised, hoping that his tone of voice would get his message across. "If you stay where you are, I won't do anything with the gun." He patted the barrel to show the monster what he was talking about. Then he decided that patting the barrel of the gun was more of an intimidating gesture than a reassuring one, and quickly shook his head. "I won't shoot this."

There was no evidence that the monster knew what he was talking about. But at least it wasn't charging at him.

Toby patted his chest. "Toby," he said. "I'm Toby." He said it more slowly, enunciating as well as he could. "*Toby*."

It was hard to tell with its sunken eyes, but the creature seemed to squint a bit. Toby had no idea what that meant.

He was starting to relax. This was probably a bad idea, considering that there was a savage beast standing not too far from him. Toby was pretty sure that he'd pushed his luck as far as it was going to go in this particular situation, and that his best course of action would be to walk away from the monster while it was relatively sedate.

"Goodbye," he told it. "I guess I'll...see you around or something."

Now came the tricky part: turning his back on it.

Toby backed up a few steps, keeping his eye on the monster, but he knew he couldn't watch both the uneven path and the monster at the same time. He turned around and slowly walked away, imagining his ears as finely tuned robotic instruments, capable of hearing the slightest movement behind him. If the monster exhaled, he'd hear it. If the monster blinked louder than necessary, he'd hear it. If the monster did anything at all...

He heard it.

He spun back around, withstanding the urge to aim the shotgun. The monster took another step toward him. It didn't look like it was trying to be aggressive or threatening—it was simply following him. Still, non-aggressive or not, Toby couldn't have a monster following him home.

"Shoo!" he said. "Go away!"

The monster stood in place. It clicked two of its talons together, and Toby felt some fresh perspiration run down his back.

"Don't follow me," Toby told it. "I'm going home. You can't come."

The monster licked its lips.

Shit.

Should he run? Should he blow a hole in its face? Should he wet himself and perish?

None of those sounded good. Well, the running part sounded good, but not on a sprained ankle.

"Stay," Toby warned. "Staaaay." God, he hoped that the monster didn't think he was being condescending.

He waited for a few moments, until he decided that the monster wasn't going to keep moving toward him. He turned his back on it once again and resumed walking. *Robot ears...robot ears...*

He made it a few steps before he heard some rustling, but when he spun around the monster was still standing there. Just normal forest rustling. No imminent peril. He returned his attention to the path ahead.

There were seven more false alarms before the monster was finally out of sight. Toby walked home, feeling relieved to still be uneaten...and absolutely exhilarated by his encounter.

5

Toby lay in bed, his injured foot elevated on a couple of pillows. His camera rested on his bedside.

He hadn't told his parents about the monster. They'd believe him—they'd *have* to, at least after he developed the picture and showed them the proof, but he just didn't feel like sharing his discovery quite yet.

It was *his* monster.

If he told people about it, he'd probably be famous, but then the government would swoop in there and capture it. They'd either throw the monster in a cage and study it, or break out their scalpels and start slicing it up. His wonderful discovery would be nothing more than strips of flesh under a microscope. Its jaws would be on display over the mayor's fireplace.

Maybe he should keep it a secret for a while longer. Why let everybody else ruin his discovery? And his forest? The best part of the forest was that nobody really ever went in the area near his house. His only close neighbor was Mrs. Faulkner, who now relied on a walker and hardly ever went outside. Some lady came in once a week to bring her groceries. If people knew about the monster, the forest would be swarmed with tourists and scientists and everybody. He'd lose his favorite place.

He could study the monster. Get better pictures. Try harder to communicate with it. And if it did attack, he'd rather be the one who shot it than some police officer. Why should they get the honor?

That's what he'd do. Enjoy the monster all by himself for now. There was plenty of time to let the rest of the world know.

"I HAD a great big bean burrito for dinner last night," Larry said, leaning in his desk toward Toby just before economics class started. "After we dunk you, you'll have to shave your head to get rid of the smell."

Despite a desperate need to use the facilities, Toby stayed out of the restrooms for the remainder of the day.

TOBY DIDN'T NEED to throw rocks after school. The monster sat on the ground, right outside of its cave. It looked up as Toby approached but didn't stand. Toby double-checked the shotgun to make sure the safety was off, and kept it pointed at the dirt as he walked forward, stopping at the same fifty-feet-away point he'd used last time.

"Hi again," he said. "It's Toby. Remember me?"

Wow, that thing had big teeth.

"Do you have a name?"

Toby wondered if there were others like it. If not, would it even need a name?

"I'm going to give you a name, if you don't mind," Toby informed the monster. "I'm sure it's not your real name, but I should call you *something*, don't you think? And you can name me whatever you want. So for now, I'm going to call you Owen." He pointed at the monster. "*Owen*. That's you. Do you like it?"

Owen—the human Owen—was the closest Toby had ever come to having a real friend. They'd met in sixth grade. Toby had been impressed by his ability to create paper airplanes that could sail all the way across the classroom, and even more impressed by his stealth in doing so without being seen by the teacher. For about three months, they went to each other's houses every day after school, and spent the night most weekends, and had a great time.

One Saturday morning, they were playing catch with what remained of a baseball that Toby had cut apart to see what was inside. Owen's throw was off-center and the baseball bounced off Toby's shoulder. In a momentary flash of fury, Toby grabbed the baseball off the grass and hurled it at Owen as hard as he could, bashing him in the face. Owen ran for home, blood gushing from his nostrils. Toby chased after him, yelling out apologies.

Owen had run inside and slammed his front door shut. When Toby knocked, Owen's mother angrily sent him away. Toby, sick to his stomach, had gone home and tried unsuccessfully to read comic books for the rest of the afternoon.

Owen refused to talk to him the next day. Toby didn't have much experience, but he didn't think this was the way friendships were supposed to work, at least with boys. They were supposed to pick up right where they left off, as if nothing had happened. Owen wasn't playing by the rules.

They didn't speak again for the rest of the year. Then Owen's dad got a job all the way over in Nevada and they moved away.

Toby had been so stupid. The baseball hadn't hurt *that* bad.

"Do you understand anything I'm saying, Owen?" he asked the monster. "If you understand me, nod your head. Nod your head like this." Toby nodded his head, slowly and emphatically.

Owen the Monster stood up.

"No," Toby said in a firm voice. "Don't stand. Nod your head." He nodded some more.

Owen raised his arms high into the air and let out a howl. Whether it was frustration or rage, Toby couldn't tell, but it was most definitely not a good howl.

"Fuck!" Toby screamed. He turned and limped away as quickly as he could.

There was another howl. This one sounded sorrowful.

Don't forget about the shotgun, you idiot!

Toby spun back around, but with his panic and sweaty hands the shotgun slipped out of his grasp. Losing his weapon concerned him for a fraction of a second. Then his concern immediately switched to his wrapped ankle as the wooden stock smashed against it, creating a fireball of pain that brought tears to his eyes and nearly knocked him to the ground. He cried out, lost his balance, and braced himself against a tree.

He didn't have a legitimate frame of reference, but based on his mother's description of the pain of childbirth, he felt like he was having a baby through his ankle.

Oh, *God*, it hurt.

Having the monster's fangs slowly sink into his flesh probably hurt worse though, so he scrambled to pick the shotgun back up. He glanced over his shoulder to see how close he was to having it take a nice generous bite out of him, and saw that Owen still stood in front of the cave.

Why wasn't it coming after him? It had some injured prey, right within eyesight. Toby deserved to get eaten, just for his ridiculous incompetence.

Owen made a coughing sound.

No, not a cough. That was a laugh. A goddamn laugh. That thing was laughing at him!

That was a lot better than it trying to rip him apart, but still...

Or maybe it had just been a regular snort. It was impossible to say. Either way, Owen wasn't coming after him, and if he wasn't attacking now, while Toby was lying there like a complete buffoon, he probably wasn't going to attack at all.

He clenched his teeth together as tightly as he could to keep from crying out again. You really weren't supposed to drop a shotgun on a sprained ankle. He wondered if he'd broken it. He stayed on the ground, waiting for the agony to subside while watching closely to make sure that Owen didn't change his mind about going on a rampage.

The pain took several minutes to fade to a manageable level. Toby grabbed a branch and pulled himself to his feet. His whole foot was throbbing. He wiped the tears from his eyes and forced a smile. "You may have to nurse me back to health, big guy," he said.

The movement was slight, and almost certainly not what Toby thought it was, but he was *positive* that Owen nodded.

It was cool, yet unspeakably freaky.

"So do you mind if I take a few more pictures?" he asked. "I don't want anybody to see them, so I probably won't get them developed right away, but I should take them now just in case you...I don't know, migrate or something."

He dug his camera out of his backpack. As long as the flash didn't scare or enrage Owen, he should be able to get some good shots before he hobbled back home. Owen leaned forward just a bit as Toby looked through the camera, but the monster had been photographed before without ill effect and it didn't seem to mind this time. Toby took eleven or twelve pictures then tucked the camera away.

"I'll come back," Toby promised. "Probably not tomorrow, since by then my foot will be the size of your entire body, but soon." It felt kind of weird to be making a promise to a creature that couldn't understand what he was saying, that had no apparent emotional attachment to him, and whose desire to devour him remained an active possibility, but he couldn't help himself.

Maybe he'd injured his brain instead of his foot.

DAD WAS ALREADY HOME when Toby got back. That wasn't such a good thing.

"Any special reason you're walking around in the woods with my shotgun?" Dad asked as he walked inside.

"Fake hunting."

"Fake hunting?"

"You know, pretending to hunt."

"You're wandering around the woods with a sprained ankle and a loaded shotgun pretending to hunt?"

Toby shook his head. "I took the shells out."

He'd left them in until right before he exited the forest, just in case Owen was silently following him and preparing to pounce, and had almost forgotten the detail of emptying the gun before he walked back in the house. He looked like less of a foolhardy idiot explaining the situation if the gun was unloaded.

"You're a strange kid," Dad said.

"Genetics."

Dad frowned.

"Sorry," Toby said.

"No need to apologize. It's all recessive traits."

Toby grinned and walked upstairs to get washed up for dinner, forcing himself to keep the limp to a minimum.

TOBY HADN'T BROKEN his ankle, but the next day it was abundantly clear that another trek into the woods anytime soon was out of the question. He'd be lucky to make it to school.

"HEY, CRIPPLE, HOW'S IT GOING?" asked Larry. Toby had been lost in thought as he took books out of his locker, and the bully's sudden appearance startled him so much that his history book fell to the floor. Larry laughed louder than merited by the humor of the situation as Toby reached down to retrieve it.

"Fine," said Toby, hoping he would just go away.

"What's that?"

"I said, fine."

"What's that? You said you were looking for somebody to kick your ass?"

This wasn't typical Larry behavior. He usually saved his intimidation attempts for more private settings. It wasn't his style to harass somebody right in the middle of the hallway—Toby's injured foot must have been boosting his courage.

"No."

"No what?"

"No, that's not what I said."

"Then what did you say?"

"I said fine."

"That's not what I heard. I heard that you want me to beat the shit out of you."

Toby sighed. Someday he'd like to get Owen on a leash, bring him to school, and turn him loose on jerks like Larry. He wouldn't be cruel—he'd pull Owen away before his jaws and talons got down to the bone.

Larry smacked him on the shoulder. Not too hard, but hard enough to jostle him a bit. "What are you looking at?"

"Nothing."

"Hey!" It was Sam Conley. He wasn't captain of the football team, but he was one of the more popular players. Toby didn't know what position he played.

Larry glared at him. "What?"

"What are you doing picking on a kid with a hurt foot? Pick on somebody who can fight back, you chickenshit."

"Screw you."

Toby glanced around. At least fifteen other kids were watching the altercation.

"You wanna start something with me?" Sam asked. "Because I'll be more than happy to finish it."

Larry stood there for a moment, trying unsuccessfully to stare him down. Then he shrugged. "Forget this. I've got better things to do."

"I'm sure you do."

Larry gave Toby a "you're dead" look and then walked away.

Toby's face felt as if a fly landing on it would burst into flame. It was almost more embarrassing to be rescued with everybody watching than to be bullied. Still, it couldn't hurt to have a football player on his side. "Thanks," he mumbled.

Sam regarded him with disgust. "Stick up for yourself, man. That's just pathetic."

Toby immediately imagined himself delivering a lengthy, profanity-laden monologue where he verbally reduced Sam to a pool of sizzling goo. Then he imagined the goo reconfiguring into the normal Sam, whom Toby proceeded to punch in the face repeatedly, accompanied by loud cheers and whistles from his classmates.

Instead, he said: "Whatever."

NEWS OF TOBY'S upcoming beating apparently reached eighty-five percent of the Orange Leaf High students before word made it to Toby himself. Reportedly, Larry and Nick planned to "meet" him right after school and administer a severe pounding as retribution for Larry's mild humiliation.

"I didn't do anything to them!" Toby protested, when a girl named Helen informed him of the afternoon schedule.

"They're still planning to get you," Helen said, in a tone that suggested "This is kind of worrisome and not nearly as funny as the idea of you having your head dunked in the toilet" but also "I plan to get good seats."

What was he supposed to do? Too many people were aware of the situation for him to sneak past the bullies after school, and getting a teacher involved wasn't an option. Unless Sam offered to do battle for him, which was unlikely, he was in serious trouble.

The rest of the day passed very, very slowly.

It wasn't as if there was a huge crowd gathered outside to witness his destruction, but there were certainly more kids lingering in the schoolyard than usual.

C'mon, Toby thought, *somebody had to have alerted a teacher to this.* Sure, given the choice most kids would opt to see a fight, but wasn't there even one peer who said something to an authority figure? Or were the teachers fully aware of what was happening and placing bets back in the teachers' lounge? He figured the odds against him were 1,500,000 to 1, but that would be one hell of a payout if he threw a lucky punch.

Toby kept his head up high and limped toward the sidewalk. Almost any other day, he gave thanks for the fact that he didn't have to take the bus. Today, he'd be more than happy to sit up front and be pelted with spitballs and boogers the entire ride.

As he walked off school grounds, he sensed that somebody was quickly coming up behind him. The amused reactions of the onlookers contributed to this perception. He didn't look back, just kept walking at his normal—that is, normal with a sprained ankle —pace, resisting the urge to run for it.

"Hey!" said Larry behind him.

Toby stopped walking and turned around. Nick was also with him. "What?"

"I didn't forget about what happened today."

"I didn't do anything."

"I think you did."

There had to be at least twenty kids watching, most of them the regulars who smoked just outside of school grounds. Normally, Larry had a look of sadistic pleasure on his face—now he just looked angry. Even a little twitchy. He clearly wasn't leaving before a punch was thrown.

Knowing that the violence was inevitable was strangely liberating for Toby. If he couldn't talk his way out of his problem, why not just say what he really felt? Yeah, it might increase the velocity and quantity of the punches, but did it really matter at this point?

"I didn't do anything," said Toby, speaking slowly and clearly. "I was at my locker, minding my own business. You walked over there and tried to intimidate me. When Sam came over, you chickened out and ran away. If you want to blame somebody for your cowardice, blame Sam, he's the one who scared you."

Toby inwardly cringed and braced himself for a punch.

Larry's look of anger deepened. "That's not how it happened."

"There were witnesses."

"Yeah, well, there are witnesses now who are gonna see me kick your ass into the ground."

"Uh-huh. They'll be really impressed. How come you have Nick with you? I weigh sixteen pounds. You should be able to handle me without a bodyguard."

"Are you *trying* to get hurt?" Larry asked.

"You've already made your decision. Your decision is to beat up somebody like me, because the only other way you'd win a fight is to start beating up girls." This sentence came out with a bit more of a self-insult than Toby had intended, but that was okay. He sensed some admiration from the spectators. Granted, there were fewer looks of admiration than looks of astonishment that he was digging his own grave in this manner.

"You weren't so brave when we dunked your head in the shitter," Larry said.

"I was trying not to laugh. When Nick was peeing, I almost lost it. I didn't know penises even came that small. It looked like one of those coffee stirrers."

Toby sensed that a very serious line had been crossed. He kind of wished he hadn't added the coffee stirrer part.

Both Larry and Nick drew back their fists at the same time.

Toby was aware of the phenomenon where time seemed to slow down at moments like these, but he'd never personally experienced such a thing. Yet time did indeed seem to slow down, and Toby imagined how this could be a turning point in his entire life.

Just before Larry's fist struck his chin, he'd block the punch with his palm. The color would drain from Larry's face as Toby wrapped his fingers around his fist. He'd catch Nick's fist in the same way. Both bullies would gape at him with their pale white faces and let out a simultaneous whimper.

"Please do not crush our hands!" Larry would beg.

But the time for pleading would have long since passed. Toby would wink at the audience of students, and then squeeze with but a mere fraction of his strength. Their hands would ooze through his fingers like Silly Putty. Nick would pass out from the excruciating pain, but Larry would hang on, eyes bugging out of his head.

"Have mercy," he'd whisper. "Please, Toby, show mercy to your inferiors."

And there would be mercy. But not for a few more minutes.

Toby's fantasy came to an abrupt end as his perception of the world—still moving in slow motion—narrowed to include only the sight of Larry's fist speeding toward his cheek.

The slow motion ended.

The punch felt like it split open the entire right side of Toby's face. He fell to the ground and instantly knew that any dignity he'd salvaged from this situation would soon be history, because there was going to be some crying involved. He couldn't even conceive of a punch to the face hurting this badly without brass knuckles involved. At least he'd only felt one punch—Nick had clearly missed.

The two bullies hovered over him. "Do you give up?" Larry asked.

Of course he gave up! Toby nodded.

Nick crouched down, grabbed Toby's arms, and pulled him to his feet. Then he wrenched Toby's arms behind him, holding him in front of Larry.

"Mess him up!" Nick urged.

Larry punched Toby in the stomach, so hard that he thought he was going to puke up his peanut butter and strawberry jelly sandwich from lunch. Instead, he dry-retched and tried unsuccessfully to find enough breath to beg Larry not to hit him again.

The next punch was to the left side of his face. There were a couple of audible gasps.

Another punch to the face. It felt like bone cracked.

Larry no longer looked simply angry. The expression on his face was wild, crazed, closer to insanity than fury. He punched Toby in the stomach again, and Toby realized that he genuinely meant to hospitalize him. Or kill him.

His protest was cut off by the blow to the jaw. Tears streamed down his cheeks, mixing with blood.

Yet another punch, and an actual scream from one of the girls watching. Spittle dangled from Larry's lower lip. He drew back his fist for another blow.

"Stop it!" Helen shouted. "This is way out of control!"

With the next punch, Toby felt consciousness starting to slip away.

"I said, stop it! You'll kill him!"

"Yeah, this is too much," said Nick, releasing Toby's arms. Toby felt as if he were floating in space for a moment, and then his face struck the ground. He just wanted to sleep.

"Fine, whatever," said Larry. He lifted his foot as if to stomp on Toby's skull, then apparently changed his mind and lowered it again. "Let's get out of here."

The bullies walked away. Toby lay on the ground, bleeding and crying and not really caring who judged him. He was vaguely aware of some classmates helping him up, and he may even have spoken to them as they helped him get home, but he couldn't be completely sure.

TOBY DIDN'T TELL his parents or the school principal who beat him up. He didn't need to. There were plenty of witnesses, and somebody (Toby hoped it was Helen, but he had no idea who it actually was) ratted about exactly who was involved.

Nick was suspended for a week. Larry was set to be expelled, but Larry and his parents made the case that Toby had instigated the conflict with his insults, so Larry's punishment was reduced to the same suspension that Nick received. He was also removed from the two classes that he shared with Toby. Toby was also out for a week—despite the sensation that his face had been mashed to frothy pulp, no bones were broken and there was nothing preventing him from returning to school except his grotesque swollen appearance. He'd tried to convince his parents that he needed another week of recovery time, but Dad thought it was best if things returned to normal as quickly as possible.

The morning that Toby returned to school, Dad took him aside.

"If you're in a fair fight, I expect you to fight fair," he said. "But if you're ever in a mess like that again, you kick that son of a bitch in the nuts so hard that they burst. Got it?"

"Yes, sir."

Toby went to school, not telling anybody that he was carrying a knife for protection.

6

Oddly enough, getting beaten almost to the point of disfigurement had a positive effect on his popularity. He would've thought that you needed to *win* a fight to gain social status from it, but apparently the Orange Leaf High student body felt that he'd sufficiently proven himself against two much stronger opponents. He wondered what would happen to him if he'd actually thrown and landed a punch. Class president?

After a couple of days, his newfound popularity faded a bit, and the number of students willing to talk to him dropped. But still, he no longer needed to leave the empty chair between himself and the people who shared his table at lunch, and J.D. stopped being such a jackass.

Two weeks after his pummeling, he felt well enough to bring some food to Owen.

HE'D FILLED his backpack with a variety of items, everything from a pork chop to a hard mint. He returned to his former vantage point outside of the cave and got the shotgun ready. "Hello, Owen!" he called out.

Nothing.

"Hello, Owen, Owen, Owen! It's me, Toby! Come on out! I've got some treats for you!"

Toby hoped he wasn't shouting at an empty cave. If Owen had moved on, that would be a serious bummer.

He called Owen's name a few more times, then moved on to Plan B. Instead of throwing rocks, he'd throw processed meat.

As he dug the package of bologna out of his backpack, Owen stepped out of the cave. The monster looked right at him, and its face seemed to light up, like Toby's grandmother when they'd visit her in the nursing home, before she died a couple of years ago. It moved forward, then stopped suddenly, as if realizing that its behavior was too intimidating. Toby kept the shotgun very much in mind, but didn't reach for it.

"Remember me?" he asked. Owen seemed to recognize him, but Toby was still pretty bruised up. Most likely that wouldn't matter—an animal like this would probably recognize him by smell. "It's your best friend Toby. Sorry I haven't been around, but for a while there, I was almost as ugly as you are."

He held up the package of bologna. "This is called baloney. It's made from parts of every animal you can think of. You'll like it." He peeled off the top slice and held it up. "I'm not sure if I'll be able to Frisbee this over to you, but we'll see." Toby decided that he probably should have tested its aerodynamic properties beforehand, so that it didn't splat onto the ground two feet in front of him and cause the monster to rush over. Fortunately, the light wind was at his back and he figured he should be able to throw it far enough to keep himself in the safety zone.

He flung the meat disc at Owen. It sailed through the air with much more accuracy than Toby would have expected, landing just a few feet in front of its target. Owen pounced upon it, impaled the bologna upon the talon of his index finger, then scooped it into his mouth.

It looked back at Toby. The message was clear: "More, please."

He threw the other slices of bologna at Owen, one after the other, with Owen stuffing them into his mouth as quickly as they landed. Toby was proud of himself—he was pretty good at the throw, and none of the slices hit trees.

When the last piece was consumed, Owen looked at Toby again. The message was even clearer this time: "More, *now*."

Toby threw the pork chop at it. "It's got a bone," he warned.

Owen chomped down on the pork chop, bone and all. He swallowed and looked at Toby expectantly.

Okay, the bologna and pork chop had been pretty safe bets. Now the real testing began. Toby took out a candy bar, unwrapped the foil, and held it up. "This is chocolate," he explained. "It's bad for dogs but I'm sure it's okay for you."

He tossed the chocolate at it. Owen devoured it with as much enthusiasm as he'd shown the meat, but then seemed to grimace.

"Not a fan of chocolate?" Toby asked. "It's good stuff."

Next up: an apple. A nice green Granny Smith one. Toby tossed it underhand to Owen, and let out a small yelp of amazement when the monster caught it. Owen held it between his fingers, inspecting it for about half a second, then popped the entire thing into its mouth. One crunch and a swallow later the apple was gone.

Owen enjoyed the other few pieces of food that Toby brought, particularly the raw bacon, which elicited what Toby took to be a smile. Owen gulped down the mint without chewing it. Toby took out his second-to-last item, a red-hot fireball candy, rolled it around in his palm for a moment, then decided not to push his luck and shoved it back into his pocket. He ended with a sure thing and tossed Owen a raw hamburger patty.

"That's all," he said, holding up his empty hand.

Owen let out a low growl. Toby wished he'd packed a little more food.

"I need to go," Toby told him. "I'll be back, though. I won't be able to bring as much stuff next time, but I'll definitely bring you a treat or two. Sound good?"

Owen continued to growl, and then licked his lips.

Toby waved. "Goodbye, Owen." He continued waving in a slow, exaggerated motion, hoping the monster would mimic him. After a few moments he decided that it wasn't going to happen and lowered his hand.

He turned and began to walk away. Then he heard shuffling behind him and knew that Owen was following him. He'd figured that this might be a risk, but hadn't quite determined how he was going to handle the situation if it happened. Worst-case scenario, he could point the shotgun at the monster again, though he'd avoid that if at all possible.

"No," he said, shaking his head. "You can't come. Stay by your cave. I'll be back some other day."

Owen gestured to his mouth. It was an eerily human gesture, although Toby wasn't familiar enough with primate behavior to know if apes or chimpanzees did this kind of thing on a regular basis.

"No more food. You ate it all." He wasn't sure what the universal gesture for "you already ate all the food" would be, so he mimed chewing and then held up his empty hands again. That didn't seem to get the point across. "All gone."

He took a step backwards. Owen took a step forward.

"Stay," Toby said, pointing at Owen. "Stay there. Or, you can have the entire rest of the forest except for the part I'm using to get home." He decided that he was saying too much and confusing the monster with his gibberish, so he repeated his previous command: "Stay."

Another step backward. This time Owen didn't follow him.

"Good," he said, continuing to slowly move away. "Very good, Owen."

When Owen was out of sight, Toby picked up his pace, just in case the monster changed its mind and tried to follow him again. On a purely scientific basis, he hadn't really learned much, except that Owen liked to eat most stuff, but it was a trip into the forest well worth making. He'd definitely be back.

———

As Toby dragged bags of kitty litter out of the grocery's stockroom, he realized that there were few things in the world more frustrating than having to work a stupid job when there was a fantastic creature in the forest just waiting for him.

"One of those bags is leaking," his boss, Mr. Zack, pointed out.

Toby looked back. The trail of kitty litter was about thirty feet long.

"Trying to mark your path so you don't get lost on the way back?" Mr. Zack asked with a smile.

"I'll clean it up."

———

He stood at his locker, trying to remember if he needed to bring home his history book or not, when Nick walked over.

"I need to talk to you," Nick said.

"You're not supposed to talk to me."

"Look, I don't blame you for being mad..."

"You don't *blame* me? Well, that's nice to know. I could barely sleep at night thinking that you might have negative thoughts about me. My conscience is cleared now."

"I'm trying to be serious. What we did went too far. Everybody knows it. We got punished."

"You got a dinky little slap on the wrist. One week suspension. Ooooooh, wow, I feel avenged!"

Nick let out a frustrated sigh. "I'm here to apologize, you little freak. Believe me, it's a lot harder for me to apologize than it is for you to forgive me."

Now Toby felt kind of bad, although it was a fleeting sensation and he quickly reverted to intense dislike. He needed more than an apology to forgive Nick. He needed bags of gold.

Still, there was no reason to get himself beat up again. "Okay, so apologize."

"I just did."

Toby was pretty sure he hadn't, but didn't dispute it. He supposed that having Nick *not* wishing him dead was better than the alternative.

"Okay. Apology accepted."

"But I need to warn you about something."

"What?"

"Larry. He's...there's something wrong with him. It's like he's obsessed or something. I'm afraid of what he might do to you."

"Seriously?" Social stigma or not, Toby wasn't going to just let Larry hunt him down. He'd tell a teacher, or his parents, or the cops if necessary, but he couldn't let fears about being dubbed a tattletale cost him his—

"No." Nick let out a mean-spirited chuckle. "He doesn't give a crap about a zit-faced loser like you. Don't be so gullible, Floren."

Toby had no response. He braced himself in case Nick intended to start throwing punches.

"By the way, somebody took a dump in your locker," said Nick, chuckling again as he walked away.

For a second, Toby considered flinging one of his textbooks at the back of Nick's head. The thick hardcover history book would leave one hell of a skull dent. But, no. It would cause far more trouble than it was worth.

He tried to think of something biting and clever to shout after him, something that the other kids would chant for the rest of Nick's high school career, but the best he could come up with was "Fatso!" And Nick wasn't overweight. So he remained silent.

Oh well. He didn't need friends like Nick anyway. He had Owen.

As Toby trudged through the forest, he wondered if considering Owen his friend was kind of sad. Even having a *human* friend who didn't talk and lived in a cave that took over an hour to walk to might be a little sad by itself. When you added the whole "monster in the woods" element, this might be absolutely pitiful. And scary.

Well...so what? It wasn't as if he and the monster were making babies. If he enjoyed coming out and throwing food to it, whose business was it of anybody else's? Except for maybe his parents, if things went terribly wrong and the monster devoured his intestines.

Screw 'em all. Especially Larry and Nick. He wished he could toss Nick's head over to Owen and see if he liked the taste better than chocolate.

Nah. If he was going to feed Owen, he should feed him something with higher nutritional content than Nick's head.

Behind him, in his peripheral vision, he thought he caught a glimpse of movement. His heart gave a jolt and he quickly looked over there, but saw nothing.

Relax. You're in the forest. Things move in the forest. Happens all the time. It's those eerie stillnesses that you've got to watch out for.

He kept walking. He had maybe a mile to go before he reached Owen's cave. Perhaps he could get Owen to relocate, find him a nice den of sticks or something.

More movement, from the same spot. He only saw the source of the movement for a fraction of a second, but it was enough to identify his follower.

Did Larry really think he was that oblivious?

Well, discounting the fact that Toby had walked this far into the forest without realizing he was being stalked...

He pretended not to have seen anything, then continued

walking. Now what? Call him out? Run after him with his hunting knife, screaming incoherently?

He decided to keep going and feign ignorance until he came up with a really good plan.

Somebody else moved. So he had both Larry and Nick after him. Crap. They must've been following from a much further distance and just now decided to sneak up closer.

No brilliant plans immediately sprung to mind. He needed something that would keep these psychos away from him forever.

Having a fanged, clawed, hairy beast jump out at them would be a pretty good deterrent against picking on him in the future, wouldn't it?

Oh, yeah.

But, no, of course he couldn't do that. Too many holes in the plan, and when it was time to reveal Owen's existence to the rest of the world, he'd much rather do it on his own terms instead of the terms of a couple of bullies with wet crotches on their pants running shrieking to the authorities.

"Toooooooby," said a ghostly voice behind him.

Damn.

"Toooooooby, why are you in the woods all aloooooone? Don't you know you can get huuuuuuurt?" It sounded like Larry, who was clearly behind a large oak about a hundred feet away.

"I'll call the cops."

"Using what? A tin can and string?" This was Nick, who was behind a different tree.

"You're not supposed to come near me," Toby said.

"We're not near you."

"You wanna go to jail? Is that it? Do you think I'm not gonna tell the cops that you followed me? Get the fuck out of here!"

"But Toooooooooby," said Larry. "That's not verrrrrrrry niiiiiiiice! You shouldn't use such ruuuuuuuuuude language!"

"I'll scream," Toby warned.

As the gales of laughter hit him, Toby wished he'd said just about anything else in the world but "I'll scream." *I'll scream?* Had those words really come out of his mouth? Not "I'll sic my monster buddy on you" or "I'll smash your heads together like overripe nectarines" but "I'll scream." Even with the potential of another severe beating looming, Toby couldn't help but focus on being absolutely mortified.

He quickly corrected himself. "I've got a knife," he said.

"You really think that scares us?" Larry asked.

"It should."

"It doesn't."

"You think I won't use it, but I will," said Toby. "It's self-defense. I won't get in any trouble."

Larry sneered. "Oh, yeah? Self-defend yourself against this." When his right hand came into view, he was holding a revolver.

7

A gun. Larry actually had a gun. What the hell was going on here? These were supposed to be bullies, not killers!

He glanced back at Nick to see his reaction to this insanity. Nick held a gun of his own, pointed right at Toby.

Toby wasn't sure how to react. To his surprise, he felt more anger than fear, although there was still plenty of fear. He wanted to simultaneously attack, cry, and, yes, scream.

Larry and Nick slowly walked toward him, guns raised, moving in such a deliberate manner that it almost looked choreographed. Should Toby run? There was plenty of tree cover, but he couldn't come close to outrunning them, and even with a lot of weaving he'd have a bullet in the back before he made it five hundred feet.

"Quit playing around," said Toby. "Those could go off. That's manslaughter."

"Only if it's an accident."

They couldn't really intend to shoot him. It just wasn't possible. The whole situation was out of control, but it wasn't *that* far out of control, was it? Though he'd brainstormed quite a few ways he could die, being hunted as human prey by two of his classmates wasn't one that had ever occurred to him.

"What are you going to do?" he asked.

"We're going to make you pay," Nick said.

"You'll go to jail."

"Not if they don't find your body."

"They'll know it was you."

"You think so? I'm not so sure. I bet you didn't think we'd come after you with guns, did you?"

"And my dad's got connections," said Larry.

They continued walking toward him. Toby wasn't even able to fantasize of a scenario where he heroically defeated the two villains. If they were serious, he was dead.

But of course they weren't serious. They couldn't be.

"Get down on your knees," said Larry.

Toby shook his head. "No."

"You know what would get you down on your knees fast? A bullet. Have you ever seen somebody's kneecap shatter?"

"There's bone and blood everywhere," Nick said.

"It's horrific."

"It's disgusting."

"And it really, really hurts."

"You won't do it," Toby insisted. "I'm not stupid."

"What's more stupid?" Larry asked. "Falling for a joke, or getting shot in the knees because you were too dumb to realize that we meant what we said?"

It was a solid point. At the same time, there was a very large chance that Larry and Nick were just playing around, and a very small chance that they genuinely intended to shoot him if he didn't comply. Before he gave them yet more fodder for ridicule, he was going to make absolutely sure that—

"On. Your. Knees." Larry's eyes looked cold and dead.

Toby knelt down on the ground. Now he was absolutely terrified.

Larry and Nick walked over to him. "Let's see how smart you are," said Larry. "Do you know what it means to put your hands behind your head, execution-style?"

Toby nodded. *Oh, God...*

"So do it."

Toby put his hands behind his neck, threading his fingers together. "There's nothing funny about this," he said. "All it's going to do is get you in a ton of trouble. You'll be expelled."

"Expelled for murder? That's not such a big punishment."

"I meant expelled for the joke."

"What joke?"

"Guys, come on..."

"Why don't you take some time to pray?" Larry asked. "That's what they do when they're about to die, right? They pray. Go on, Toby, pray."

"Out loud," said Nick. "We want to hear it."

Toby hesitated, then spoke in a whisper. "Dear God, who art in heaven, hallowed be thy name, please let these assholes realize the error of their ways..."

"Oh, now, see, you messed up a perfectly good prayer," said Larry. "Now we want you to beg."

"No."

"Beg for your life."

"I'm not doing that."

"I bet you will," said Larry, pressing the barrel of his gun against Toby's forehead. Toby felt like he was going to throw up but choked down the urge. "Beg me not to kill you."

"No."

"Do it." Larry raised his voice to a falsetto. "'Oh, please, Larry, don't shoot me in the head.' Say it."

Toby remained defiantly silent.

"Then how about 'Oh, please, Larry, don't shoot me in the stomach, because that would hurt a lot worse.' I bet you can say that."

"No."

"No. No. No. You sound like a broken record. If you don't want to say anything, that's fine. Just close your eyes. Close your eyes and count to ten."

"No."

"*Stop saying that!*" Larry shouted with enough ferocity that Toby nearly lost his balance. "*I've got a goddamn gun to your head, and you need to start taking this seriously! Now close your eyes!*"

Toby didn't close his eyes. He just couldn't.

"On the count of ten, you're going to die," said Larry. "Are you ready?"

"Let's do it on five," Nick suggested.

"Okay, five. Five seconds left to live. That's got to be scary."

"Five..." Nick began.

"Four..."

"*Threetwoone!*" Nick shouted. Both of them pulled the triggers at the same time. Both guns clicked.

Both of the bullies howled with laughter. Larry placed his foot on Toby's shoulder and shoved him onto his back. "I can't believe you fell for that! You actually thought we were going to blow your head off! How stupid can one person be?"

Toby was so relieved not to be dead that he was having trouble being furious. But as they continued laughing, Toby felt his relief fading and his rage rising. He sat up.

"I'm going to the cops," he said.

That made Larry and Nick laugh even harder, if such a thing was possible.

"I mean it."

"Yeah? Will that be before or after you run home crying to Mommy?"

Nick, who was practically doubled over, cackled as if that was the most hilarious insult ever to pass somebody's lips. Toby couldn't remember ever having felt such rage. He wanted to gouge his thumbs into Larry's eyes and rip his head right off his body.

Instead, he settled for tackling Larry. He didn't care if it meant he was going to get beat up again. He needed to get in one punch. Just one good punch.

"Hey, whoa," said Larry, still laughing as they crashed to the ground. "Kind of violent there, aren't you?"

Toby punched him.

It wasn't that hard of a punch, and it got Larry in the shoulder instead of the face, but it definitely made Toby feel better even as his fist exploded with pain.

Larry's return punch got him right in the nose. The *crunch* and immediate gush of blood proved that Larry's punch had done a lot more damage than Toby's. The pain was so intense that Toby's vision blurred.

He slammed his fists down upon Larry, as hard and quickly as he could. Larry seemed far more amused than hurt, and deflected the countless blows with minimal effort. Nick apparently thought this was the funniest part yet, and even Larry continued to chuckle.

Larry grabbed Toby's nose and gave it a pinch.

The laughter suddenly stopped.

Toby didn't remember taking out the hunting knife, or pulling it out of its leather sheath. But Larry now looked really frightened.

Gripping the handle with both hands, Toby slammed the blade deep into Larry's chest.

For a fraction of a second, it felt almost euphoric. Then the reality of what he'd just done struck him, and he cried out in horror. "*Oh God, I'm sorry...I didn't...oh God...*"

Larry lay there, eyes wide open in shock, body twitching. Toby wasn't a doctor, but he knew exactly where he'd plunged the blade, and you didn't survive when you had an eight-inch hunting knife protruding from your heart.

"*Oh God...oh Jesus...*"

He looked up at Nick, as if for help. Nick had his hand over his mouth and looked as if he were hyperventilating. There was no more scorn in the bully's eyes—just pure panic. Toby knew his own panic was even worse. He just wanted to curl up into a tight little ball and scream and scream and scream.

But he couldn't do that.

Larry was dying. He couldn't be saved. Maybe not even if there was an ambulance parked ten feet away, and definitely not all the way out here in the woods. No matter what he did to try to fix things, he'd *murdered* somebody. There was a bloody corpse on the ground next to him and *he'd* made it.

Nick was the only one who knew what he'd done.

If he let Nick leave this forest alive, Toby was going to jail.

He couldn't spend the rest of his life in prison. Not for somebody as cruel and worthless as Larry.

Toby wrenched the knife out of Larry's chest. He couldn't look at the blade, couldn't see the blood or he'd go insane and not be able to do this.

There was no time for apologies or explanations. He had to move fast, get Nick while he was still in a state of shock. Toby rushed at the larger boy, feeling his rage return, rage at Nick for making this happen, for destroying his life. The rage felt a lot better than the fear, the helplessness.

Nick turned and ran.

In a voice that sounded muffled, as if he were speaking from inside a casket, Toby reassured him, promised him that everything was going to be okay, that he wasn't going to hurt him, that Larry was fine. As Nick got further away, Toby pleaded with him, did the begging he'd refused to do at gunpoint, said things that made no sense.

Nick fell to the ground.

Had Toby thrown the knife? No, it was still in his hand. Nick had just tripped, that's all.

Toby couldn't even feel his foot as he ran over to the fallen boy. He swung down at him, jabbing the blade into the open palm Nick held up to defend himself. Toby stabbed again and again, the blade slashing Nick's arms, his chest, his face. It took Toby a long time to stop.

He was covered with blood. Dripping with it. If he watched this scene from the outside, he'd be filled with revulsion at the boy with the knife. The deranged boy. The ghoulish boy. The psycho boy, drenched with red, the murderous little animal that should be shot in the head and dragged away, so that the sight of him wouldn't horrify onlookers.

Finally he crawled away from Nick, leaving the knife in the bully's throat, and vomited.

What had he done?

It hadn't happened. There weren't two dead kids lying in the woods with him. There was no possible reality where that could be true.

He was a killer.

He'd murdered Larry and Nick. It wasn't even self-defense.

Toby looked back at Nick's body, waiting for Nick to sit up, wipe the fake blood off his chin, and let out a shrill laugh at the uproarious practical joke they'd played. "Stop being so gullible, Floren! We aren't really dead! A little runt like you could never kill us!"

Nick remained dead on the ground.

Toby rubbed his hands in the dirt, trying to get the blood off. He scooped up a handful of dirt and rubbed it on his arms and on his face, desperate to hide the red. He wiped off the mud but a crimson stain remained on his skin.

Why had he brought the knife? Why had he even brought the fucking thing in the first place?

He bit down on his wrist to keep from screaming. Screaming was bad. Screaming brought people.

He just wanted to die.

No. No, he didn't. He'd get through this.

Larry and Nick were horrible people. They deserved to die. Even worse than the way they had. A slow, lingering, agonizing death was the way they should have gone, so Toby was doing them a favor. The world was better off without them. They contributed nothing but misery. It was their own fault. Stalking him through the woods—you take a huge risk when you do something like that. You put your life in danger. It wasn't his fault.

And they deserved it. They completely deserved it.

He was a murderer. A cold-blooded murderer. A criminal.

He took a deep breath. He had to calm down. Had to figure this out. It was done—he couldn't take it back, so now he just had to figure out how to get away with it.

The blood-splattered boy. The crazy-eyed boy. The cackling, maniacal, don't-let-your-children-get-too-close boy.

Think.

Did anybody know where they were? If you were following some kid into the forest with a gun, unloaded or not, would you tell your parents where you were headed? Unlikely. They'd want to be able to deny it later. So they'd either not told anybody, or they lied. This was good.

His nose was still bleeding, but he just let the blood flow.

The boy they should put in a cage, so people could poke him with sticks.

Had anybody seen them go into the forest? No way to know. If they cut through his yard and his mom was in the living room, she might have seen them, but only if she happened to be facing the window. She knew what Larry and Nick looked like and what they'd done—she wouldn't let them just wander into the woods without saying something.

So there was a very good chance that nobody knew where they were.

The demonic boy. The hellbound boy.

Stop it!

If he hid the bodies well enough, he might be okay.

This was a vast forest. Millions of places to hide a body.

But could he hide it well enough to keep it from the police and their dogs? If he buried them deep enough, maybe, but...

What if he fed them to Owen? Owen would probably pick the bones clean, if he didn't eat those as well. And, worst-case scenario, if the bones were found, the authorities would think that Larry and Nick met their ghastly fate at the claws and jaws of a never-before-seen monster.

You can't let Owen take the blame for this. He's your friend.

Jesus Christ, what was he thinking? Of course he could let Owen take the blame for this! He was a wild animal.

Anyway, the remains would never be found. He'd make sure of it. It was far from a foolproof plan, but it was the best he had for the moment, save for marching over to the police station and confessing everything. That wouldn't end well.

If he had time to sit around, mulling his options in a leisurely fashion, he'd probably come up with something better, but right now he had to move quickly. He couldn't do this in the dark, and he couldn't risk leaving the bodies out overnight. Larry and Nick would be missed by bedtime. So the best course of action was to feed the corpses to Owen.

Could he even bring himself to do such a thing?

Yeah. If he could stab them to death, he could feed them to an animal.

There was a problem with the plan, though. Well, there were lots of problems, but one particularly big one: He couldn't drag their bodies out to the cave. Not even one of them by sundown, much less both. So he had to bring Owen to them.

He needed bait.

TOBY WALKED DOWN THE PATH. He held the bottom of his shirt out in front of him, like a little girl carrying blueberries that she'd picked. Piled in the makeshift sack were twenty severed fingers.

The fingers had been difficult to cut off until he got into the

73

proper rhythm, and he'd originally wanted to use simple strips of flesh, which were easier to slice away. But the first strip leaked badly and came apart in his hands. He needed something firmer, to avoid leaving traces along the path to the cave. So he went with fingers.

Bite-sized, he thought, but was unable to amuse himself.

When he reached the cave entrance, there was no sign of Owen. It was going to be a pretty rotten night if the monster had finally moved on to greener pastures, but he'd remain optimistic.

He held his shirt up with his left hand, and selected an index finger—Nick's, he thought—with his right. His gag reflexes kicked in, even though he thought he would've been over that by the sixteenth or seventeenth digit he cut through with the hunting knife. He flung the finger at the cave, but the throw went wild, landing a good twenty feet off the mark.

He stared at the spot where it landed, marking it clearly in his mind. He'd have to make sure he retrieved it later. He'd do it now, but he didn't want to walk that close to the cave until he was certain of Owen's whereabouts.

"Owen!" he called out. "I'm here with food!" He should've announced himself before the first throw. He couldn't afford to waste fingers.

Owen emerged from the cave, looking sleepy. Toby hurriedly selected another finger, a ring finger this time, though without an actual ring on it, and tossed to him. Owen caught it in his hand, stared at it for a second, then popped it into his mouth.

"Was it good? Was it delicious?" Toby asked, slowly backing away. Owen seemed to agree that it was indeed delicious and followed him. Toby's hope was that Owen would follow him at the same pace that he was walking, and not stampede over to him to get the rest of the fingers. There was a definite level of trust here. And probably stupidity.

He tossed Owen another finger as he continued moving backwards along the path. The monster caught this one in his mouth. He was pretty good at that. If he got caught, maybe he could pay for his legal defense by charging people to watch Owen do tricks.

Focus. Concentrate. This is serious stuff.

Owen followed him, step by step, for about twenty feet. Then Owen let out a soft growl. Toby tossed him another finger. At this rate, he wasn't going to make it anywhere close to where the dead bodies lay. He had to ration them.

He couldn't walk backwards the entire way back, obviously, so he switched to a sideways step that allowed him to keep track of Owen and the uneven ground. After another twenty feet or so, Owen let out another growl.

"Not yet," Toby said. "You'll get more, lots more, I promise. Just be patient."

Owen growled louder.

"No." Toby shook his head. "Don't growl. Just follow."

He kept moving without throwing another finger. Owen followed him at the same pace, and didn't seem ready to pounce upon him to get the meal sooner.

"Good boy," Toby said. "Very good. Keep this up and you'll get all kinds of scrumptious, yummy treats."

The plan worked well enough that by the time Toby reached the bodies, he still had four fingers left. He tossed them to Owen, one after the other. His stomach never stopped churning.

"Here," he said, pointing to Larry's mutilated body. "Dinner for you."

He quickly moved back, giving Owen plenty of room. The monster walked toward him a few steps, as if unsure what Toby was trying to say, and then saw the corpse. Owen dropped down to all fours over the body and thrust his face down onto Larry's stomach.

Toby quickly turned away. It wasn't enough. The sounds of ripping and chewing made him fall to his knees, dry heaving.

Could Owen eat all of this?

Not in one sitting, but he didn't think that a creature so obviously hunger-driven would leave the bodies to rot. He'd take them with him, right? Toby had no idea. He might have totally screwed up his plan by doing this, but he sure as hell wasn't going to try to take Owen's meal away from him.

There really wasn't anything he could do at this point except hope that Owen liked to clean his plate.

8

———————

Toby lay in an excruciatingly cold creek, letting the water rush over him for several minutes, hoping it would take the blood away.

———————

HE COULDN'T THINK of a good way to explain away his appearance beyond "I fell in a creek." Fortunately, Mom and Dad were in the kitchen when he came through the back door, and Toby hurried across the living room before either of them saw him.

"Toby...?" Mom asked.

"Gotta go to the bathroom! It's an emergency!" Toby said, rushing up the stairs.

He wadded his wet clothes up in a tight ball and hid them in the back of his closet. Tomorrow he'd burn them.

The broken nose he explained as a nasty fall. Mom and Dad both looked doubtful and questioned him relentlessly, but he insisted that it was a result of his own clumsiness, and that nothing would make him happier than to have them give Larry and Nick's parents a call if the bullies had been the ones to injure him, but this time it was his own fault. They seemed to reluctantly believe his story.

He didn't expect to have an appetite for dinner, but instead he was ravenous. He also didn't expect to be able to sleep, but exhaustion beat out guilt and he was asleep minutes after climbing into bed.

The nightmares, however, were rapid-fire images of knives and blood and sharp teeth.

NEWS OF LARRY and Nick's disappearance had spread through the student body before classes even started for the day, and Toby wasn't surprised to find himself pulled out of first period history within two minutes of the bell. Mrs. Pendle, the secretary, took him into the principal's office, where two police officers sat. One had a thick mustache and a friendly smile, while the other was clean-shaven and wore a scowl. Good cop, bad cop.

After some polite introductions by the good cop, the bad cop spoke: "When was the last time you saw Larry Gaige?"

"Yesterday after school, when he broke my nose."

The bad cop raised an eyebrow. Toby had decided that trying to hide his adversarial relationship with Larry and Nick would be a mistake. Everybody knew about it. Pretending that they were friends would raise suspicion. Better to be open about his dislike— after all, he wouldn't be telling the cops that he hated the dead kids if he was the one who stabbed them to death, right?

If his parents discovered the discrepancy in his story, he'd just say that he'd been embarrassed to admit that he'd been beaten up yet again.

"And why did he do that?" asked Bad Cop.

Toby shrugged. "Because he and Nick are jerks." He'd mentally rehearsed this on his way to school. *Are* jerks. Not *were* jerks.

"You saw him with Nick Wyler?"

"Yeah."

"When?"

"After school. They came into my backyard, started threatening me. Then Larry punched me."

"Did you fight back?"

"Not really." Toby tried to look suitably ashamed of his own physical inadequacies. "They're big guys—both of them. If I'd had a baseball bat I would've bashed them in the face, but I didn't, so… well, there's a reason guys like that pick on guys like me."

"It doesn't sound like you liked them very much."

"I don't. They're bullies." *Not gonna catch me using past tense, Bad Cop.* "You heard about what they did to me before, right?"

Bad Cop nodded. "We did. Why do you think they did that, Toby?"

"I just said why. They're bullies. That's what bullies do. Didn't you have them when you were in school?"

Bad Cop ignored the question. "What else can you tell me about what happened?"

"Not much. I was outside doing my homework, they came up and started saying 'You're dead, Floren!' I tried to get back inside but they wouldn't let me pass, and then Larry punched me. They laughed their asses off and left."

"Any idea where they might be?"

"Antarctica, hopefully. Don't get me wrong, I don't wish them dead or anything like that, but I'm not going to sit here and tell you that we got along and that I hope everything is fine. They've made my life pretty miserable."

The officers nodded, although Toby couldn't tell if it was a nod of understanding or a nod of "We've got our killer." "One last question," Bad Cop asked. "Did Larry say anything about his parents?"

"Not to me."

"Okay. If you think of anything else, tell your principal and she'll get in touch with us. We'll let you get back to class now. I know you've got a test this morning."

Crap! He'd forgotten about the history test!

"Thanks," he said, and returned to class. He was amazed at how easily the lies had come, considering that he usually couldn't even successfully lie about drinking one of Dad's cans of Coke. He wasn't proud of this, but he was certainly relieved.

Right before third period, everybody was marched into the assembly room. The principal explained that two students had gone missing, and that anybody who had any information should share it with her as soon as possible. Then all of the students were asked to close their eyes and silently pray for Larry and Nick's safe return. Toby took that time to pray that his crimes wouldn't be discovered.

By lunchtime, Toby had heard most of the story. Larry and his parents had been fighting in a big way ever since he got suspended. For years he'd been threatening to run away to New York City, and he'd apparently left a note on the kitchen table saying that he'd done just that. Two guns were missing from his dad's collection.

Wow. So he and Nick had probably stopped by Toby's place for one last bit of cruelty before running away from home. That would explain why they were willing to risk pointing guns at him in the woods, even empty ones, knowing that they'd almost certainly get expelled for it.

What did Larry want in New York City? To be an actor? A singer? To just wander the busy streets? He'd never envisioned Larry as having any ambitions beyond beating up kids smaller than him.

Why was Nick going with him? They must have had a pretty strong friendship.

Screw them. Screw both of them. They deserved to be digesting in Owen's stomach right now. If they were going to run away to New York City, then they might as well have been killed by Toby, who had a legitimate grudge against them, instead of some random drug dealer.

Justify it all you want. You're still a murderer.

Toby spent the rest of the day lost in fantasies where the knife got stuck in its sheath. Larry and Nick pointed at him and laughed while he fumbled around, trying unsuccessfully to withdraw the blade. They left him in the woods, enjoying a good hearty chuckle at his incompetence.

He called in sick at the grocery and walked out into the woods, hoping that the bodies were gone. *Please, please, please let Owen have cleaned up my mess.* It didn't have to be flawless—he just didn't want to find dozens of body parts strewn amongst the trees.

Except for some bloodstains, Larry and Nick were gone. Toby almost cried with relief.

Though he wanted to walk to Owen's cave to investigate, he also wanted to spend as little time in the woods as possible until things calmed down. Thanks to the "runaway" element, the police wouldn't be searching the forest for corpses. They'd be trying to find motorists who might have picked up a couple of unpleasant hitchhikers. Toby was far from safe, but he was much better off than he was yesterday. He walked back through the woods into his backyard.

Then he remembered the severed finger he'd left behind, cursed, and headed back into the forest.

It was still there. He felt intense revulsion as he picked it up, despite having handled severed fingers galore yesterday. It just wasn't something you got used to, and now the finger had a fairly rank odor. He brushed off the tiny ants that swarmed over the parts that had no skin, and then—

Owen stood in the cave entrance, looking at him.

This was the closest Toby had ever been to the monster. Not

close enough for Owen to reach out and slit Toby's throat with one of his talons, but close enough that Owen could be upon him in seconds. Close enough that he could see that one of Owen's talons was split, and that he had a tiny bare patch over his left eye.

Toby was much less scared than he would have anticipated. "Hi, Owen," he said.

The monster rushed at him.

Dear God, he hadn't fed it enough. Even two dead bodies weren't enough to quell its ancient hunger. Toby was going to be ripped to shreds, scraps of flesh flying high into the air as Owen tore him apart, hunting for the tastiest pieces. His skeleton would be dragged away and dumped into a bone pit. And because he was a double murderer, he was hellbound for certain.

Owen stopped just inches from Toby. The monster lowered its head, and then rubbed its forehead against Toby's chest. Affectionately.

Toby didn't know what to do, so he stroked the fur on Owen's arm. Owen made a sound that wasn't exactly a purr, but was definitely a *happy* sound. It was kind of like a growl without hostile intent.

"You're welcome for the food," Toby said.

THE SENSE of guilt was huge, almost unbearable at times, but no matter how bad the nightmares got, and no matter how much it felt like something was eating away at his stomach from the inside, he couldn't deny that life at school was much more pleasant with those creeps dead.

He could go to the restroom without fear. He wasn't constantly worrying about being humiliated. If he could go back in time and change his murderous actions, he would, no doubt about it, but still, not having Larry and Nick around was kind of nice.

And after about a week, he started to realize that he just might get away with it.

He'd been questioned once more, this time by the good cop working alone. It wasn't much of an interrogation, just a couple of follow-up questions that didn't even require Toby to lie. No, he hadn't seen Larry or Nick in the past week. No, they hadn't tried to get in touch.

It poured rain three days that week, almost as if the heavens were trying to help wash away the evidence.

Soon, Larry and Nick stopped being a daily topic of conversation at school. Though the "Missing" signs with their pictures stayed up on telephone poles, the signs faded and weren't replaced. Toby wanted to tear them down so he wouldn't have to see them, but didn't dare take the risk of somebody seeing him. A transfer student took Larry's empty seat in economics class.

He still saw blood on his hands that wasn't really there. But overall, it was a better world without those bullies.

"What are you drawing?" asked J.D.

Toby shrugged. "Nothing."

J.D. reached across the table and snatched Toby's notebook. "Ooooh, a big scary monster! That's what I used to draw when I was in first grade, too! Hey, Elizabeth, check this out..."

9

"Don't look at me like that. You know I can't get out here every day. It's not my fault you don't have any other friends. If you'd get out of the cave once in a while, you might get to socialize more often, you know? Meet a nice elk or something, get some interspecies lovin' going on. Where's your Owenetta?"

Owen patted his belly.

"You ate her? Really? That's pretty darn rude. You're not supposed to eat your mate, unless maybe you're a black widow or something."

Owen patted his belly again, more insistently this time.

"Okay, okay, I was only kidding. Jeez. I know you're hungry. And today I've got a special surprise for you." Toby tapped his foot on the blue cooler. "You'd better like it, because this ice was *heavy.*"

He took the lid off the cooler, pushed aside some of the ice cubes, and pulled out the carton of ice cream. "This is Neapolitan," he explained, "so you get chocolate, vanilla, and strawberry all at once. You'll love it."

Owen reached for the carton. Toby slapped his hand away.

"Not yet. We've got to do this right." He took a pair of ice cream cones out of his backpack. "All right, one of them broke, but since I'm such a nice person I'll give you the unbroken one." He dug around until he found the metal scoop, then opened the carton. Owen growled.

"Have a little patience. Good things come to those who wait. How many monsters in the woods do you think have people bringing them ice cream? Not many. You are a fortunate soul, Owen, and when you taste this delicious treat, all of your problems are going to fade away."

It was jacket weather, but no snow had fallen yet, and even in the cooler, the ice cream was starting to melt. It was easy to get out a nice big scoop. Toby made sure he got all three flavors, and then plopped it onto the cone.

"Here you go, sir," he said, handing the cone to Owen. "Don't eat it too fast or you'll get a headache."

Toby was somewhat less than surprised when Owen popped the entire cone into his mouth. Owen's eyes widened, as much as his sunken eyes were capable of widening, and then he gave Toby an enthusiastic thumbs-up sign.

"Yeah, it's good stuff, isn't it?" asked Toby. "It's better if you savor it, though."

He prepared himself a cone, just strawberry, and slowly licked it. "See? Lick. It's way better like this, and it lasts more than a third of a second."

Owen made a grab for Toby's cone, but he held it behind his back. "No. There's more, but you have to wait until I'm done with mine. You know that."

Owen patted his belly.

"Seriously, you need to chill out about this whole food thing. I'm hungry, too, but you don't see me trying to shove you around to get fed. We need to develop your gourmet tastes. Any animal can just shovel food into its mouth. You should learn to appreciate fine cuisine. Like this ice cream cone." He turned it in a slow circle as he licked.

Owen watched him carefully, not taking his eyes off the cone.

"Stick your tongue out," Toby said, sticking his tongue out as far as he could.

Owen continued to stare at the ice cream.

"Come on, do it," Toby urged, his words garbled because his tongue was sticking out. He waggled his tongue and pointed at it with his free hand. "Let's see that tongue!"

Owen tilted his head a bit, and then stuck out his tongue.

"Good job!" said Toby. He handed his ice cream cone to Owen. Owen tossed the entire thing into his mouth.

Toby prepared himself another ice cream cone. "Lick," he said. "Just lick. Savor the smooth, creamy goodness." He slowly licked the ice cream. "Like this. See how I'm doing it?"

Owen moved his tongue in a licking motion.

"That's right! You've got it!" He gave Owen this ice cream cone as well. "Now remember: Lick."

Owen ate the entire cone in one bite.

After one more try, Toby gave up and just let Owen eat the rest of the ice cream directly from the carton.

"Wow, THIS IS REALLY GROSS," said Toby, trying to pull a comb through Owen's thick matted hair. "You've got bugs in here. Did you know that? Bugs. How can you not be constantly itching? This would drive me crazy."

It took all afternoon to get Owen's arms into decent shape, and Toby wasn't sure that he was ever going to get the tangles out of the monster's back. "I think that once we get this done the first time, it won't be that tough to keep it up," he said. "But right now I'm thinking we should just shave you."

Owen continued his semi-purring. He clearly enjoyed the

process, except for the moments where the comb tugged his hair too hard.

"By the way, I've told you this before, lots of times, but your aroma isn't everything it could be. It's a level of reek you don't usually get from things that are still alive. Next time I may bring some shampoo. And some mouthwash. That might take care of your romantic problems, don't you think? There's nothing that can be done for me, but I think an Owen that doesn't stink to high heaven might attract the lady monsters. We'll see."

The comb caught on a particularly gnarled section of fur, but Toby carefully and patiently worked the teeth through until the knot was gone.

"'THE BULLETS TORE through the side of the armored car like it was tissue paper,'" said Toby, reading aloud from the thin paperback. "'The driver flopped over, bleeding from three different head wounds. Outside of the now out-of-control vehicle, the hostages screamed as it hurtled toward them, tires squealing.'"

Toby was sure that Owen didn't understand the plot, but he seemed to enjoy being read to, particularly when Toby laced the reading with sound effects. He mimicked the sound of an armored car plowing into a crowd of six tied-up hostages.

THEY MADE up lots of new games. Owen had trouble understanding most of the rules, but even something generic like Twenty Questions was a lot more interesting when playing it with a hideous monster. Tag was a little too dangerous and was discontinued after one session.

88

"Let's try it again. *Owen. Owe-wen.* Say it."

Owen silently stared at him.

"C'mon, you can do it. *Owen. Oooowwwwen.* Say your name."

Owen contorted his mouth and made a low, growly noise that sounded nothing like his name.

Toby gave him a thumbs-down sign. "You're not getting it. *Owen.* Just start with '*Owe.' Owe.*"

"*Ahh-ehh.*"

"Better, sort of. A little disturbing, but definitely on the right track. Let's keep trying. *Owen. Owe-wen.*"

"You know what he did?" Toby asked. "So I'm sitting there at lunch, and he asks to see what I'm writing, like he always does. You'd think he'd have outgrown that by now—we're sophomores, right? But no, he tries to grab my notebook, and I yank it away, and I knock over my can of root beer. And everybody in the cafeteria starts applauding, and J.D. is laughing as if it wasn't his fault! I wanted to make him eat the can. I swear, Owen, sometimes I'd like to just bring you to school and turn you loose."

Owen walked back into his cave.

"Oh, well, gee, *that's* not rude or anything! Sure, just walk away while I'm sharing my personal misery with you."

He'd never quite worked up the nerve to walk back into Owen's cave. He was very comfortable around Owen, but still...walking into a dark, narrow cave with a monster didn't seem like a particularly good idea. Out in the open, he at least had some potential for running to safety if Owen went wild. In the cave, he was dead for sure.

"Okay, well, I guess I'll go home now," he announced. "Thanks for lending a supportive ear. I appreciate it."

Owen walked back out of the cave. He held a skull.

The lower jaw was missing, and there was a pretty large crack in the center of the cranium, but apart from that the skull was intact. Any flesh or hair that might have been on it was completely gone. Toby had no way to be certain exactly whose skull it was, but he was pretty sure that he could narrow it down to one of two people.

Owen extended the skull toward him.

"Uh-uh," said Toby. "That was a one-time thing. I mean a two-time thing. It's never going to happen again."

He could do it, though. Figure out a reason to lure J.D. out into the woods, show him the cave, and let Owen have another hearty meal. Then Toby could draw whatever he wanted in peace.

Owen tapped the skull against Toby's chest, as if urging him to take it. Toby recoiled.

"Stop it. You don't get to eat anybody else. I'm lucky I'm not in prison right now, and you're lucky you're not in a zoo. Why do you still have that thing? Bury it or eat it or something, okay?"

Owen prodded him again.

"Not a chance. I'm not going to bring anybody to you, and I'm sure as hell not going to stab anybody again. Do you want to know how often I see their bloody faces? Every goddamn night. I used to have cool fantasies. I used to pretend I was zapping aliens. Now I just keep thinking about what I did. Did you know that I can hardly even think about girls? I'm serious. I'm not sorry they're dead, don't get me wrong, but I'm going to be dealing with this for the rest of my life. So find your own meal."

He yanked the skull out of Owen's hand. He couldn't trust his friend to properly hide it again. He'd just bury it on the way home.

"I'm sorry, I don't mean to flip out on you, but that part of my life is over, okay? Still friends, right?" He forced a smile and gave Owen a thumbs-up gesture.

Owen tapped the skull with his talon.

"Friends, right?" Toby repeated.

Owen returned the thumbs-up gesture.

"Good. I have to get home. See you tomorrow."

As Toby walked home with the skull, he realized that he'd most likely inadvertently communicated to Owen that yes, he would indeed bring another human for him to prey upon. Damn it.

"WHEN ARE WE GONNA GET THERE?" J.D. asked, as they walked through the forest three weeks later. It was a slow process now that there was snow on the ground, but it hadn't snowed in the past few days so Toby's path was still there, making it easier.

"In a while."

"I swear, if you're dragging me out here to go all homo on me, I'm going to tell everyone."

"Just shut up until we get there."

"Why are you being such a dick? You're the one who wanted me to come with you."

"Look, we've been enemies for long enough. I think it's time we should try to be friends, that's all."

"You already said that," J.D. noted. "You're a creepy little bastard. Did anybody ever tell you that?"

"Come on. You're slowing down."

"I'm going to stop is what I'm going to do. I have way better things to do than let you lure me into the woods in the freezing cold and then whip it out."

"It'll be worth it when we get there, so quit whining."

"I'm not the one behaving like a elementary school kid. 'Waaah, we should be friends, let's go out and play, waaah!' What a complete waste you are."

"Then why are you here?"

"Because I'm curious about how much of a loser you are. You're probably taking me out to see your art collection. Ooooh, robots and monsters and fairies and shit!"

Toby couldn't wait to watch Owen bite into this jerk. Hopefully he wouldn't kill him on the first chomp—Toby would have to somehow encourage him to start with the extremities.

Scream loud, J.D. We'll be too deep in the woods for anybody to hear you.

He stopped walking.

What the hell was he doing?

"Go back home," he said.

"What?"

"Go away. We're done."

"Seriously? You dragged me out here for nothing?"

"Yes. Fuck off."

J.D. snorted in disbelief. "I can't believe you. You are a creepy, nerdy, zit-faced little freak. Go back to the circus."

"I will. Fuck off and die."

"God, you're a loser," J.D. muttered as he walked back the way they came.

Toby knew he was a loser. He was fine with that. But the fact that he was ready to feed another classmate to Owen scared the hell out of him.

10

1963. Age 18.

Toby tossed his graduation cap high into the air, hoping it would get caught in a wind stream and sail away, never to be seen again. It didn't, it landed on the grass right in front of him, but that was fine because school was *over*.

No more school! No more books! No more teacher's dirty looks! No more cretins who test your resolve not to commit the act of murder again, or at least lead them to their violent deaths!

Mom and Dad watched proudly from the bleachers. They would've been prouder if he were going to college, but Toby had no interest in that. It was hard to believe that there was an era when he didn't consider school a waste of time. He'd applied to a few universities just to play along, and been accepted into two of them despite his lackluster grades since freshman year, but that wasn't where his life was headed.

He wasn't sure *where* his life was headed, exactly, but it wasn't more school. Without Orange Leaf High hogging up all of his weekdays, he could get in a lot more hours at work, make a lot more money, and get his own place. No dormitory with a roommate for him. He was headed for freedom.

"AND THAT'S IT. I never have to see that place again. I mean, I guess I have to drive by it sometimes, but I never have to set foot in that stupid awful building ever again. It's a day of celebration. Now I can finally figure out what I want to do. I guess you're supposed to figure that out in school, but I think it's one big distraction in your life. It doesn't leave time for anything else. But now it's all over!" He did a merry little dance with his arms folded, like he'd seen some Russian dancers do on television, then frowned. "What's up, Owen? You don't seem all that excited."

Owen had appeared happy when Toby showed up outside his cave, as the monster always did, but his eyes were glassy and his energy level was low. "Are you sick?" Toby asked. He mimed throwing up to clarify what he meant. "Sick?"

Owen gave him a thumbs-down.

"Does that mean no, you're not sick, or is that just a thumbs-down to the way you're feeling?"

Owen lowered his head. It was difficult for a creature with oversized jaws to look pitiful, but Owen pulled off the feat.

"Here, let me feel your forehead." Toby brushed some of Owen's hair away and pressed his palm against his forehead. "You're kind of hot, but I honestly don't know how that compares to your usual temperature. You don't look like you're dying, at least. Maybe you should get some rest." He tilted his head and placed his hands together under it, miming sleep.

Owen slowly wandered back into his cave.

Poor guy. This was the first time Toby had seen him feeling bad, but he had to get sick *sometime*, right? Everybody got sick. There was plenty of stuff in the medicine cabinet at home, but Toby had no idea how it would react with Owen's body, so giving him human medicine was probably a bad idea. Rest was the best answer. And maybe orange juice.

What if his friend was dying?

He wasn't dying. That was stupid. Glassy eyes and low energy did not mean that the Grim Reaper was chopping down your door with his scythe. Owen would be fine.

Still, Toby should at least make sure that he got into bed safely. They'd been friends for three years. Owen wasn't going to rip him apart in the cave, especially when he wasn't feeling well. Toby dug his flashlight out of his backpack, turned it on, and walked into the cave after him.

Owen pushed through some vegetation that hung in the corner —the secret passage that Toby had missed all those years ago. "Fancy," Toby said. "It's almost like you've got a beaded curtain. I hope you tidied up the place for my visit."

Toby pushed through the "curtain" as well, stepping into a room that wasn't much larger than his own bedroom. There were bones everywhere. As Toby shined the flashlight beam around on them, he was relieved to note that none of them looked human, not that he could necessarily tell a human rib from a deer rib at first glance.

"Nice place," he said. "Not the decorating scheme I would have gone for, but it works. The scattered bones give it sort of a homey feel."

A large pile of bushes, arranged almost like a nest, rested against the far wall. Owen lay down in it and closed his eyes.

"Don't worry, buddy," said Toby. "I'll take care of you."

He looked around some more. Not much to it. He hadn't expected Owen to live in a nicely furnished luxury suite with fine china and a butler, but a bunch of bones and some bushes to sleep on seemed kind of sparse. The next time he came out here, he'd bring a picture of himself to tape up on Owen's wall. Give the place a little more character.

"Hey, Floren, it's kind of hard to breathe under here," said a voice from within the pile of bones.

"So come out. You don't need my permission."

Larry pushed his way out of the bones. He was looking bad. He always looked bad, but this was a particularly gruesome day for him. Each of the stab wounds still had a knife imbedded in them. The blades wobbled as he got to his feet.

"These hurt," he noted.

"They would."

"I can't pry them out."

"You did last time."

"That was different."

Larry's appearance changed each time. Sometimes he only had one knife in him, usually in his chest. Sometimes he had no knives, but was covered with hundreds of stab wounds, far more than Toby had caused. Sometimes the cuts leaked. Sometimes they glowed. Sometimes they weren't there at all. Once, Larry had just been a pool of reddish ooze—Toby knew it was him from the hazel eyes floating in it.

Nick hardly ever showed up. When he did, his body was filled with gaping holes and he didn't talk much.

Larry tugged at the knife in his chest. "You stuck this thing in deep."

"I was angry."

"I'm really sorry about what we did. We should have been nicer to you while we were alive. I think, deep inside, we were just insecure about ourselves. We just wanted to be loved." He chuckled. "A dumb way of showing it, right?"

"Okay, nobody wants to hear that," said Toby. "Go back to the bones now."

"I don't want to."

"Then melt."

Larry shrieked as his skin began to bubble and smoke. There was a sizzling sound as pieces of flesh curled and dropped off his body, bursting into flames as they hit the ground. Within seconds

Larry was nothing more than a knife-filled skeleton. Then the bones fell apart and he collapsed back into the pile.

Good. Toby had control over his imagination today. That wasn't always the case.

"You know what would be funny?" he asked Owen. "If you didn't exist, either. I could be out here talking to myself. The people at the looney bin would love that."

Owen opened his eyes, looking sort of annoyed that Toby was still making noise when he didn't feel well.

"If that were the case, though, I'd be a cannibal. I may be crazy, but I'm not *that* far gone." He knelt down next to Owen and stroked his fur. "You're not going to die on me, right? If you ever leave me, I'll...I don't know. I'd just be really sad, I guess. I'll stop talking now."

He sat with Owen until the monster fell asleep, and then went home.

———

Toby had hated his senior year of high school, but he had to admit that his senior photo was pretty good. If nothing else, it was the best picture taken of him in at least a decade. His parents wouldn't miss a 5x7 print. Tomorrow he'd take it to the cave and give Owen something to remember him by when he wasn't around.

Or...maybe he'd decide instead not to be a complete idiot.

Owen was his best friend, but he'd also devoured two humans. Maybe, just maybe, it wasn't in Toby's best interest to have his picture posted right there on the cave wall. That might be a challenge to explain to the police.

As a double murderer who was buddies with a flesh-eating monster, it was very important that he not do stupid things. What he should do, right now, was make a list of dumb things to avoid. A mental list, though—if he wrote it down, it could be discovered, and that would be spectacularly dumb.

No pictures of himself on Owen's wall, obviously.

Always leave in enough time to get home before dark. He'd screwed that up a few times. Yeah, he always carried a flashlight and had spare batteries in his backpack, but still, he should avoid walking in the forest at night. What if Owen had relatives?

Don't talk to hallucinations. To be fair, he'd only done that once outside of the forest. Larry had sat down next to him at the library, and Toby had told him to go away. Not a big deal. Nobody had heard. But still, the "talking corpse" versions of Larry and Nick were figments of his imagination, and speaking to them outside of his mind was dumb. He did it fairly often when he was hanging out with Owen, only because he was so used to talking to somebody who didn't talk back, but that needed to stop.

Don't think about feeding people to Owen. Well, that wasn't necessarily something he could control. He thought about it a lot. But after that one time sophomore year when he'd lost his mind and tried to lure J.D. out here—God, how could he have let himself get that far out of control?—he'd never done anything like that again. And he never would. So it didn't need to be on his list.

Don't get too comfortable. He messed this up all the time. He just couldn't conceive of Owen hurting him. But there were a lot of lion tamers missing limbs because they stopped being cautious around their beasts, and he needed to remain aware that Owen was dangerous. He didn't want to find himself lying in a hospital bed without his arms thinking "Wow, I really should have been more careful around the creature with claws and razor-sharp teeth."

Never tell anybody about his friend. This was the hardest one. It was no longer a case of just wanting to share his cool discovery. He had a friend—his only friend—and didn't dare tell anybody about it, for his sake and for Owen's. Every time Mom or Dad asked what he was doing out in the woods all the time, he was tempted to tell the truth, but he never could. They were worried. They didn't think it was healthy to spend this much time alone. If they knew the truth, they'd think it was even *less* healthy.

Those were the rules. Those were the dumb things he had to avoid. There was nothing on that list he couldn't handle. And if he broke the rules...well, then he deserved whatever ghoulish fate was in store for him.

11

GLIMPSES
1964

"We brought you a housewarming present!" said Mom, excitedly walking through the front door. She held a large present wrapped in shiny orange and green paper, big enough that she had to wrap her arms around it as if giving it a hug.

"What is it?" Toby asked as she set it on the otherwise bare dining room table. He always asked that when he got a present, which was silly because the whole point of having it wrapped was to hide the surprise until he opened it. It was similar to the way he said "Hi, it's me," when he called his parents on the telephone. Who else would it be?

"You'll have to open it and find out," Mom said, as always.

While Mom and Dad watched, Toby tore off the wrapping paper. "A sewing machine?"

"That's just the box."

He ripped open the taped lid and looked inside. He pulled out another wrapped present, this one in shiny blue and purple paper.

"Obviously, your mother has a lot of time on her hands," Dad said.

It took eight wrapped boxes to get down to the real present: a top-of-the-line coffeemaker that he absolutely loved. Although he'd bought Mrs. Faulkner's house when she passed away, so Mom and Dad were right next door, and having his own coffeemaker now gave him one less reason to visit, so maybe it wasn't such a great present.

While he was cleaning out his room, he'd found the undeveloped roll of film from when he'd taken pictures of Owen. He'd kept it hidden in his bottom drawer. The set of drawers went with him to his new house, and he left the roll of film where it was. He'd probably never take the pictures in to be developed, but he liked having it as a souvenir.

1965

"Toby. *Toby.* Toe-bee."
Owen growled.
"No, that's not even close. Just say Toe. *Toe.*"
Another growl.
"Maybe I could learn to growl in your language."

1966

"That's...that's great news," said Toby with much more enthusiasm than he felt.

"He won't say anything, but your father is so excited he can hardly see straight." Mom grinned. "He's been hoping to get this job for going on six months now. It's the opportunity we've been waiting for since before you were born."

"Well, congratulations."

"We're going to miss you like crazy. You could come with us."

"I think I'm kind of old to be moving across the country just to be close to my parents."

Mom gave him a kiss on the cheek. "You're never too old. It also works out great because your Aunt Jean is out there, so we've got somebody to scope things out while we make the moving arrangements. It'll be nice to see her more than once a year."

"Yeah."

"You look upset."

"Well, I am, kind of."

"It's going to be hard, but it really is a great thing for your dad. And don't worry, I'll make him keep a bedroom open for you. And we both know he'll complain about it, but I'm going to put up all of your posters and toys and everything."

"You don't have to go that far. Just put them up right before I get there and pretend you had the room that way."

"Are you okay with this?"

"Yeah, sure, of course. It's great news. Seriously."

"We can't wait."

"Wow. Las Vegas. That's…not close."

"We'll come back to visit. I promise."

1967

"Hi."

Toby stood there until the awkward silence became unbearable. "Hi," he finally repeated.

"Sorry. I thought you were talking to somebody else."

"No, just saying hi."

"Do I know you?" the woman asked. She took a long drag from her cigarette and blew the smoke out slowly.

"No, not yet. I was just seeing if you wanted to dance."

"With you?"

"Maybe."

"Maybe?"

"Yes."

"This is your first time talking to a woman, isn't it?"

"No, not at all. I'm just, you know, nervous."

"Well, I need a man who's confident."

"Oh. Okay. Sorry to have bothered you."

"I wasn't ruling you out. I was just saying that you have to be confident."

"Do you want to dance?"

"You're really not very good at this."

"I guess not."

"Practice. But on somebody else."

1968

Toby opened the February issue of *Argosy* magazine and flipped to the page he wanted to show Owen. "This kind of looks like you," he said, holding up the Bigfoot photographs taken by Roger Patterson and Bob Gimlin. "His fur is a lot darker, and your face is different, and you've got claws, but...I don't know, I think there's a resemblance."

No.

"You don't think so?" Toby looked back and forth, comparing Owen to the photographs. "Yeah, I guess you're right. This was in California, anyway."

"I QUIT."

"No, you don't," said Mr. Zack.

"I'm pretty sure I do."

"Nope, you don't. Do you know why?"

"Why?"

"Because you, Toby, are what is considered a 'valuable

employee.' Therefore it's not in my best interest to let you quit. And so we will begin what experts refer to as the 'negotiation process,' wherein I make a counteroffer and we go back and forth until a mutual agreement is reached. How does that sound?"

"It sounds like I need to watch your every move."

"That's a good tactic regardless of the situation. So you've asked for a ten percent raise. You knew coming in here that you weren't going to get ten percent. I'll offer you two percent."

"I quit."

"Seriously, I can give you five."

"I deserve at least eight."

"Can't give you eight. Do you have a wife or kids to support that you haven't told me about?"

"I've got a pet."

"Cat or dog?"

"Neither."

"I can give you six. And you'll take six because you love working here and I love having you work here and it's generally pleasant for everybody, and also because most other bosses are a lot meaner and less entertaining than I am."

Toby thought that Mr. Zack often tried a little too hard at the "entertaining" part, but he was right, there were probably a lot worse bosses out there. At least Toby never got yelled at or pushed around here at the grocery.

"Seven."

"Six and a smile."

"Seven and a punch in the face."

"Seven and a smile. See? That's much better than being unemployed." Mr. Zack patted Toby on the shoulder. "You're a good kid. I'm surprised some fine young lady hasn't scooped you up."

"I don't get out much."

1969

"Where have you been? Do you know how worried I was?" Toby demanded.

Owen just stared at him.

"Three days! Three days you've been gone! I thought you'd gotten hurt or moved away! I don't expect you to write me a note, but you could have done *something*!"

Owen pulled apart his lips, showing his teeth.

"Oh, so you're mad at *me* now? I'm not the one who disappeared for three days. Where were you?"

Owen pointed to the left.

"What were you doing?"

Owen made doggy-paddle motions.

"You were swimming? You went swimming for three days?"

Thumbs-up. *Yes.*

"You were not swimming for three days. Where would you even go? Did you find a pond or something?"

Yes.

"You didn't need to be gone that long. You could have figured out a way to leave a message, or at least told me beforehand that you were leaving. You know, it's not that short of a walk out here. I've got a lot of better things I could be doing than trekking all the way out here just to find an empty cave."

Owen tapped his heart with two talons. *I'm sorry.*

"Well, you should be. I don't have anybody else, you know."

Owen furrowed his brow and curled his index finger.

"No, I'm not mad. Not mad *anymore*. Just don't do that to me again, okay?"

1970

"It's a brand new decade, Owen. Everything is going to change. The world is ours for the taking, buddy. I can't believe I brought this party hat all the way out here and you won't wear it."

1971

"Listen to me," Toby said. He tapped his ear. "Listen. What I have to say is very important. Do you understand?"

Yes.

Toby felt sick to his stomach. He should have confessed this years ago. Or he shouldn't confess it at all. What if it destroyed everything?

"You remember that day, right? A long time ago? When I fed you?"

Owen curled his hand into a fist and licked the air.

"No, no, not ice cream. I mean way back. Well, maybe your first ice cream cone was before this, but I mean that time I gave you other food. People food. You know, not food that people eat, but people food. Kids like me. Remember that time?"

Yes.

Toby felt his eyes welling up with tears. "I need to share something with you. You have to promise not to get mad. Do you promise? You sure? You have to promise."

Owen promised.

"When I did that, when I led you to their bodies, I wasn't thinking about you. I was going to blame you for what happened to them." Toby let the tears fall. "I wouldn't do it now. If the police found out, I'd confess everything, I'd let them know that you had nothing to do with their deaths, but at the time I was scared and I didn't know you and I just wanted a way to get rid of them where they wouldn't be discovered."

There was no reaction.

"I'm sorry, I shouldn't even be telling you about this. You may not even understand me. I just—I've felt bad about this for a long time, and I needed to get it off my chest. It was a horrible thing to do. We weren't friends back then, but even so, I would've let them gas you or whatever they would've done. But not anymore. I swear."

Toby bit the inside of his cheek and looked into Owen's eyes.

He couldn't always tell what Owen was thinking. Usually he could make a guess, but this time he had absolutely no idea. He didn't know if Owen was ready to wail in misery, bite his face off, or shrug and return to his cave.

"Can I have a hug?" Toby asked.

Owen gave him one.

1972

"Damn it! You little bastards get out of here!" Toby shouted after the laughing, fleeing kids. He could understand them egging and toilet-papering his house if it was Halloween or April Fool's Day, but it was Lincoln's Birthday, for crying out loud!

"Bye, weirdo!" one of them shouted back.

Weirdo. Yeah, that was appropriate, but he wasn't sure how he ended up being treated like a crazy old man. He wasn't even thirty.

One of the kids, Joey, had ridden his bike over a couple of times to talk about baseball. Toby had no interest in or knowledge about baseball, but he faked it. Then the kid's mother had told Joey to stay away from him.

He got a towel from the linen closet and went outside to wipe off his front window. He grimaced at the smell. These eggs had gone bad quite some time ago—you almost had to admire their commitment to keep them around that long.

Almost.

"Little bastards," he muttered under his breath as he wiped away the slime.

"*TOBY.*"

"Oh my God! It's your first word!"

1 2

1973. Age 28.

As Toby lay in bed, the night before his parents were coming to visit for Christmas, he realized that he hadn't seen Larry in over a week.

He didn't see Larry every single day, but in thirteen years he was pretty sure that he'd never gone two consecutive days without a visit. These weren't always the long, nightmare-inducing, sanity-questioning visits—usually he'd think about the horrible act he'd committed, his unforgiving imagination would conjure up an image of the bully (or bullies), and he'd spend a few minutes trying to get rid of them. Sometimes it was just a few seconds. Sometimes it lasted all night. Sometimes he was terrified, sometimes he was disoriented and confused, and sometimes the visions of Larry and Nick made him so angry about the ongoing torment that he wanted to stab them to death again.

But if he remembered correctly, the last time Larry had haunted him was during dinner last Monday. Toby had envisioned poking a fork in his eye and he'd gone away.

Last Tuesday, Toby had met Melissa Tomlinson. Neither Larry nor Toby had returned since then.

This wasn't a coincidence.

Of course, now that he was thinking about the fact that he hadn't thought about Larry, the son of a bitch showed up, but Toby made the image dissipate quickly, before it could even say anything. It was time to get over this crap. Time to move on with his life.

Melissa was his new co-worker at the grocery. A cashier. Twenty-three years old. The most beautiful woman he'd ever seen. Perhaps not in a traditional way; in fact, Andrew, one of the baggers, had asked "Who's the new dog?" Toby had resisted the urge to suffocate him with one of the bags.

Her long, straight black hair was unevenly cut, and she had sort of a crooked smile, but it wasn't like she was missing a nose or anything like that. Not everyone could be on the cover of *Playboy*. As far as Toby was concerned, she was a goddess of beauty.

It helped that she was nice to him.

She'd never worked a cash register before, and Annette, who she would be replacing, was immediately exasperated, even though from what Toby could tell she was picking it up quickly. People weren't *born* knowing how to use a piece of man-made equipment. Toby wanted to walk over there and tell Annette this, and he almost did, but Melissa seemed to be handling everything fine, and her smile never vanished.

Then Mr. Zack asked Toby why he was loitering out here, and he sheepishly returned to the stock room.

He spent the morning lifting boxes and working up the courage to ask her to sit next to him at lunch. Or the courage to sit next to her, wherever she decided to sit. Either one of those would be fine.

Melissa went home for lunch. Apparently she lived only two blocks from the store.

Toby spent the afternoon mopping floors and trying to decide if he would be risking severe humiliation by asking her to go to a movie with him. *Robin Hood* was still playing, though he didn't know if she'd want to go see a Disney cartoon. The only other thing playing was *Serpico*, which might be kind of violent for her.

His hands were so sweaty that he dropped a box of Tide when he tried to put it on the shelf. Fortunately, Mr. Zack didn't see him.

"Hi," Toby said, walking over to her as their shifts ended. "I'm Toby. Mr. Zack introduced us this morning."

"Yep, I remember." Toby wasn't sure if her smile actually got bigger, but it might have. "What's up?"

"How was your first day?"

She shrugged. "Not too bad. Annette tries to make it a lot more difficult than it really is. I think she's embarrassed by how easy it is. You don't even have to add up the numbers yourself. At least your job requires strength."

Toby grinned. "Well, not *that* much strength."

"More strength than pushing buttons for eight hours." She lifted her hand and stared at it in mock agony. "Oh, my poor, poor, delicate fingers!" She had long fingernails, painted with bright red polish.

"Do you want to go to a movie tonight?" Toby asked. He hadn't planned to just blurt it out like that, but at least he didn't screw up the words. He'd half expected to say something like "*Tonight want go movie-thing me come too?*"

"Ooooh, I can't tonight."

"No problem."

"I can tomorrow, though, but we have to see *Sleeper*. Have you heard of that?"

"No."

"It's about a guy who wakes up in the future. It's a comedy, though. It looks hilarious."

"I didn't know it was even playing."

"It's not in Orange Leaf. We'd have to drive about forty-five minutes. Is that okay?"

"Of course!"

"How about we leave right after work? I'll drive."

"I've got a car."

"Yeah, but I'll drive. Are we set?"

"Definitely."

———

Toby went out and bought a new shirt and jeans for the date. He pretty much only wore the same five shirts, so everybody at work would know that he'd bought something special just for this occasion, but he didn't care. He didn't have any reason to downplay his excitement.

"Nice shirt," said Annette. "You look good in green."

———

"I should let you know that I investigated you," said Melissa, as she pulled out of the grocery store parking lot. She was dressed simply—faded jeans and a yellow t-shirt—and Toby had never seen anything more radiant.

"You did?"

She nodded. "I just asked people around work if you were safe. Apparently you're extremely quiet and keep to yourself most of the time."

"That's probably accurate."

"Except Mr. Zack said that you can be a smart-ass."

"That's probably accurate, too."

"And everybody was surprised that you asked me out."

"I was kind of surprised, too."

"I'm glad you did. I really want to see this movie and I didn't want to go by myself. And I promise that I'm not a serial killer if you promise that you're not one."

"I promise."

"And I'm not a political activist or a religious nut."

"Neither am I."

"Good. So we're not serial killers, political activists, or religious nuts. I think we'll at least be able to make it through the trailers without any problems."

They talked and laughed all the way to the movie theatre. Owen was his best friend and that would never change, but it was *so* nice to have an extended conversation with somebody he could fully communicate with. This was natural. This was right.

Sleeper was the funniest movie Toby had ever seen in his life. He laughed until tears streamed down his cheeks. They shared a popcorn and a package of red licorice, but they were still hungry when the movie ended, so they went to get a burger and fries. They laughed some more and quoted their favorite lines from the movie, over and over.

Toby didn't know what being in love felt like, and to be honest he thought that it probably involved a more dramatic shift in his outlook on life than what he was currently feeling. Still, there was no question that he really, *really* liked Melissa. Maybe more than he liked anybody besides Owen.

Right now, she was his favorite human being.

They got back into her car. She didn't start the engine. She looked over at him and raised an eyebrow. "Do you get high?" she asked.

"Sure," he said, though he didn't.

"Do you have anything with you?"

"No."

"I've just got some weed. Wanna go somewhere?"

Toby felt himself begin to perspire and hoped that she didn't notice. Yeah, he wanted to "go somewhere" with her, but not to do drugs. How was he supposed to explain this? *Sorry, Melissa, I appreciate the offer, but I have these disturbing images in my brain that I can't always control, and if I try a mind-altering substance I have no idea what I'll see or say.* He'd kept his secret too long to risk sharing it while he was stoned. He could just imagine himself, rolling around in a giggling fit: "*And then I cut off their fingers! It was the funniest thing I've ever done!*"

"I can't."

"You don't trust me?"

"Oh, no, I trust you completely."

"You shouldn't. Because one of the things I said I wasn't isn't true." She poked him in the chest. "Vote Democrat."

He sensed that she was trying to let him off the hook, but he wanted to explain himself, even if his explanation was completely made up. "It's just that my parents are coming to visit for the holidays, and my mom is as anti-drugs as you can possibly get, and if she even thinks she smells pot she will absolutely flip out."

Nice. Smooth. His great excuse for not getting stoned with Melissa was that his mom might not approve. Wow, she was going to think he was simply the coolest person who'd ever lived in the entire history of the universe.

"That's too bad," Melissa said. "Pot makes me horny."

Toby felt like an entire bathtub's worth of sweat suddenly gushed from every pore in his body. Maybe he'd just smoke a little, or fake the inhale.

No. He knew what would happen. One kiss from Melissa and he'd forget himself, suck in a deep lungful, and then chase imaginary bullies around the room with a hunting knife.

"Well, *you* can smoke it."

"Nah, it's okay." She started up the engine. "Was there anyplace else you wanted to go?"

Toby shook his head. He'd screwed everything up. He always screwed everything up. He tried to maintain his composure, but inside he was trying to strangle himself.

"Don't worry," Melissa said. "There are other ways to get me horny."

"You're coming in, right?" she asked, as they pulled up in front of her apartment complex.

"I kind of have to," Toby said. "You drove."

"Yeah, you're trapped with me. What a scary position to be in. I'll try to be gentle with you, but I can't promise that there won't be broken bones."

After they parked and got out of the car, she took him by the hand and led him to her second-floor apartment. She put a finger to her lips as she unlocked her door, indicating for him to be quiet. "We don't want to wake my roommate," she whispered.

She led him through the dark apartment into her bedroom, quickly shutting the door behind her. She turned on a blacklight, illuminating posters of Pink Floyd, Led Zeppelin, and Blue Oyster Cult.

The kiss happened so quickly that Toby nearly yelped in surprise. She threw her arms around him, kissing him with incredible fervor.

I can't believe this is finally happening, Toby thought.

Don't analyze it! Enjoy it!

They'd been kissing for less than thirty seconds before she took his hand and pressed it against her breast. He squeezed it.

"Ow. Not so hard."

"Sorry."

They kissed some more.

"Harder than that, though."

He stroked her nipple with his thumb, feeling it quickly harden underneath her shirt. The shirt was gone seconds later, as she pulled it over her head, tossed it aside, then unfastened her bra.

"You gonna do it with your clothes on?" she asked as she began to tug down her jeans.

Toby shook his head and took off his shirt as well. His heart was racing and he was trembling a bit and he wished that things were moving a bit more slowly—not a *lot* more slowly, but enough to let him better take in the experience.

She sat down on her bed, naked. "Are you a virgin?" she asked.

Toby considered lying, but decided against it. "Yeah."

"Seriously?"

"Yeah."

"Wow. And you're twenty-eight?"

"I'm a loser, I know."

"Nah, you're not a loser. I think it's great. I've never deflowered anybody before. If you have any objections, you'd better get them out in the open now, because once I'm done with you, you will never find that cherry again."

Toby had no objections.

———

"STOP LOOKING SO GRUMPY. I'm sorry I woke you up." Toby continued shining the flashlight in Owen's face. "This wasn't something that could wait, and you don't have a phone out here. I've got news to share!"

Owen waved him away.

"Guess what it is. Give up? I just had sex."

Toby told him the whole story, leaving out the premature ejaculation but using gestures to make sure that Owen understood that they did it three times.

"I may be in love with her, I don't know, but it was an incredible evening."

Then he told the story to Owen again, from beginning to end. It was a great story.

———

THE NEXT EVENING they skipped the movie and went straight to her bedroom.

Mr. Zack explained that neither of them would be fired, this time, but that such indiscretions at work were completely unacceptable, and that he would never get the image out of his head.

"Mom loved her. I can't tell what Dad thought. I'm sure he liked her, too. But we're sitting in the living room talking, and Melissa says 'Hey, Toby, I think there's something wrong with your toilet.' And I knew exactly what she had in mind, because of the way she said it, you know? You wouldn't think you could say something like that in an erotic way, but she did. And I'm almost positive that Mom knew what she had in mind, too. Isn't that gross?"

"*Toby.*"

"Yep, I'm Toby. So I don't really want to do anything with my parents in the house, but I can't just ignore a broken toilet, right? I go in there, and Melissa drops down to her knees. Now keep in mind that the bathroom is only one door down the hall from the living room where they're sitting, and the door isn't closed all the way. So I'm trying to be quiet, but Melissa isn't, she's just slurping away, and I'm trying to finish quickly so we don't get caught. Of course, when we go back Dad wants to know what was wrong with the toilet, and being the master liar that I am I said 'Oh, we just needed to jiggle the handle,' and I guess that sounded dirty because Melissa went into complete hysterics. Then we all sat down and Mom told us about Aunt Jean's hysterectomy."

Owen signaled. *Big fun.*

"Yeah, it was fun. I don't think I'll ever be able to look Mom and Dad in the eye again, though. I'm glad they're leaving tomorrow."

Toby lit the marijuana cigarette and stared at the rising curl of smoke. Melissa had brought up the subject multiple times in the past month, and though she always seemed to be sufficiently horny without drugs, at some point Toby was going to have to cave in.

So he sat alone in his bedroom. He'd test it out. See what happened. Maybe it would kill some brain cells that he *wanted* dead, and banish Larry and Nick from his mind forever.

He inhaled deeply.

He didn't really remember most of the experience, but Larry and Nick didn't go anywhere.

13

1974. Age 29.

"It's not her best picture," Toby admitted. "We've got other ones that you aren't allowed to see."

Owen looked at the photo of Melissa. His talon was poking through the corner, but Toby didn't say anything about it.

"Pretty nice, huh?"

Owen gave him a thumbs-up.

"You probably can't even judge. But we're still together, which is pretty amazing, don't you think? We're not having as much sex, but there's still plenty, I mean, I have no complaints."

Toby didn't think that Owen understood the concept of sex, even in an animalistic mating sense, but he knew that Owen understood that he was in love. Owen seemed very happy for him.

"You'll get to meet her soon," Toby promised.

"So when do I get to meet Owen?" Melissa asked, gently stroking him.

"I don't know."

"Well, you spend enough time with him that it's time for me to meet him. I'm starting to think that you have another girl on the side." She winked, then took him into her mouth, ending her part of the conversation.

"You will someday. I keep telling him that I'm going to bring you over."

He'd told Melissa that his best friend Owen lived in a small cabin in the woods, and that he was horribly disfigured. His older brother had splashed a pot of boiling water on his face when they were kids. Owen was entirely home-schooled, had no friends, and never went out.

"It's great that you're so nice to him," Melissa had said.

"He's nice to me, too. We don't feel sorry for each other. I like hanging out with him."

"How bad is his face?"

"It's awful. You wouldn't even know he was human."

"Wow. That's really tragic. Nobody should have to live like that, no matter how they look."

Toby brushed her hair out of her face as he felt his orgasm approach. He did this every time. It somehow seemed more romantic than saying "Just thought I should let you know that I'm about to come in your mouth."

As always, she pulled away and finished him off with her hand. They'd cuddle and talk for a while, and then when he was ready they'd move on to intercourse. They were in something of a rut, he had to admit, but as far as ruts went it was a pretty enjoyable one.

"So tell him I want to meet him."

"I have."

"Tell him again."

"I will."

"He's probably in desperate need of some action. Maybe I'll let you guys double up on me."

Toby gaped at her, horrified. The visual image this brought to mind was immensely distasteful, even in a brain that was filled with unpleasant images.

"I was *joking*!" she said. "Wow, Mr. Serious, I think you need to lighten up. You're the only stud for me. But while we're on the subject, Tina said that you're massively hot and asked if I'd share you with her sometime."

"Really?"

"No. That's two threesome jokes you've fallen for in about ten seconds. You make this way too easy, Toby."

"Yeah, I know."

"This is her sweater," Toby said, handing the garment to Owen. Owen let the red sweater dangle from his talon, apparently unsure what to do with it.

"Smell it." Toby took the arm of the sweater and pressed it to his own nose to demonstrate. "Take a big whiff. You're going to meet her and I want you to know her scent."

Owen pressed the sweater against his face and inhaled.

"Nice, huh? She always smells great. Remember that Melissa is a friend. *Friend.* Not food. Don't show her your teeth. If the two of you get along, maybe you can have somebody else to spend time with. Wouldn't that be wonderful?"

Yes.

Toby took out his Polaroid camera. "Say cheese. Don't smile."

Toby figured that, considering the delicate nature of the situation, he couldn't just lead Melissa out to the cave and hope that she was okay with the idea of Owen being a hideous beast instead of a burned human. He knew Owen would never do anything to harm somebody that Toby cared about, but still, having their first meeting start off with a shriek of terror would be undesirable.

He wasn't sure if he should tell Melissa the true story before or after sex. Probably after. She'd be more relaxed.

"There's something I need to tell you about Owen," he said, kissing her neck afterward.

"He doesn't exist?"

"No, he exists. He's just not what I told you he was."

"He's a ghost?"

"I'm being serious. Owen is...he's sort of like a pet, except that I don't own him or anything like that. He isn't a person. I don't know exactly what he is, but he doesn't live in a cabin, he lives in a cave, and he doesn't leave the woods because he's a...I don't know, I tend to think of him as a 'monster,' but that's not a good way to describe him. He's an animal."

"What?"

Toby sat up. He knew this conversation was going to be awkward. "Owen is a big hairy creature with claws and fangs. He can't talk except for saying my name, but we can communicate through hand signals, sort of like sign language except that we made it up."

Melissa pulled the sheet up over her chest. "Your friend is a big hairy forest creature?"

"Yeah. Sort of. No, not sort of, it's completely accurate. Yeah."

"Is this a joke?"

"Is it funny?"

"No."

"That's because it's not a joke."

"So, what, you befriended a talking bear? Come on, Toby, you told me you've been spending time with your disfigured childhood friend. What the hell kind of conversation are we having? Did you start smoking pot? If you started smoking pot without me I swear I'll rip your heart out."

"No, I'm telling you the truth." He got out of bed and pulled on his underwear. "I know how it sounds, and you probably think I'm totally weird and creepy, but when you meet Owen you'll understand." He picked his blue jeans off the floor and took a folded Polaroid out of the back pocket. "I didn't expect you to believe me right away, so here's a picture."

Melissa took the photograph from him. "Holy shit, Toby! What *is* that thing? Is that a mask?"

"No. It's real."

"Fuck you. You are *not* friends with that thing."

"I am. I swear."

"Come on, Toby, end the joke. There is nothing about this that I believe. If you've been cheating on me, just fess up to it instead of making us both look like idiots."

"I'm not cheating on you. I lost my virginity at twenty-eight—do you think I have a lot of opportunities?"

"What's that supposed to mean?"

"What?"

"Are you saying I'm ugly?"

"Huh? No. No, that's not what I meant at all. It was just a joke."

"This seems to be the day for failed jokes. Well, Toby, I'm sorry that your love life sucks. Hopefully in another twenty-eight years you'll find a non-repulsive person to have sex with."

"That's not what I meant! What the fuck? This discussion isn't about anything like that! I'm trying to unload a gigantic bombshell about my monster friend!"

"You should leave."

Toby had expected that the conversation might spiral out of control, but not in this particular manner. "No! Get dressed! We're going out to see Owen. He's a big scary monster and you need to meet him. He's real. We haven't been dating that long in the grand scheme of things, but we've been together long enough that you know I'm just not going to take you out into the woods and have a friend jump out at you with a monster mask, right?"

"Do you love me?"

"Okay, listen, I refuse to let this turn into an argument about the state of our relationship. I refuse. You hear that? Complete and total refusal. The only thing we should be discussing is the lie I've been telling you about my grotesquely burned friend! By telling you the truth, I'm trying to take our relationship to the next level, so I guess the answer to your question is yes, I do love you, but that's not what the fuck we're supposed to be talking about right now, okay?"

"Why couldn't you tell me you loved me before?"

"Okay, you know what, I'm going to hang myself. I'm going to find a noose, throw it around my neck, and step right off a chair. Then I'll be dead, and the madness will be over, and we can all be happy again!"

"Maybe we should continue this tomorrow."

"Yeah, let's do that."

Toby's DOORBELL rang at sunrise.

"I'm ready to meet Owen now," Melissa said.

"How can he stand the cold?" Melissa asked, as they trudged through the snow.

"I don't know. I guess that's just what animals do. He's pretty hairy."

"You should buy him a space heater or something."

Toby chuckled, although he wasn't in a particularly humorous mood. He was nervous as hell. If you really stopped to think about it, which he had at length, this had the potential to be the single worst idea of his entire life.

On the other hand, it had the potential to be the best idea.

He'd be careful. He'd keep everything under control.

And he had a pistol in his jacket pocket. He had absolutely no intention of using it, and almost had left it at home...but, no, Owen was still a dangerous creature. He hadn't killed Larry and Nick, Toby had, but Owen had eaten them. What if he went berserk over the opportunity to taste more human flesh? Toby needed to have the gun with him. If things looked like they were going to get out of hand, he'd point it at Owen, Owen would cower away, and he'd get Melissa out of there.

He saw a real future with Melissa, and he needed to share this part of his life with her. It would all work out okay. Sure, there'd be some rocky points in today's encounter—gasping, looks of disbelief, maybe some accusations that Toby's mental state wasn't everything it could be—but it would be a huge relief to finally have everything out in the open.

Except the murders, of course. Those were staying well hidden.

"Remember that thing I did last Friday?" Melissa asked.

"Which one?"

"The show. With the toy."

"Oh, yeah. Of course. I'll never forget it."

"Keep it in mind, because if this does turn out to be a prank, you'll never see anything like that again."

"I completely understand."

They were at the final uphill portion, starting to get close to the cave, and Toby was beginning to feel physically ill. Maybe they should come back some other day, after he'd given Owen more time to prepare for the meeting. Maybe he should call off the whole thing. Or, instead of being a complete chickenshit...maybe he should see it through. Change his life for the better in a big way.

"You should wait here," he said. "I'll go up ahead and make sure everything's cool."

"No way. You're not leaving me in the woods by myself."

"I'm not abandoning you. Just checking things out."

"Toby, we're out here under the pretense that there's a giant monster living in this forest. Do you really think that I'm going to let you out of my sight?"

"Okay, that's fair. We'll stick together."

Before too much longer, the cave entrance came into view. Toby no longer threw rocks into it—these days he just walked up and called out Owen's name, but this time he thought he should be quite a bit more cautious and stay a safe distance away. "Owen!" he shouted. "I'm here with Melissa."

Melissa grabbed his hand. "All right, all of a sudden I'm really scared."

"Don't be. I'll protect you. But you won't need to be protected."

They waited.

"Owen!" Toby repeated. "Come out and meet her!"

"Are you sure he's in there?"

"No. He goes out sometimes. He also sleeps a lot, though. But do you see the tracks in the snow?"

"Yes. That's why I'm scared."

"You call him."

"I don't want to."

"Nothing's going to hurt you, I promise. Just call him."

Melissa hesitated, and then cupped her gloved hands around her mouth. "Ooooooowen! Ooooooowen!"

Owen emerged from the cave.

Melissa screamed.

"No, no, don't scream!" said Toby. "It's fine!"

"Oh my God!"

"It's fine, it's fine, I promise. He's not coming at you."

"We need to go, Toby, we need to go."

Toby held up his hand. "Stay back!" he told Owen. "Just stay where you are!"

Owen looked hurt and confused. He signed: *Friend?*

"Yes. Friend. But you're kind of scary for her. It'll be fine. Everybody just stay calm. Melissa, don't run."

"I wasn't going to run." She stood there, staring at Owen. "That's not a mask. Holy shit, that's not a mask."

"You're right, it's not. But you see that he's not doing anything, right? He's not trying to hurt you. He's just staying there." He reached into his jacket pocket. "I'm going to give you the gun, but do *not* point it at him unless you have to, okay? I'll go over to him, and you'll see that it's completely safe, but you'll have the gun. How does that sound?"

"I don't want to be here," Melissa said.

He took the gun out of his pocket, making sure the barrel remained pointed at the ground. "Here, take it."

She shook her head.

"Okay." He put the gun back into his pocket. "Just stay where you are. I'm going over to him, and when you feel comfortable, you can join us. If you don't feel comfortable, we'll go home and try again some other time."

"Let's try again some other time."

He smiled and gave her a quick kiss, then slowly walked toward Owen. "How've you been, buddy? This is my friend that I've told you all about. She's beautiful, isn't she? She's really wanted to meet you, and I think you two are going to get along great."

"Toby, be careful!"

"I am, don't worry." He returned his attention to Owen. "See, Owen, you probably thought I was making her up, didn't you? You thought Melissa was a fictional character. I had to drag her all the way out here through the snow to prove to you that she existed."

He stood right in front of Owen. Owen gave him a big hug.

"Yeah, I missed you too."

"He's hugging you," said Melissa.

"Yep, he does it all the time. He's pretty affectionate for such a horrific monster."

"Are you sure it's safe?"

"Positive. Owen, show Melissa how you feel about people who I care about. Care. Show her care."

Owen balled his fists together and put them over his heart.

"That's right. And who's your best friend?"

"*Toby.*"

Melissa gasped. "He talks!"

"Kind of. Not really. That's pretty much his whole vocabulary. But we're working on other stuff. I tried to teach him to say Melissa, but it hasn't worked yet. Owen, can you say Melissa? Melissa?"

Owen gave him a thumbs-down sign.

"Try it. Melissa."

No.

"That's okay. It's not your fault, is it?" He looked back at Melissa. "I think he likes you."

"How can you even tell?"

"Oh, I can read him pretty well. You like Melissa, right? Do you like Melissa?"

Yes.

"See?"

"That's incredible," Melissa said. "You taught him that?"

"Yeah. It's been slow, but it helped that I didn't have any other friends. He doesn't learn new signs that well anymore. I think his brain is full. Is your brain full, Owen? Do you have a full brain?"

"I can't believe it. This is the most amazing thing I've ever seen."

"You don't want to miss out on your chance to pet a monster, do you?" Toby asked.

"No. Actually, I don't."

She slowly walked over to join them.

1 4

"Don't freak out if he hugs you," Toby warned.

"I guarantee you I'll freak out if that happens."

With about ten feet separating them, she hesitated.

"It's okay," said Toby. "He's totally calm, see?"

Melissa took several deep breaths, the cold air misting in front of her face, and then walked over to them.

"Melissa, this is Owen. Owen, this is Melissa."

"Can he understand you?"

"Yeah, some of it." He gave Owen the *friend* signal, and Owen did the same.

"Have you told anybody else?"

"No. You're the first ever."

"And when did you meet him?"

"It depends when you start keeping track. But talk to him instead of me—I think you're confusing him."

"Hello, Owen." Her voice was quivering, but she didn't look as if she were going to lose control.

Owen placed his hand on her shoulder.

"Oh, shit."

"It's okay. He won't hurt you."

"His claws are huge."

"So are your fingernails. You're kindred spirits."

"We need to go now."

Toby nodded. "That's fine. Owen, let go."

After a moment of apparent indecision, Owen removed his hand from Melissa's shoulder, and then lowered his head.

"He wants you to pet him."

"I can't."

"You don't have to."

Melissa clenched and unclenched her fists several times, and then removed one of her gloves and stroked the top of Owen's head. He let out a soft, contented growl.

She slid her hand over his hairless cheek. "It feels weird."

"Well, he's a monster."

"No, I mean it feels almost like a human. I didn't think it would be this soft."

"He's cuddly."

"Yeah."

"He really likes you."

"I can't believe I'm doing this."

"It's cool, right?"

Owen smiled, showing off all of his teeth.

Melissa flinched in terror, scraping her fingernails across his cheek.

Owen grabbed her arm.

"Tell him to let me go," she said, her voice rising in panic.

"Owen, let her go."

"Let *go*!" She pulled her arm away before Owen had a chance to release her.

"It's okay, it's okay," Toby insisted. "Everything's fine, right, Owen?"

Owen signed: *Hurt.*

"I know, but she's your friend. Tell her that she's your friend. Friend, Owen. She's my friend, and she's your friend."

Owen signed: *Friend hurt.*

"She didn't mean it. She just got scared. Show her that you're still friends."

After a moment of hesitation, Owen reached out his enormous arms to give Melissa a hug. She shrieked and slashed her hand across his face. This time her fingernail scraped his eye.

Owen howled in pain as Melissa pulled away from him.

Toby screamed, "You hurt him!"

Owen lashed out, his claw smacking the side of Melissa's head. She cried out and fell down into the snow.

"No! Owen, stop it!" Toby reached into his jacket pocket, fumbling around for the gun. "Just stop!"

Owen growled, the loudest, most ferocious growl Toby had ever heard from him.

"Get him away from me!" Melissa screamed.

Toby pulled out the gun and pointed it at Owen. Owen squealed in fright and covered his face with his hands.

"Get out of here," Toby told Melissa. "Just go!"

Melissa got up and ran.

Owen moved his hands away from his face. Blood trickled down his cheek. He howled in misery, and then lunged forward and slashed Toby across the chest, his talons ripping through Toby's jacket, exposing the cotton insulation.

Toby pulled the trigger.

Blood sprayed from Owen's arm. The monster howled again and dropped to his knees.

"I'm sorry, I'm so sorry!" What had he done? How could he shoot his best friend? What kind of horrible, heartless person was he?

Owen looked enraged. Animalistic.

Toby ran after Melissa, calling her name. He'd been so stupid.

This could never have worked. What sort of lunatic brought his girlfriend out into the forest to meet a goddamn monster with jaws?

Movement behind him. Coming fast.

The impact knocked him to the ground, landing face-first in the snow. Owen's claws dug into his back. He cried out, barely feeling the pain but knowing that all ten talons pierced his skin. He deserved it, but didn't want to die.

Owen withdrew his talons, then raced ahead.

"No! Owen! Don't hurt her!"

Toby got up. His arms were numb and the gun dropped into the snow. Owen pounced upon Melissa. She screamed as he let out a roar, opening his jaws wide. He thrust his head down at her.

Toby stumbled toward them.

Melissa put up her arm to defend herself, and Owen's teeth sunk into her arm. He tore away, ripping off vinyl, cotton, and flesh. Blood rained onto the snow.

"Owen, *please!*"

Owen looked back at him.

"Don't kill her. It's my fault. I shouldn't have brought her out here. But if you hurt her I'll never come back and you'll be alone forever." They didn't have a signal for *I'll never come back* but he prayed that Owen understood him.

Melissa kept screaming. Toby knew that they were deep enough in the woods to be out of earshot, but he still worried that everybody in town could hear her.

Owen hesitated.

Then he tore another chunk out of her arm.

Toby spun back around. He needed the gun. He had to shoot Owen before he killed Melissa. Toby was feeling sick and dizzy but he needed to end this, and Owen was no longer listening to him. He couldn't let Melissa die.

He picked up the gun and fired. The shot went wild, knocking some snow off a tree branch. Owen looked back at the source of the noise, and Melissa wriggled free and ran off, cradling her mangled arm.

Toby aimed the gun more carefully, but his fingers wouldn't work.

Owen didn't seem scared by the gun anymore.

Toby switched to his other hand. Fired another shot that didn't even come close. If he kept this up he'd shoot Melissa by accident.

Owen looked back and forth between Toby and Melissa, as if trying to decide which one to attack. Good. If he came after Toby, he could get a better shot. "Here!" Toby said, gesturing toward himself. "Come get me!"

The monster rushed at him.

Toby squeezed off two more shots in rapid succession. Neither one hit. He didn't think he was trying to miss on purpose, but maybe subconsciously he—

Owen leapt at him.

They both slammed onto the ground.

Toby hit him in the face with the gun. If he couldn't shoot straight, he could at least use it as a bludgeoning weapon. Owen yipped like a hurt puppy. Toby struck him again, and the gun dropped out of his grasp once more.

"I hope she blinded you!" Toby screamed. He threw a punch at Owen's face, thumb extended, trying to gouge out his uninjured eye—

—and then his hand was pinched between Owen's jaws.

Toby stopped moving. Owen could bite his hand off with almost no effort, pop that thing right off and gulp it down.

They locked eyes. Owen's eye had a small cut in the iris, and he kept blinking.

"Owen, please don't," Toby said, forcing himself to remain calm and soothing. "Don't hurt me. You don't hurt your friends."

Within Owen's mouth, Toby felt a warm tongue slide over his palm.

He desperately hoped that Melissa was running fast, putting

plenty of distance between them, getting the hell out of this deadly forest.

Toby's hand remained attached, so Owen hadn't gone completely feral. He could still be reasoned with. They were still friends.

"Let me go," said Toby, softly.

Owen continued to lick his palm. A sign of affection...or gauging the taste?

Then he opened his jaws, just enough for Toby to pull his hand free. Toby did so and then flexed his fingers, as if testing to make sure they were really still there and not inside Owen's stomach.

Owen gave him a look that Toby couldn't decipher, then sprung to his feet and raced in the direction that Melissa had gone. Toby got up and went after them.

Melissa hadn't gotten far. The trail of red snow ended just around the corner, and she leaned against a tree, bracing herself as she tried to catch her breath. God, she'd lost so much blood.

"Toby, please, call him off!" she wailed. "You said—!"

Owen got her.

He bit into her shoulder, ripping off and devouring a chunk of flesh that went down to the bone. The next bite ended her screams.

Toby stood in place, watching. Now he just felt numb.

He should have tried to scare Owen away from Melissa's corpse, but the idea of the monster defiling her body didn't matter to him, now that his girlfriend was dead. It wasn't Melissa anymore. It was food.

He just watched Owen eat.

Owen watched Toby as well, as if daring him to come closer.

"Why did you do it?" Toby finally asked, but not loud enough to be heard over the chewing sounds. "She didn't hurt you that bad. It wasn't on purpose."

Owen's meal went on, uninterrupted.

Toby wiped away tears and collapsed against the same tree he'd used to brace the shotgun all those years ago. "You shouldn't have done it. I wish you hadn't done it."

HE SNAPPED BACK TO REALITY, as if awakening from a trance. There was blood everywhere, staining the snow and the trees and the rocks. Melissa lay in a gory, half-skeletal mess. Owen remained hovered over her, his teeth stripping her right leg.

"Get away from her," he whispered.

Owen didn't acknowledge him.

"*Get away from her!*" he shouted. He looked around and saw the gun lying on the ground. He picked it up and pointed it into the sky, firing off four or five shots before the clip was empty.

Owen ran, not looking back as he charged off into the depths of the forest.

Toby walked over to what remained of Melissa. He stared at her with an almost detached curiosity.

And then he let it all out, screaming in primal anguish, punching and kicking the trees, cursing the heavens, vowing to hunt down and kill the murderous beast, and sobbing over his loss.

This morning, he'd had two friends. Now he had none.

15

"Burn the whole forest down," Larry suggested. "Just pour gasoline over every square inch, light a match, and watch this place go inferno."

"I might," said Toby.

"Yeah! We'll dance in the flames! It'll be the party of the century! Burn, burn, burn!"

"You want to know the best part?" asked Nick. "Watching Owen run through the woods with his hair on fire. Total body burn. I'll cheer for that. Hopefully I'll even have a bucket of water in my hand that I can refuse to throw on him."

"It wasn't Owen's fault."

"Oh, of course not, his claws aren't bloodstained at all. Somebody else grabbed his jaws and opened and closed them on Melissa's arm. Owen's just a big furry puppet."

"You know what I mean."

"I don't know crap about what you mean, Toby. I just know that you should destroy that thing. Get a machine gun and pump six thousand bullets into its chest. Flay the skin right off its bones. Better yet, get the army involved, have them drop a whole atomic bomb right smack-dab on his cave. Turn Owen into a pile of glowing white ashes."

"Not painful enough," said Nick.

"I don't even care about making him suffer. I just want to see something spectacular. Flames or an atomic blast. Wipe him off the map."

"He's my best friend."

"Are you still clinging to that? Toby, I know you don't think of me as a father figure, but I'm going to share a piece of wisdom with you: When somebody tears your girlfriend apart and scatters her guts all over the ground, he ceases to be your best friend. He ceases to even be a pleasant acquaintance. It's pretty much mortal enemies territory."

"But he's the only thing I've got."

"Well, yeah, *now*. Because of *him*. You don't have to open the valentine with the time bomb just because it's the only one in your mailbox. If you're that needy, move to California and live by your mommy and daddy again."

"I don't need your advice."

"You know what's sad? We're dead, and Melissa's dead, but you're talking to us instead of her. That's pretty fucked up. Where is she?"

"I don't know. I can't find her."

"Priorities, man. She was ugly, but she was a lot better looking than this guy." Larry pointed at Nick. "And she was a great lay. Even without a basis for comparison you know she was a great lay."

Nick nodded. "That toy thing was sensational."

"Both of you, just shut up and go away."

"No, I want to see how you deal with this mess. It's snowing, so that's a point in your favor. Cover the tracks. Cover the blood. What are you going to do with the body?"

"I don't know."

"Won't be easy to bury her in frozen ground. You'd need some heavy machinery. You may have to take her home with you."

"I'm not doing that."

"Yeah, I suppose keeping a mangled rotting corpse at your place is a bit morbid. And the cops might find that kind of discovery fairly interesting if they search your house. So you can't bury her and you can't take her home. I think you're pretty much left with dragging her off the main path and building a nice little makeshift above-ground grave."

Toby whispered infinite apologies to Melissa as he carried her through the woods. She was so light. Half of her face remained, though her eyes were gone, and there was no expression. No scream, no grin, nothing to show what she'd once been.

He gently placed her on a pile of snow. She sunk down into it a bit, not enough to hide his crime, but enough to bring fresh tears at the sight of her moving away from him.

He pushed snow over her, burying her.

There should be some kind of marker. A cross or something to memorialize her.

"Don't even think about it," said Larry.

Of course, he was right. There was no place here for honoring his dead girlfriend. This was about covering up a horrible crime. Nothing else mattered.

He couldn't leave her out here forever, but the forest was huge. Nobody would find her before the snow melted. Not even Owen.

He was freezing to death. Could be hypothermia. He needed to go back home, take a long hot bath, and try to get his mind working again so that he didn't miss any important pieces that might send him to jail.

I didn't kill her.

But he had. He'd put her in this situation, promised her that everything would be fine.

Leave guilt out of it. From a purely practical standpoint, even if they blame her death on a wild animal, having her body discovered means that the police might link her death to the deaths of Larry and

Nick. Those you did *do. Don't let yourself get caught. Don't go to prison. You're only twenty-nine, you still have plenty of living to do.*

Or he could put a bullet in his skull and make things better for everyone.

"Don't do it," Larry said. "Even I don't think that's the way to go, and I hate your fucking guts."

There'd be no suicide. Toby wasn't going to be found dead in his living room with his brains decorating the wall like abstract art. He did dumb things all the time, but he wasn't a complete moron, and he'd figure out a way to get through this.

Toby eased himself into the hot water. It felt wonderful on his frozen extremities, but it ignited the claw-marks on his back.

The antiseptic hurt even worse.

"That bitch," he said.

Mr. Zack glared at him. "Stop it. That's completely inappropriate."

"I know, I'm sorry, I just didn't think she'd actually do it."

"What exactly did she say?"

"She said she'd met this guy, she refused to tell me his name, and she said she was in love. I thought she was just pissed at me for some reason."

"Did you have a fight?"

"Not a serious one. Things weren't going as well as they used to, but I really thought she'd be here at the store when I came in this morning."

"THANK you for speaking with us, Mr. Floren."

"No problem."

"The last person to talk to Ms. Tomlinson, besides you of course, was her mother, two nights ago. I don't mind telling you that she shared a somewhat different view of your relationship with her daughter."

"What do you mean?"

The cop, Detective Dormin, smiled, though it was only with the corners of his mouth. He looked about forty and Toby had disliked him immediately.

"Apparently Melissa told her that things were going extremely well. She was in love with you. Thought you might even be The One."

Toby chuckled without humor. "Just like a woman, huh? One day she's madly in love, the next day she's running off with some stranger."

"Interesting that she didn't tell her mom about this."

"Do you think something else happened to her?"

"No, we're not ready to call it foul play quite yet. A girl that age doesn't have her head screwed on completely straight. I did find it interesting to go back through some files and see your name attached to another disappearance. Two disappearances, actually. You know who I'm talking about, right?"

"Of course I do."

"Apparently they ran away, too. Were never heard from again. You didn't get along with them very well, did you?"

"You're right. Fifteen years ago I was questioned about two missing kids. Dear Lord, it's a killing spree!"

"Hey, watch the lip. If you think this is a joking matter you're going to be very disappointed when I slap some cuffs on you. It was more like fourteen years, and there's no statute of limitations on murder."

"If you're accusing me of murder, I'd like a lawyer."

"I'm not accusing you of anything yet. When I do, I'll have all my ducks in a row. I hope you do as well. Tell me, Toby, if I may be so informal as to call you Toby, did you hear any gunshots last night?"

"Yeah. A bunch of them. I hear gunshots all the time. That's what happens when you live in a rural area."

"Again with the lip."

"Am I free to go?"

"You are, but I'd recommend that you stick around and answer as many questions as I've got for you. And I've got a lot of them. You're what we like to call a 'person of interest,' and I've got something of an obsessive personality. You don't want to be my pet project."

"Fine. What do you want to know?"

"Start from the beginning again. Be detailed."

IT'S A HUGE, vast forest. They'll never find her.

Toby's story held up to close scrutiny. It had to. Nobody would know he was out in the woods with Melissa. He couldn't imagine that she would have told anybody about Owen beforehand. If she had, and somebody came forth, he'd worry about it then, but for now he was just going to assume that his secret was safe.

He wondered how Owen was doing.

How much blood had he lost? Was he okay? How did a wild animal tend to a bullet wound?

Was Owen as lonely as he was?

Was Owen even still alive?

He wanted to go out into the forest to see him, just a quick glimpse, just to satisfy his curiosity, but of course he couldn't. He couldn't go back into the woods until he knew for certain that the police were no longer watching.

Anyway, he hated Owen now, right?

142

"HELLO, Mr. Floren, so sorry to drop in on you unexpectedly like this." Detective Dormin handed Toby a piece of paper. "This is a handy little search warrant. Judge Baird's number is on the top if you'd like to give him a call. I'll wait."

"That's okay."

"Great, I'm glad that you won't be giving us any problems. You've got some puffy eyes, Toby. Doing a lot of crying, have you? Guilt or sorrow? Maybe a little of both?"

"I lost somebody very close to me. I don't need you giving me crap about it."

"You're right. That was unkind of me. Nice place you've got here. I recommend that you find yourself a good book to read and a comfortable spot, because we're planning to be here for a while."

TOBY THREW up into the toilet. He couldn't keep any food down anymore.

Melissa. He missed her so much.

"HAD YOURSELF A NICE LITTLE BARBECUE, did you?" Detective Dormin asked. "Seems kind of cold for that sort of thing, but I'm not one to judge. Fresh ashes in there. The lab boys, they said they don't really look like charcoal. They say, and you're going to think this is the strangest thing, that it's fabric. Isn't that odd? Why would somebody be burning fabric on their barbecue grill? I'm a smart fellow, and I'm having trouble wrapping my mind around that."

"Am I under arrest?"

"Do you think you deserve to be?"

"Don't treat me like I'm a kid."

Dormin leaned across the table. "Do you know what I hate most in the world, Toby? Liars. I hate liars more than I hate murderers and rapists. It's a little quirk in my personality, I guess. So I'm not that fond of you. The fact that you cooked your clothes, that's suspicious to me. Why does a man burn his clothes? It's just peculiar. Now, I'll be honest with you, my wife has threatened on several occasions to burn my favorite pair of socks, the ones I still wear even though they've got holes in them, but you're not married, are you? You don't even have a girlfriend anymore. Unfortunately for me, my hunch that you burned your clothes to hide evidence because you wore them when you were murdering Melissa Tomlinson isn't enough to arrest you. But it's enough for me to ensure that you have some long, uncomfortable days. So why did you kill her?"

"I didn't."

"Yep. Some long, uncomfortable days."

"IN LOCAL NEWS, Hector Smith, age 78, was found deceased in his backyard by his grandchildren last night. Smith had reportedly gone out to investigate a disturbance, and awoke several neighbors, who called 911 to report screaming. Smith was apparently savaged as if by some sort of large animal. Chief of Police Martin Rundberg had this to say."

"At this time we do not know exactly what kind of animal attacked Hector Smith. We urge local residents to use extreme caution when venturing outdoors, until this thing is captured. Though we had men on the scene minutes after the call was made, Hector Smith's head was torn from his body, so obviously we're very alarmed and concerned about the situation..."

16

Toby trudged through the snow, miserably cold and—he had to admit—more than a little scared. There was a reason he rarely ventured out into the woods at night. The flashlight provided no real feeling of security, nor did the newly loaded gun in his pocket.

He had no plan of action. He didn't know if he was going to shoot Owen, given the chance, or just plead with him not to murder anybody else.

Kill anybody else. It wasn't murder when an animal did it.

He knew it was a terrible risk to go out into the woods when that detective could be watching his every move, but he had to talk with Owen. He couldn't sit at home, watching TV, and let the monster kill people.

It was unbearably cold. He didn't remember it ever being this cold, or snowing this hard.

Melissa's body was out here. Frozen solid. He wondered how she would have looked at him if she'd been told that someday he'd leave her mutilated corpse out in a pile of snow. He tried to picture the look of betrayal and hurt but couldn't.

Then again, was it worse than a mortuary keeping a body in a freezer?

Uh...yeah.

By the time he reached the cave, his face felt like it was completely frostbitten. There were no tracks. No imprints where the falling snow might have covered them up. It didn't look as if Owen were here.

Instead of calling out or tossing a rock, he walked into the cave unannounced.

Empty.

He shone the flashlight around, searching for traces of blood that would indicate that Owen had been inside. There was nothing. Owen had abandoned his home.

Toby sat on the icy ground and waited for him to return.

Owen didn't come back, of course. It was ridiculous to think that he would have. There was no magical connection between the two of them, where Owen would just happen to sense Toby's presence in the cave and hurry back there to reunite with his friend. He'd probably gutted another human being while Toby sat there for hours, staring at the empty cave exit.

Toby's joints ached and he really just wanted to curl up and go to sleep, but he forced himself to get up and begin the long cold trek home.

Toby wandered the streets all night, as he'd done for the past seven nights. Mr. Zack had given him paid leave "until things got sorted out," and he'd taken this opportunity to become nocturnal.

He didn't know what he was expecting to find. In a town of twenty-five thousand people, he wasn't likely to just stumble upon

Owen, hanging out in somebody's backyard. But it gave him a sense of purpose, feeble as it was.

Gave him something to do before Detective Dormin threw his ass in jail.

THE NEXT VICTIM WAS A JOGGER, a young woman who'd just turned eighteen. Her parents had begged her not to go jogging alone, but she'd laughed them off, insisting that she'd be perfectly fine.

They didn't find much of her. Just enough to identify her by three of her fingerprints.

"I NEED TO START DRINKING," Toby said, staring into the nearly empty refrigerator. That sounded like a fine idea. Guzzle some booze, get good and plastered, and forget his problems. Become the town drunk. And if he started babbling to complete strangers about his monster buddy in the woods, hey, nobody would believe him.

It was the best plan he'd concocted in his life. First thing tomorrow morning he'd go stock up on beer, or maybe whiskey, and get right into it. Drinking alone was supposedly a depressing activity, but it couldn't be more depressing than anything else in his life.

Something slammed against the kitchen window.

Toby quickly glanced over there. Total darkness outside. He shut the refrigerator door, then went over to the switch and turned on the light to illuminate the backyard.

Through the kitchen window, he saw Owen standing outside his house.

He immediately shut off the light, in case anybody was watching. He paced back and forth for a moment, trying to figure out if he should bring the gun or not, and decided not to. He threw on his bathrobe, opened the back door, and walked outside.

Owen turned toward him, head hung. Through the indoor light, Toby could see the blood caked on his arm. His left eye was also closed, the lid swollen.

"We both really screwed up, didn't we?" Toby asked. "I've already got gigantic skeletons in my closet, but that wasn't enough, I had to go and hang a few more in there."

Owen signed: *Friend hurt.*

"I know, I know. Your arm looks awful. I wonder if that's gangrene? Wouldn't surprise me. How did you know where I live?" He pointed to his house. "How did you know?"

Follow.

"When?"

Owen didn't answer. It didn't matter. Toby had walked the path from his house to Owen's cave hundreds of times, and though he always made Owen stop walking with him as soon as they were a mile away, it wasn't a stretch that Owen would have followed the path the rest of the way and figured out where he lived. He hoped to God that Owen hadn't pounded on anybody else's kitchen window first.

Owen tapped his eye.

"There's nothing I can do for you, Owen. You need to run away. People are hunting for you, and they're going to kill you. You need to run as far away as you possibly can. Never come back."

"*Toby.*"

"Go. If you come back here, I'll shoot you myself. You're lucky I'm even giving you a warning. I never want to see you again."

Owen signed: *I'm sorry.*

"Yeah, I'm sorry, too."

Owen tapped his eye again.

"I know you're in pain. I already said there's nothing I can do about it. This is your fault, too. You took Melissa away from me. Did you know that I was going to ask her to marry me? Did you?"

Owen hung his head even lower.

"Okay, that's not true—I don't know why I said that. But it was great to have somebody, you know what I mean? You're my best friend, but it's not like we can go to the movies or go get some french fries or anything like that, right? I needed to have part of a normal life, and you ruined that. And now you're killing people."

No.

"Bullshit. Don't lie to me. Why are you doing it?"

Owen rubbed his belly. *Hungry.*

"Then you can eat deer and squirrels and everything else you've been eating your whole life. You don't need to eat people. Those people had families, Owen. They had friends. The old man had *grandchildren*. What does that make you?"

No response.

"It makes you a monster, Owen. It makes you an awful, horrible monster. It makes you the goddamn Boogey Man. So you need to go back into the woods, run away, run to another state, and live like an animal instead of a nightmare."

Hurt.

"Stop saying that. I don't care."

Miss you.

"So what?"

Scared.

"Me too."

Toby sighed. He couldn't just send Owen away. If nothing else, he might go out and kill somebody else. There were only so many deaths he could have on his conscience before he went completely, genuinely insane and started seeing spiders crawling around on the inside of his eyelids.

"Okay, I'll help you. I'll try to make the hurt go away. We can't do it here, though. You need to go home." He signed: *home.*

Owen signed *home* back.

"You go there. I'll be there in a bit."

No.

"In a bit. I promise. It won't be long."

No.

Toby stood there for a long moment. Then he sighed again. "Okay, let me go get some things, and then I'll walk back with you."

———

THEY WALKED THROUGH THE WOODS, not speaking. Owen looked beaten, almost ashamed. *He should*, Toby thought.

The thing is, best friend or not, Owen wasn't human. He was an animal. And when he got hurt, he was going to react like an animal. If Toby got a fingernail in his eye, he'd probably go berserk, too. He just didn't happen to have claws and sharp teeth.

Melissa was gone forever. Why did Owen have to be?

Because he was a killer.

So was Toby.

But Toby had killed a couple of worthless bullies. Owen had killed two innocent victims and a girl who meant a lot to Toby. You couldn't compare them.

Owen's killings were based on hunger. On fear. On confusion. Toby's killings were based on rage.

What kind of friends was he going to make after this blew over? All of his life he was a social outcast. Did he really think that he'd start forging healthy new relationships after burying his girlfriend in the snow? Was banishing Owen from his life going to make things better, or create a gap that he had no chance of filling?

"You know," Toby said as they walked. "All friends have fights now and then. Usually there aren't dead bodies involved, but this isn't exactly a normal friendship, is it?"

He couldn't believe he was going to forgive Owen. Maybe the spiders were already squirming around, spinning webs in his eyeballs and he just couldn't see them.

"You have to promise me something. If anybody comes out here and it's not me, you need to run. Find a new place to live for a while. You're in a lot of danger if they find you. Do you understand?"

Owen didn't seem to get what he was saying, but by the time they reached the cave, Toby thought he'd made his message clear. Then he took the antiseptic and bandages out of his backpack, hoping that the process wasn't *too* ugly. If Owen was to go on another pain-related killing spree, having the alcohol rubbed on his wounds would be the thing to induce it.

OWEN'S HOWL of agony seemed to echo through the forest, loud enough to awaken the entire world.

TOBY WAS NO DOCTOR, or anything even close, but he thought he'd done a pretty good job of cleaning out Owen's wounds. It hadn't been an especially precise process—he mostly just splashed on the antiseptic and then ran for cover, but though the pain was clearly excruciating, Owen had made no attempt to attack him.

If the bullet was lodged in his arm, it was just going to have to stay there. Trying to dig it out with a knife couldn't end happily, even if Toby thought he had the surgical skill to do such a thing.

Owen gave him a hug.

Sorry.

"I can't believe we let this happen," said Toby. "We're friends forever, right? It's almost like we let a woman come between us. That stuff, it's all temporary. This—" He patted his chest, and then Owen's. "—is the real thing. They can't break our bond. They might think we're the most fucked up friendship of the 20th century, but they're not going to drive us apart. No matter what, we're together forever."

Yes.

"But you can never leave the forest again. Never. Not for anything. Promise me you'll never walk out of these woods for any reason."

Promise.

"And, also, don't kill anybody else, okay, buddy?"

"THERE'S something I hate worse than a liar," said Detective Dormin, lighting up a cigarette. "We found your girlfriend, but I'm sure my co-workers told you that when they were driving you here. Her body looked bad. I bet you can envision what I'm talking about, can't you?"

Toby remained silent.

"We don't see a lot of murders in Orange Leaf. Last one was, oh, about six years ago. Nothing fancy, just a good old-fashioned robbery. Wild animal attacks are something brand-new. If you exclude dogs, I don't think we've got any on record. So you can understand that there's a lot of pressure to find the thing that's out there killing folks. Not so much pressure on me personally, it's more of an animal control issue, but I tend to take a lot of responsibility that isn't necessarily mine."

"What's your point?" Toby asked.

"Sorry, I do tend to ramble on, don't I? My point, Mr. Floren, is that we know that the animal that chewed up Hector Smith and Janine McDouglas is the same one that chewed up your Melissa. I think you were there for it. I think you saw the whole thing. I think you watched that animal kill your girlfriend, and you couldn't save her, so you lied about the whole thing. Now why would you do that?"

"I have no idea."

"It's not something people lie about unless they've got something to hide. Just like people don't burn their clothes unless they're trying to hide something, like bloodstains. I have a pretty vivid imagination, so I can see it clear as day. Out walking in the woods with your girlfriend. Everything's nice and romantic. Maybe you're thinking you're going to get some, against a tree. Then something attacks her. You're close enough that you get her blood on your clothes. But you don't try to save her. If you tried to save her, you'd tell everybody what happened, wouldn't you? No, you left her there. Before you knew she was dead you left her there, and you ran to save your own skin. Now how far am I from the truth?"

Toby tried to summon some tears. He thought of Melissa, screaming on the ground while Owen bit into her, and the tears arrived with little effort.

"Do you know what I hate worse than a liar? A coward."

"It wasn't my fault."

"Get out of my sight. And try to live with what you've done. I hope it's a happy life."

TOBY SAW on the news that they'd found the cave.

It was empty. One of the men in the group caught a glimpse of something hiding in the bushes nearby, but it ran off before he could get a good look. His quick glimpse did match the description Toby had given to the police.

He hadn't described Owen in detail ("It was so dark, I could barely see anything!") but he'd offered up a general sketch of what their culprit might look like. At this point, why lie? What was somebody going to say? "Look! There's a giant hairy humanoid beast roaming around the neighborhood! But, no, wait, it doesn't match the description Toby Floren gave. Must be a different monster. Let this one go."

The mob—well, technically not a mob, but that's how Toby chose to think of it—gave pursuit for a while. It was hard to run in the deep snow, though, and they finally gave up.

The Chief of Police, not hiding his annoyance at the reporters' questions, explained that they couldn't search the entire forest for one animal, but that cops would be working double shifts to protect their citizens.

"We're out there, doing our best, but just be aware of the risk until this situation is resolved."

Toby gave it a long, excruciatingly slow week before he went out to the woods to look for Owen. He called out his name. So what if somebody heard him? It wasn't like Owen wore a nametag.

Nothing.

Owen had followed his instructions, which was a good thing, but Toby wondered if he'd ever come back.

17

1975. Age 30.

"Thirty. I'm old."

"Thirty is *not* old," Mr. Zack assured him. "Do you know how many sins I'd commit to be thirty again?"

"Wouldn't the whole point of being thirty again be to have the energy to commit more sins?"

"Well, different sins, anyway."

TOBY SAT OUTSIDE THE CAVE, running his fingers through the melting snow.

"You were supposed to come back."

"I CAN'T DO THIS ANYMORE."

"I understand. The problem is, you're a great employee, probably my best, but not everybody is cut out to be a manager."

Toby nodded. "I know. We've talked about it lots of times. For that kind of thing, you need social skills."

"I'm not saying that you don't have social skills, I'm saying—"

"You can say that I don't have social skills. It's all right."

"You don't have the skill set that would make you a good manager. How about that?"

"I understand. That's why I need to leave."

"I'm not going to hold you back. You're getting a gold-plated reference from me."

"Thanks. I appreciate it."

Mr. Zack shook Toby's hand. "I wish you nothing but the best. Maybe you'll be able to hire me someday, when you're a fabulously wealthy business owner."

"Maybe." He shook his head and chuckled. "Thirty years old. How did that happen?"

"HE'S NEVER COMING BACK," said Larry.

"Yes, he is."

"He's off having himself a hot summer fling with some other forest monster. How's that for irony? He destroys your love life and then goes off and enjoys his own."

"What if he got hurt?"

Larry considered that. "That seems reasonable. The lynch mob might have tracked him down. Skinned him, made bandanas out of his fur, sliced him open neck to groin and played 'keep-away' with his insides. Then they felt bad about reverting to primal savagery and all took a vow to keep it a secret."

"That's not what happened."

"His arm and eye did look pretty bad. You cleaned it up, but you can't expect to just rinse out a bullet wound and have everything heal up like a paper cut. Think of the infection. How much pus do you think leaked out of his eye before he couldn't take it anymore? Do you think his arm just sort of rotted off by itself, or is it still dangling there, flopping around, always getting in his way?"

"It's time for you to go now."

Larry shrugged. "Whatever. You're the boss."

Toby envisioned the ground splitting open. Withered hands grabbed Larry's feet and pulled him beneath the surface. He looked kind of bored while they did it.

"Do you know what's really sad?" Toby asked out loud, to nobody in particular. "Larry is probably my best friend at this point."

"I'M GOING to be blunt: this isn't working out."

"Why? What do you mean?"

"You're not getting along with the others in the mailroom."

"*What?* I haven't had any problems with anybody!" Toby insisted.

"They say that you make them uncomfortable."

"That doesn't make any sense!"

Toby's new boss, John Rydelor, frowned and looked nervously toward the door of his office, which was ajar. "Please lower your voice. You were hired on a six-week probationary period, and like I said in the interview, I believe that the only way to achieve success in business is through teamwork. The other members of the mailroom team have issues with you, and I'm going to respect their wishes."

"OWEN, you son of a bitch, how could you leave me? See what I did? I swept out your cave. It's the first time your cave has been swept in fifteen years! Come on, Owen, I really need to talk to somebody!"

———

HE'D RESISTED the idea of taking the roll of film, which had remained hidden in his bottom drawer, in to be developed. But if he couldn't have his monster, he could at least have pictures from their first encounters. He'd just tell the employee at the photo booth that it was a guy in a mask.

It didn't matter. The film was too old and couldn't be developed.

———

"HELLO?"

"Toby, it's Mom."

"Is everything okay? What's wrong?"

"Your father's had a stroke."

———

THEY CELEBRATED Thanksgiving in the hospital, three weeks early. It was always Dad's favorite holiday. Toby wasn't sure if Dad could smell the turkey or the mashed potatoes, but Toby liked to think that, at least in his mind, his father enjoyed the meal right along with them.

Toby wrote a wonderful speech for the memorial service, heartfelt yet amusing, but succumbed to uncontrollable tears after a few sentences and left the podium.

———

"DO YOU HAVE TYPING SKILLS?"

"I don't, but I can learn."

"We're not really a 'learn on the job' environment."

1976

"*Happy birthday to me...*"

"You don't want to come back? Fine! There's nothing to come back to!" Toby smashed the hammer into the side of the cave. He struck it again, harder this time, and shards of rock sprayed into the air.

He bashed at the stone wall again and again, bellowing with frustration. He refused to stop. Even when his arms ached so badly that they felt like the hammer had been smashing them instead of the wall, he kept at it.

He didn't quit until the hammer slipped out of his hands and he was physically unable to pick it back up.

Then he started kicking.

"Hello?"

"Toby?"

"Aunt Jean...?"

It didn't surprise him how thin she was. Aunt Jean had told him on the phone that she didn't have much of an appetite since Dad died. He'd told her that she needed to eat, and she promised him that she'd try, and she'd say something like "Your aunt is making me a milkshake right now," and then the next week she'd admit that she just wasn't very hungry.

He'd offered to move to California, to stay with her, but she'd laughed away the idea. He had his own life. She loved hearing him talk about it every Sunday. A great job, a serious girlfriend, lots of friends who got into wacky misadventures...she couldn't let him put everything on hold for her. She'd be fine. She just wasn't very hungry these days.

It wasn't her physical appearance that upset him when he walked into the hospital room. It was the bandages around her wrists.

"Do you want to be alone with her?" Aunt Jean asked.

"Yeah."

Aunt Jean nodded and left the room.

Toby sat down on the edge of the bed and patted her hand. "Why did you do it, Mom?"

"I really don't know." He could barely hear her.

"That's the kind of answer I'd give you when I was a kid. You wouldn't let me get away with it, either."

She gave him a weak smile. "I guess I just felt like your father was the only thing keeping me...sane."

"What do you mean?"

"I was sitting there in the bathroom, on the edge of the tub, and I was crying. I didn't feel bad about it. That's what you do when your husband dies—you cry."

Toby wiped his own tears from his eyes.

"And while I sat there, I suddenly thought that I didn't want to live without your father. And I knew there was a pair of scissors in the medicine cabinet, that I'd used to cut his hair the last time. I got them out, and I opened them up, and I didn't make a sound when I used them."

"God, Mom..."

"I didn't do it right, though. You shouldn't do it across the

wrist. You should do it up the arm. That's why I'm still here today."
She sighed. "I hope I'm not here tomorrow."

"Don't say that. That's horrible."

"I miss him so much."

"I know, but you can't just give up."

She looked straight at him. "I'm not giving up. I'm making a decision."

"I'll stay with you, Mom. I'll take care of you."

"No. You'll use up all of your vacation time."

———

THE NEXT MORNING she was gone.

———

TOBY LAY IN THE CAVE, staring at the ceiling. There were no stalagmites. Any good cave was supposed to have stalagmites. Or was it stalactites that hung from the ceiling, and stalagmites that grew from the floor?

It didn't matter. The cave didn't have either.

This was sure a small cave. No wonder Owen left. You couldn't live in a tiny little cave like this for your entire life.

1977

"I was told this job had upward mobility."

"It does."

"It does not! I'm still scraping rust stains off the floor!"

"You don't just climb the ladder automatically. It needs to be earned."

"I have earned it. I work my ass off here. Three people who started after me have moved out of The Pit."

"It's not all about hard work. Part of it is attitude. You want to work your way into an office, you need to start shaking some hands and building some skills. I've watched you, Floren. Sitting by yourself in the lunchroom is no way to work your way out of The Pit. What else are you good at? I don't know. Show me."

TOBY KNELT in front of Melissa's tombstone.

"I don't even know what to say to you. I'll just sit here and be quiet, if that's okay."

"*SLEEPIN' in a cave, oh yeah, I'm sleepin' in a cave. I'm feelin' pretty brave, 'cuz I'm sleepin' in a cave. I think...*"

What rhymed with cave? Fave. Pave. Save. Rave. Wave.

"*I think it is my fave, to be sleepin' in a cave. The path outside I'll pave, so I can get inside my cave. My money I will save, 'cuz the rent's really cheap when I'm sleepin' in a cave, except when I've still got a mortgage payment because I still usually sleep at my real house. About it I will rave, the love for sleepin' in a cave. When you walk outside please wave, to me sleepin' in a cave...*"

"HE'S ONLY BEEN HERE a week! How did he get out of The Pit before me?"

"Are you kidding? Look at his hair!"

"YOU SHOULD BASH your head against the wall until it's completely splattered," Larry suggested. "I mean, hit it *really* hard. I bet if you put your mind to it, you could crack that skull in under five hits. Go on, prove me wrong."

Nick giggled. "Put your mind to it. That's kind of funny."

"Ha! I didn't even plan that! Go ahead, Toby, put your mind to it and splatter your mind! I want to see your thoughts trickling down the wall."

"Both of you, go away."

"I don't think we're going anywhere for a while."

"OF COURSE I'll take you back," said Mr. Zack. "You're always welcome here. You know that."

"Thank you, sir."

"You don't have to call me sir. Who put those crazy ideas into your head? Sir. When I hit a hundred years old, you can call me sir. Until then, it's Mr. Zack. This is great timing, because guess who just announced that he's retiring?"

"Who?"

"Mr. Koerig. How would you like to become a butcher?"

TOBY KNEW that spending this much time in a cave was unhealthy, both physically and mentally. Even prehistoric cavemen probably didn't spend this much damn time in caves. It was a sign of a sick, sick brain.

He couldn't help himself.

He just knew that if he waited long enough, someday Owen would walk through that cave entrance.

And one day, he did.

18

"Where in the name of fuck have you been?" Toby demanded. "You selfish, inconsiderate, uncaring dickhead. Do you think I can even describe what I've gone through waiting for you?"

Then they hugged.

"I can't believe you're back. You haven't gone completely wild, right? You're not going to kill me?"

Owen gave him the thumbs-down sign.

"You still remember! Can you talk now? Do you speak fluent English? Where have you been? You've got a lot of explaining to do."

Owen signed: *Home.*

"Yeah, you're home now. Or are you just surprised that I'm in your home? I've taken pretty shitty care of the place, as you can see." Owen's eye seemed to have healed just fine. His arm had a bare patch and a scar where the bullet had hit it, but there was no indication that he was having any problems using the limb.

Owen tapped his belly.

"You're asking me for food? Fifteen seconds after you get back?

Get your own damn food."

Owen tapped his belly, then pointed at Toby.

"You want to give *me* food? I don't want to eat anything you would scavenge. Where the hell have you been?"

Owen repeated the *food* gesture.

"Don't get impatient with me. You're the one who's been gone for a couple of years. You want me to get food?"

Yes.

"Food for me?"

Yes.

"So you want me to get food for myself? You mean pack food, like for a trip?"

Yes.

"Why?"

Come with me.

"Are we going somewhere far?"

Yes.

"Okay, I'll go home and get some stuff. Will you still be here when I get back?"

Yes.

"Do you promise?"

Yes.

"What are you going to do while I'm gone?"

Sleep.

"Fair enough."

TOBY FILLED his backpack with food, mostly granola bars that had probably gone stale in his pantry but which he assumed were still edible and nutritious. They were certainly a lot healthier than the crap he'd been eating for the past couple of years. He refilled the Thermos with water, and double-checked the first-aid kit that he always carried. He'd used up quite a few of the Band-Aids from chips of cave wall hitting his arms and face, so he added a few more from the bathroom supply.

Toilet paper, a poncho, a spare set of shoes, and he was ready to go.

There was a carton of chocolate ice cream in the freezer. Owen would love that. He probably hadn't enjoyed a treat in years. But it would melt before Toby got back to the cave, and he didn't want to drag an ice chest out there along with his heavy backpack.

And, most important, Owen didn't deserve ice cream. Why even consider such a thing? What Owen deserved was a great big punch in the nose.

Still, he was elated to have him back.

HE HIKED BACK out to the cave, half expecting Owen to have abandoned him again. But the monster lay on the ground, curled up, fast asleep. Toby lay down next to him. He couldn't fall asleep —he still had concerns about his personal safety—but he did snuggle with the monster until sunrise.

AS THEY WALKED, Toby realized that he'd regained his appreciation for the beauty of the forest. Sunlight streamed through the canopy, illuminating a world of green. Birds chirped. Flowers bloomed. The entire forest was filled with the potential for discovery, for adventure.

And, yeah, it all sounded like a bad greeting card, but Toby didn't care. Despite a lack of sleep, he was wide awake. He was as excited about this journey as if he held a skull-and-crossbones-adorned treasure map, leading him to the location of a long-buried pirates' stash of gold, silver, and jewels. He was in a cobweb-filled corridor of a pyramid, avoiding poison-tainted death traps while seeking the sarcophagus of an ancient emperor. He was seated in the cockpit of a plane he'd built himself, flying over the South American jungle, searching for a lost tribe.

Owen led, of course. Sometimes Toby spoke to him. More often, he remained silent, lost in happy thought.

He got tired more quickly than Owen, and insisted on more rest breaks. When Owen balked, Toby reminded him of the whole "gone for two years" issue and Owen relented. They never rested for very long. Toby was too excited to resume their journey.

As darkness fell, Toby built a makeshift shelter out of some branches. It was about as makeshift as you could possibly get, but it only collapsed once during the night. This time, Toby had absolutely no trouble falling asleep. He dreamt of his mother making him a peanut butter and strawberry jelly sandwich, her wrists unscarred.

THE NEXT DAY they came upon a large pond. They splashed around in it for nearly half an hour. Owen jabbed a fish with his talon and threw it into his mouth whole, chewing it rapidly and then offering Toby a scale-tainted smile.

"You could have at least left me the tail or something," Toby said.

After a few minutes of effort, Owen hooked another one. Toby built a small fire, used a branch as a skewer, and cooked the fish up perfectly. He ate most of the meat. Owen ate the head, tail, and bones.

They swam some more, until Owen indicated that it was time to leave.

THE BUGS SEEMED a lot worse in this part of the forest, but Toby buried his face into Owen's back and was still able to get a decent night's sleep.

—————

"How far do you think we've come so far?" Toby asked, as they walked side-by-side. It had to be at least fifty miles. Maybe closer to seventy-five. "Are we almost there?"

Yes.

"This is going to be worth the trip, right? It's not going to just be a slightly larger cave? Because by 'long trip' I kind of thought you meant a few hours, and I never asked Mr. Zack for the time off. I'm in the butcher department now, so we spend a lot of time around knives. Just thought you should know."

—————

Toby took a bite of his tasteless granola bar. Even with raisins, or what purported to be raisins, it was pretty bland stuff. He hadn't really researched it, but he assumed that Magellan had much better cuisine during his travels.

"You need to hunt us a deer," Toby said. "A nice big plump one. Venison. Lots of venison." His stomach growled.

Owen began to jump up and down, almost like a baboon. Toby had never seen his friend act this excited. They must be getting close. Owen pointed ahead, jumped up and down a few more times, then raced off, leaving Toby behind.

Toby hurried after him.

He ran out into the clearing, and then froze. "Oh my God…"

There was another pond. Three creatures relaxed in the water. Long brown hair. Sunken yellow eyes. Enormous fangs. Sharp talons.

Toby didn't know if he should be awestruck or terrified.

Owen looked back at him, and frantically gestured for Toby to follow.

That didn't seem like a good idea. This was the kind of social encounter that one eased oneself into, perhaps over the course of weeks.

Were these Owen's relatives? Or had he just somehow found more of his own kind?

Were they going to welcome him as one of their own, or have a family feast?

What if Owen had lured him all the way out here to be dinner for his new friends? "You want human flesh? Oh, I can get that for you, no problem!"

Shit.

The monsters all looked over at Toby, and then began to quickly emerge from the pond. He should run. He should definitely run.

Instead, he stood there, forcing himself to stay as calm as possible, and let the monsters approach. They moved rapidly at first, until Owen waved them back, after which they carefully crept toward him, watching him with intense curiosity.

Toby couldn't be certain, but the monsters looked like a mother, a father, and a child.

They surrounded him. He shuddered as they gently poked at him, smelled him, tugged at his shirt, and ran their fingers through his hair. Any of the three could easily open up his scalp with one of their talons, and they didn't, so he supposed that he should feel safe. Such a feeling eluded him.

No nibbling. Please no nibbling.

Owen talked to them in a series of grunts and growls. They talked back. Toby didn't have the slightest clue what they were saying to each other, and Owen wasn't paying attention to his attempts to signal, but at least things didn't appear to be moving in a "Let's snap the wishbone" direction.

This went on for several minutes. One of them, the child, did indeed nibble at Toby's elbow, but after a loud growl from Owen he stopped.

Finally the crowd dispersed, leaving Toby standing there, drenched with sweat. The others went off into the trees.

"Is this your family?" Toby asked Owen.

No.

"They seem nice."

Owen led him to the pond. They waded out into the water, waist-deep, and just stood there, enjoying the sunshine. Owen still wasn't off the hook for being gone so damn long, but Toby was thrilled for his friend. He'd often considered that there might be other creatures like Owen out there, but he'd never expected to actually find them, or be smelled by them.

A moment later, the three creatures dragged a deer carcass near the pond. They waited expectantly as Toby and Owen walked to shore, and then all four creatures stared at Toby.

Aw, crap. He was pretty sure that they were waiting for their guest of honor to take the first bite.

"You know that I like my meat cooked, right?" Toby asked Owen. Of course, his friend conveniently had no idea what Toby was talking about. This seemed like a scenario where offending his hosts could be fatal, so Toby reached into the carcass, tore off a small chunk of meat (which didn't come free easily), and reluctantly shoved it into his mouth and chewed.

As if he'd fired a starter pistol, the monsters dove into the dead deer, burying their faces in the raw meat and ripping off huge pieces with their teeth. Owen gestured for Toby to join them, and he held up his hand and tried to make an "I'm full" gesture. Owen didn't insist, probably figuring "More deer for me!" and resumed the dining frenzy.

After the feast, the other three monsters crawled off, presumably to sleep. Toby and Owen sat alongside the pond, feet in the water. Owen yawned.

"You can go take a nap. There's no way in hell I'm falling asleep anytime soon."

No.

"So, pretty nice setup they've got. Are you their Uncle Owen or something?"

Owen didn't understand the question.

"It doesn't matter."

Stay.

"Me?"

Yes.

"Oh, no. It's nice out here, but I can't live out in the woods like this."

Or could he? He could spend the rest of his life hanging out by the pond, catching fish and teaching these creatures the art of not eating raw meat. Never shave or get another haircut—just let his hair grow out like Rip Van Winkle. Speak in grunts.

It was an appealing concept.

But, no, of course he couldn't do that. He'd be dead in a week. Any life spent out here would be a life spent making frequent treks into town, shoplifting supplies. He'd gotten away with murdering Larry and Nick, but he'd probably go to jail for swiping a toothbrush.

And he'd spent years building up a bond of trust with Owen—a bond that had, incidentally, resulted in a violent death. He couldn't just assume that these other three fanged clawed monsters weren't having carnivorous thoughts about him.

It *was* kind of cool that he'd found himself in a position where he *could* live with a quartet of monsters, should he choose to do so. Most people weren't given that particular opportunity.

He shook his head. "Can't do it, Owen."

Please.

"No. I appreciate that you made the trip to come get me—a couple of years late—but there's no way I can stay out here. I'm human. I'm bad at it, but I'm human."

Owen looked at him sadly.

"It'll be okay. You can stay out here with your friends. I'm much happier with this idea than the idea of being abandoned, you know?

I don't know how the hell I'm going to find my way back home, but I'll be okay."

No.

"It'll be fine. Stay with your own kind. I want you to be happy."

Come with you.

"I can't let you do that. You shouldn't be living in a cave all by yourself. What kind of life is that? You spend your days waiting for a loser like me to show up and entertain you for a couple of hours. You should stay here. Be with the kind of people you should actually talk to."

No.

"What kind of friend would I be if I let you go back to Orange Leaf? It's the worst place in the world. I'm going to miss you like you wouldn't believe, but you need to stay here."

No.

"Don't argue with me. I'll come visit. There's this shitty saying, 'If you love something, set it free,' and that's what I'm doing."

The thought of losing his best friend again, so soon after rediscovering him, made Toby heartsick, but he was speaking the truth. He couldn't let Owen come back with him. Not if he'd found a better life here.

Come with you.

"No."

Yes.

"Okay, we don't communicate well enough to have this kind of argument. So you win. We'll both go home." He repeated the signal: *Both go home.* "We'll leave first thing in the morning."

His plan was simple. As soon as Owen and the others fell asleep, Toby would sneak off and begin the journey home by himself. He couldn't stop Owen from following him, but hopefully Owen would get the message and stay here by the pond.

Or...he could inadvertently lead three extra monsters to Toby's hometown. That would be problematic.

Nah. They wouldn't leave this nice pond in favor of a crummy little cave. Owen had never before abandoned his dwelling since Toby knew him, so whatever kind of creatures they were, they liked to stay in one place. He wouldn't be able to get the other three to uproot themselves just to hang out with a skinny pink-skinned idiot. Right?

And if Owen did follow him back, great. He'd have his friend back with a clear conscience.

As evening approached, he spent a short amount of time making a rickety shelter out of branches. He was capable of doing much better, he was certain, but this one didn't need to last long. As he lay the branches together, he watched Owen play-wrestle with the child in the mud near the pond.

Toby had named the child Scruffer. The female (he thought) he named Esmerelda. The male (he knew) he named Brutus. There was no hidden meaning to these names; he just thought they were appropriate.

After dark, the creatures went into their den and went to sleep.

Boy, was it dark. Toby couldn't remember ever having been in such complete, enveloping darkness. He couldn't even see the moon through the trees. There could be thousands of snakes slithering only inches from his body. He had a flashlight, which he'd use when he got far enough from their camp, but maybe this was better as an "early in the morning, before they wake up" plan than a "late at night, right after they go to sleep" one.

And he was exhausted. Not a good idea to walk through the pitch-black forest when you were exhausted.

He'd sleep for a couple of hours and decide the best course of action from there.

⸻

HE WOKE to Owen prodding him.

No, wait, *was* it Owen…?

A clawed hand grabbed his ankle, squeezing tight.

19

Toby screamed as he was dragged out of the shelter. It fell apart around him, branches scraping his face as the monster pulled his leg. He heard a hungry growl—it had to be Brutus.

He grabbed a branch—hopefully a long one—and jabbed it forward. Felt like a direct hit. But the roar sounded like fury, not pain.

He jabbed a second time. Missed. His other arm brushed against his backpack, so he grabbed that by the strap and swung it as hard as he could. There was a satisfying *smack* as it struck its target. The claw released his ankle.

Brutus's roar was still all fury.

He swung the backpack again, bashing Brutus in what he hoped was the face. Some warm wet drops hit his stomach. And then Brutus' talons raked down his leg, not scraping deep, but enough to rip through his jeans and almost certainly draw blood.

"*Owen!*"

He kicked. Something gave way beneath his shoe, and Brutus

175

let out a sharp whine like a hurt dog. Toby scooted backwards, wincing as his hands came down on rough branches. He thought he might have knocked out some of Brutus' teeth, but he couldn't be sure.

The talons wrapped around his ankle again.

He bashed his free foot against them. This time he knew without seeing that he'd broken off at least a couple of the talons. Brutus howled.

Toby scrambled back until he collided with a tree. He immediately turned around, grabbed a branch to help pull himself to his feet, and began to climb, the backpack dangling from his shoulder. He'd never seen Owen climb anything, so maybe—

Brutus yanked him off the tree.

Then something yanked Brutus off of him.

There was hissing and tearing and chaos but Toby tried to focus entirely on climbing the branches. Get up the tree, further than Brutus could reach. Keep himself from being shredded just long enough for Owen to make everything all right.

A roar of pain. Owen.

Toby grabbed for the branch he'd been pulled from. Found it in the dark. Used it to steady himself as he stepped up onto the lowest branch and started to climb again. In his panic, he tugged so hard on the next branch that it snapped free and he nearly lost his balance, almost plunging into the bedlam below.

He kept moving.

The tree shook as both monsters slammed into it.

Toby climbed up a few more feet, just to be sure he was high enough. His left hand stung like crazy—he'd really gouged it bad on one of the branches.

He held on tight, trying to catch his breath as he watched the two black figures struggle. His eyes had only barely begun to adjust to the darkness, not enough to let him make out any details, but the sounds and the shapes were enough to prove that neither creature had any intention of letting the other live.

A wail from further away. The child?

Toby let go of the tree with his bloody hand and unzipped the backpack, fishing out the flashlight. He turned it on and shone the beam downward, just in time to catch a glimpse of Brutus' talons tearing across Owen's chest.

Owen howled and returned the vicious favor.

They circled each other, snarling. Brutus dove at him, and both monsters rolled on the ground, clawing, growling, biting.

Toby watched the spectacle with horror. *Please don't let Owen die...*

But a small part of him, a part that remained an eight year-old boy, watched in amazement, unable to believe that he was actually getting to watch two bloodthirsty monsters battle it out in a death match.

Then he cringed as Brutus jammed his talons deep into Owen's side.

Owen threw back his head and let out a sound of such intense distress that it felt like a crossbow bolt piercing Toby's brain. Toby screamed Owen's name, wishing he could do *something* to save his friend.

Owen clearly had no intention of giving up the fight. He lowered himself into a crouch, then locked his jaws onto Brutus' leg. The other monster bellowed with pain and tried to shake him off, but Owen's teeth remained deep in his flesh, not coming loose until Owen tore off six inches of bloody fur.

Toby threw the only thing in his backpack that had any real weight—his thermos. It was a perfect throw, cracking against the back of Brutus' skull, but it didn't seem to phase the monster.

Though Toby couldn't see Brutus' eyes, he could imagine them, bloodshot and red with rage. Brutus slashed Owen across the chest with his claws once, twice, three times.

Toby didn't know what he could do to help, but he had to try something. He couldn't just hide in a tree and watch Owen get ripped apart. Better to die on the ground. If he had to, he'd beat Brutus to death with the goddamn flashlight.

He climbed down a couple of branches, then jumped all the way. The light beam shifted as he landed, clearly illuminating Owen's face. Owen gaped at him as if to say *"What the hell are you doing?"*

Brutus looked at him as well. Despite his blood-soaked fur and a protruding bone, the monster still appeared hungry.

Owen grabbed Brutus by the wrist and swung him into a different tree. Brutus' elbow collided with the trunk, his arm snapping backwards, bone bursting through fur.

And then Owen's hands were in Brutus' mouth, and he was pulling, Brutus' teeth were imbedded in his palms but Owen kept pulling, and Brutus' tongue lashed back and forth, and blood dribbled between Owen's fingers, and Owen's eyes were squeezed shut and his jaws were closed tight as he struggled and struggled and then there was a wet *rip* as Brutus' cheeks tore apart and a *crack* as the top half of his head was wrenched backwards.

Owen released his grip, and the dead beast dropped to the ground.

Another wail.

Toby swung the flashlight beam around. Esmerelda and Scruffer stood there. Scruffer moved first, but within seconds both of them were cradling Brutus's limp form.

Owen stared at them. He raised his palm over his eyes as Toby flashed the light in his face. Toby thought he'd caught a glimpse of a tear.

Toby took Owen by the wrist and quickly led him through the woods, away from there.

———

"I'M SORRY," Toby said, after they'd gone far enough that the howls of sorrow could no longer be heard.

Owen said nothing.

————

IT WAS A LONG JOURNEY HOME. They were both tired and hurt and, though Owen became slightly more communicative after their first afternoon nap, the monster seemed depressed.

Toby wondered if Owen would have followed him back to Orange Leaf, had Toby's plan to sneak off in the middle of the night been successful. He liked to think that Owen would have. And at least then it would've been Owen's choice, instead of the way it was now, where he was banished from a society with a known population of three.

"We'll really fix the cave up nice," Toby said. "We'll dig our own pond. How long can that take with claws like you've got? We'll build ourselves a luxury resort right out there in the woods. What do you want to call it?"

Stop.

"Stop what?"

Stop talk.

"Fine. Whatever."

————

"I KNOW you're busy being all sad and stuff, but I would like to take a moment to point out how unbelievably cool it was when you ripped that thing's head in half," Toby said.

That seemed to cheer Owen up a bit.

————

"Do you know what makes you such a good friend?" Toby asked. "The fact that without you, I'd be dead now. I'm not talking about you saving my life, because I definitely would have done that for you if our roles were reversed. Oh, yeah, I would've grabbed that thing by the jaw and tore its chin right off, mark my words. But what I appreciate most in our friendship right now is your animal instinct, because I never thought that this whole voyage was supposed to be a one-way trip, and so I wasn't leaving any breadcrumbs to mark my way home. I'd be dead right now. Completely dead. Wolves would be snacking on me, and forest monkeys would be tossing my clothes around. So thank you, Owen, for your innate sense of direction."

Yes.

"Damn, but you're a good conversationalist. Time to change your bandages."

———

"Know what you need? A last name. I think you've earned it. Owen Smith? Owen White? Owen Jones? Owen DeathTeethBiter? When we get home, if we ever do, we'll just march right into City Hall and demand the necessary paperwork to give you a last name. How does that sound?"

———

"Are we there yet?"

No.

"Are you sure?"

Yes.

"Are we there yet?"

No.

"Are you sure?"

Yes.

———

THE THERMOS WAS LONG EMPTY, and they hadn't found a stream or a pond or any water at all since yesterday. Toby was no longer sure that Owen was taking him back the same way. This could be really bad.

THE SOUND of a car driving past.

Toby rushed up ahead, and emerged from the forest next to a paved road. He recognized the graffiti on the "Curve Ahead" sign, and returned to Owen.

"We're *fifteen* miles off," he announced. "I really wish you could hitchhike. I take back my compliments about your sense of direction."

They continued walking through the forest together, following the road but staying deep enough in the woods that no passing vehicles would see the man and his monster.

THE CAVE DID NOT ACTUALLY GLOW with an otherworldly golden aura, but it seemed to for a moment. Toby changed Owen's bandages again, gave the monster a hug, and then left him to get some desperately needed rest.

When Toby got home and looked at himself in the mirror, he nearly ran screaming from the house. Wow. That must be what feral people who'd been raised by wolves looked like.

He showered until the hot water was gone.

Then he slept.

Then he tried to figure out how exactly he was going to explain his absence from work.

"I DON'T BELIEVE YOU," said Mr. Zack, folding his arms in front of his chest.

"What?"

"I'm sorry, Toby, I don't believe you."

"How can you not believe me? I'm all beat up!"

"Because when people are in car accidents, they call. Not necessarily the first day, but by the seventh day they usually think to pick up the phone."

"I was in Maine!"

"They have phones in Maine. I've seen them. If you bring me a note from your doctor in Maine that says that you were in such bad shape that you couldn't even make a phone call, or ask somebody to make a phone call for you, then I'll reconsider. Otherwise, I have to follow my gut instinct that you're lying. I'm happy to cut you lots of slack, you know that, but I can't have people working for me who are unreliable. You can goof off and mouth off and boink your girlfriend in the stock room, but..." He trailed off. "I'm sorry, I shouldn't have brought her up. That was horrible."

"It's okay."

"But you understand what I'm saying, right? You can't disappear for a week and expect a job to be waiting for you when you get back."

Toby nodded. "I understand. I'm sorry."

"I'm sorry, too."

TOBY SAT ON HIS COUCH, newspaper open to the classified ads. He'd circled a couple of items, but there wasn't anything that came close to singing out to him.

He skimmed the ads again, just in case there was something amazingly exciting that he'd missed.

Nope.

He flipped back to the funny pages. Yeah, the comics were way more interesting than the classifieds. Even the ones without punchlines like *Gasoline Alley.*

He liked to draw. At least, he used to.

Maybe it was time to restart his hobby...

20

GLIMPSES
1978

"And here in the last panel, he says 'Glub, glub' as they dunk him into the toilet." Toby pointed to the carefully rendered artwork. "What do you think?"

No.

"But it looks like a toilet, right? Do you know how hard it is to draw a toilet and make it look three-dimensional?"

No.

"It's a pain in the ass. I really wish you had a better sense of humor, because I need to test these gags out on somebody who can laugh at things other than me hurting myself."

"Perfect!" Henry Lynch, an editor at the *Orange Leaf Times*, held up Toby's work and examined it closely. "Absolutely perfect. Yes, you're hired."

Toby grinned. He'd cut himself pretty bad with the razor blade, trying to cut the newspaper copy to the exact specifications, and he'd gotten hot wax all over his sleeve when he did the layout, but he didn't tell that to Mr. Lynch.

"I need to hire older people more often. Kids today, they have no patience for the art of newspaper layout."

"Thank you, sir."

"OKAY, which do you like better? This—" He held up the drawing of Rusty with a mustache and goatee. "—or this?" He held up the drawing of Rusty, clean-shaven.

Owen offered no immediate opinion.

"Please don't poke this one with your claw."

WHEN TOBY COMPLETED his twenty-fifth satisfactory comic strip, he celebrated by making a homemade banana split with extra hot fudge, extra strawberries, extra pineapple topping, extra whipped cream, and three maraschino cherries.

He felt a little sick afterward.

Then he re-read the strips in order and decided that none of them were even remotely funny. Instead of throwing them away, he taped them up on his bedroom wall, where they could haunt him and provide a constant reminder to do better.

"LOOK what I've got here. Oooooh yeah." Toby took the Styrofoam container out of his backpack and popped open the lid. "Two New York strip steaks. One medium well, one rare. Mr. Zack still cuts me a special deal."

HE ERASED the pencil drawing of Pugg's hand for the tenth or eleventh time. It was incredibly difficult to draw a dog holding a telephone receiver. Paws weren't meant to hold telephones, he supposed.

After another half an hour, he got the details just right, and reached for the ink.

"NOT THAT YOU ASKED, but I still don't have a title. *Peanuts* doesn't actually mean anything, as far as I know. Maybe I'll call it *Tomatoes.*"

1979

"What do you know about proofreading?" Mr. Lynch asked.

"Uh, nothing, but I can learn."

"Can you learn today? Helen's having her baby early and I'm kind of stuck."

"SO WHAT DO you think of this? The strip wasn't working out, but I did these five as a single panel. I think they're pretty funny. I couldn't get Rusty's hair right so I got frustrated and added a cowboy hat, but it makes him more visually interesting, don't you think? No? Do you even understand art?"

TOBY REACHED for his glass of apple juice, spilled the bottle of ink all over the seventh version of the drawing he was working on, and used several words that he could never include in the comic itself.

"I'M CALLING IT *RUSTY & PUGG*. Not inventive, I know, but it has a nice rhythm to it, right? *Rusty & Pugg. Rusty & Pugg.* I'd read it, wouldn't you? Also, I'm going back to the strip format instead of the single panel."

MR. LYNCH TOSSED the newspaper on his desk in front of Toby. "I got three different complaints about this typo. It's right in the headline. Makes us look stupid."

"What's wrong with it?"

"Raccoon has two c's."

"It doesn't have to. Both spellings are correct."

Mr. Lynch frowned, then grabbed a dictionary from the corner of his desk and flipped through the pages. "I'll be damned, you're right. What the hell is wrong with these idiot readers?"

"I KNOW there aren't any monsters in it, but it's pretty good, don't you think?" asked Toby, flipping through the pages one by one.

Yes.

"I'm going to mail the samples off to a few syndicates tomorrow. Wish me luck, buddy."

Happy.

"Me too."

1980

"Do you know what today is? I bet you have no idea. Exactly twenty years ago, I discovered your cave. Can you freakin' believe that? We've known each other for twenty years! That's crazy! It's more than half of my life! And we've both got some grey hair to show for it."

He scratched Owen behind the ear, which is where most of the monster's grey hair had sprouted, though he also had small tufts on his shoulders. Toby hadn't really noticed his own until his last haircut, when he looked at the pile of hair on the barbershop floor and saw more grey than black.

"To celebrate twenty years of friendship, I've decided that this bullshit about me walking four miles each way to your cave has got to stop. So look what I drew for you."

Toby unfolded a large piece of paper and handed it to Owen. The talon of Owen's index finger tore through the center.

"That's okay, it's just a copy. That's the plan for your new house. Shack, to be more accurate, but it'll be nicer than what you've got here. I've picked out a nice spot maybe a mile from my house, we're going to cut down some trees, and we're going to build you a nice new dwelling."

———

"HEAR ANYTHING YET?" asked Mr. Lynch.

"Not yet."

"Not from anybody? How long has it been?"

"Nine weeks."

"Well, if *Rusty & Pugg* gets picked up, I'll happily cancel *Hagar the Horrible* to make room."

———

"WHAT ARE YOU DRAWING?" asked the woman, pausing to glance

at his table as she walked to her own booth. Her tray had a single burger and fries—maybe she was having lunch alone.

"It's a comic strip."

"Oh, are you a cartoonist?"

"Trying to be." Toby tilted the strip, which didn't really help her see it better but gave him something to do with his hands. "The dog is Pugg and the human is Rusty."

He sat there, watching nervously as she silently read the strip, which involved Rusty getting a letter from the IRS. She looked a couple of years younger than him, had curly red hair, and had eyes that were such a beautiful shade of green that they seemed almost otherworldly.

Would she laugh at the punchline? Or at least smile?

He could imagine her smile. Radiant. Perfect white teeth.

"Hmmm," she said, showing no sign of amusement as she looked away from the strip. "Interesting. Good luck with it." She walked to her own table and sat down to eat.

Toby crumpled up the strip.

TOBY HAD FOUND a spot where he could make sufficient room for Owen's new home by only cutting down three trees, which he was pretty sure he wasn't actually supposed to be doing, so he hoped nobody would hear the crashes.

It was unlikely that anybody would. Somehow Toby and Owen's forest had escaped the notice of the evil logging industry all this time (Toby liked to think that the loggers would *love* to ravage the land, but were frightened away by whispered tales of a deadly monster that lurked within) and he'd never seen a single human being out here during his walks, so he figured the risk of Owen being discovered was extremely low.

All of the exercise was keeping him in good shape, but he was getting to the age where sometimes he was a little sore after getting back home from his visits. In another decade, he'd be thankful he'd built the shack.

He was a little concerned about bringing Owen closer to the populace...but, what danger was he really creating? If Owen wanted to leave the forest, he would, whether he was four miles away or one. As far as Toby knew, he'd never left the woods again after the...incidents, and was unlikely to leave it ever again.

"*Dear Mr. Floren, though we reviewed your materials with great interest, we regret to inform you...*"

As Toby chopped up the logs, Owen dragged them out of the way. Owen was strong and pretty good at basic manual labor but he wasn't much of a tool-user, or else Toby would have made him chop up the logs himself. Putting a sharp bladed weapon into his claws seemed like a potential descent into unnecessary amputation.

"Now, don't expect indoor plumbing or electricity or anything like that," Toby said. "We probably won't have windows either—I don't think you want any hikers peeking into your living room. Basically just think of it as a wooden cave that's closer to my house."

Like cave.

"I like the cave, too, but this is seriously overdue. Anyway, you'll have a door, just like civilized people."

This envelope was thick. Too thick to just be his samples back.

How thick was a syndication contract? With all of the complicated merchandising rights and stuff, he could easily see a contract being ridiculously thick.

Don't get too excited, he warned himself. *This could be a hundred pages of detailed description of how much they hated my submission, followed by a demand for me to never submit them another piece of work for as long as I live, followed by a restraining order, just in case.*

It wasn't.

It was, however, just a form rejection, along with a free catalog from their parent company.

"YOU LIKE IT?"

No.

"Remember, it's just the frame. It's not the completed shack."

Love it.

"THAT WAS INCREDIBLE," she said, as Toby rolled off of her. "I just can't even describe it. You made me feel like a woman again."

"Thanks."

"I'm in a state of shock at how good that was. We need to do this again. You'll call me, right?"

"Do I get a discount next time?"

"If you become a regular, we'll see."

She fixed up her makeup as Toby got dressed. It was hard to be flattered by her confessions of bliss when he knew that he'd been laughably bad in bed, and when he knew she'd overcharged him but he'd been too embarrassed to negotiate.

And he knew the feeling of self-loathing would kick in as soon as he left the hotel room. But he also knew that it would fade by morning.

THREE BILLS. Four pieces of junk mail. No self-addressed stamped envelopes.

Damn.

"OWEN, hold it! Hold it, Owen! Owen, I'm losing it! Owen—!"

The entire north wall crashed to the ground.

"You're a jerk, Owen."

At least he could incorporate this into a comic strip.

"I'D LIKE to start writing articles," Toby said.

"That's a great idea. I was thinking the same thing." Mr. Lynch searched around his desk for a few moments, found a manila folder, and handed it to him. "Write up these obituaries and have them to me by three."

TOBY AND OWEN stood in the clearing, looking at what they'd accomplished.

The shack looked...well, it looked like crap. But it was sturdy, moderately furnished (including a mattress that Toby had dragged all the way out here, nearly throwing out his back), and—most importantly—a lot closer to Toby's house.

"Welcome to your new home. Try not to bring too many bones in here."

"*DEAR SIR OR MADAM, thank you for your recent submission. Unfortunately, we longer review unagented queries...*"

1981

"I'm not deluding myself, right? This is good stuff, isn't it? I'm not saying it's brilliant, but it's better than a lot of the strips out there. You'd think somebody would read it and laugh. You're not just humoring me, are you? I mean, I know you're not the best person to judge punchlines, but you like the artwork, right?"

Pretty.

"Thanks, but it's not supposed to be pretty. It's supposed to be wacky and funny. I just don't want to spend this much time on it if it's not something that people are going to enjoy."

IN THE DREAM, Owen slashed at the old man with his claws, slicing a red crisscross pattern across his entire body. The pieces of flesh tumbled to the ground as his grandchildren screamed. Then Toby was sitting in the front row of the funeral he hadn't attended outside of his dreams.

"Whose fault is it when a wild animal goes berserk like that?" asked a woman seated directly behind him. Her voice had an almost musical lilt.

"Why, it's Toby Floren's fault, of course!" the man next to her replied.

"I agree. It's every bit as much his fault as if he'd stabbed a knife into that poor old man and that poor young woman."

"He should be severely punished," the man said.

"You don't understand...it's not my fault," Toby protested. "We're friends. I don't own him. Whatever he does, no matter how bad it is, is out of my..."

He realized that he was no longer dreaming and was in his bedroom, talking out loud. He wished that he could just wake up screaming, like a normal person did—at least in the movies.

Dear Toby,

Thank you for your submission of Rusty & Pugg, *and our apologies for the delay in our response. Your talent as an artist is very evident from these sample strips. Unfortunately, though we enjoyed the art very much, we felt that the humor was weak and often confusing, and that neither Rusty nor Pugg had a strong enough personality to make the strip a success.*

We wish the very best of luck in your future endeavors.

"I got my first personalized rejection!" Toby shouted.

Two self-addressed stamped envelopes were in Toby's mailbox the same day. A thick one and a thin one. The last two. Wouldn't it be hilarious if he'd been waiting all of this time, and got two acceptances the same day?

He tore open the first envelope, the thick one, and pulled out the cover letter: "*Thank you for your submission. Unfortunately—*" This one didn't even have a salutation.

Okay. Down to one.

He opened the envelope, took a deep breath, and then wondered if he should take the letter to Owen's shack so they could read it together. If this was good news—and Toby couldn't help but feel that it was—they should share the joy. How awesome would it be to get the very last response, walk it all the way to the shack, and have it be an acceptance? They'd scream so loud that the walls of the shack would blow apart.

The envelope was only thick enough to contain a letter. They hadn't returned his samples.

He should definitely walk it over to Owen.

Screw it. He couldn't wait that long. He pulled the letter out of the envelope and unfolded it.

"*Dear Sir, thank you for your submission. However, we regret to inform you that your material, while interesting, doesn't meet our present needs. We wish you—*"

Damn.

He wasn't going to give up, but this was disheartening in a big way. He supposed that most cartoonists went through this process for several years before getting the big "Yes," but he was off to a late start. Christ, he was almost forty.

He looked at the letter again, as if the message might have changed.

"*—doesn't meet our present needs. We wish you the best of luck with* Mom & Runts, *and if you create other projects in the future, please feel free to send them.*"

They'd put the wrong letter in his envelope.

Holy shit.

He quickly hurried into the kitchen and picked up the telephone. He dialed the number on the letterhead and chewed on his fingernails—a habit he just now acquired—while he waited for the receptionist to put him through to the secretary who could answer his question.

The secretary's intern answered, and apologetically explained that the secretary had left early today and that he wasn't sure how to research the issue, but that she'd be back tomorrow—no, wait, she'd be back the day *after* tomorrow, and if Toby called then, she'd happily answer his question.

TOBY LED OWEN a few miles into the forest, and his friend joined him in several minutes of the loudest frustrated bellowing that Toby had ever engaged in.

He felt better when they were done.

196

THE SECRETARY APOLOGIZED—SHE had indeed put the wrong letter in Toby's envelope, and his letter had gone to the creator of *Mom & Runts.*

Toby's letter was also a rejection, but without the offer to review future projects.

1982

Toby n' Owen, a wacky strip about two aliens stranded on earth, fared no better.

1983

"You believe in me, right?"
Yes.

1984

When Toby checked the mail, there was a self-addressed stamped envelope inside.

And a check.

The Blender, a small press magazine, had bought one of his comic strips for five bucks.

He practically danced the entire way to Owen's shelter.

21

1985. 40 years old.

The woman in turquoise, who said her name was Sarah Habley, looked at the linoleum floor and shifted uncomfortably in her seat as she spoke. "It's been almost four years, and I still cry at weird times, just out of nowhere. I feel like I should be over it by now. Not *missing* him, but crying over him like that. And that part I can deal with, I guess, but sometimes I can only remember him the way he was at the end, not the way he used to be. I can look right at our wedding pictures and still only remember those last few months."

She didn't cry now, though she held a Kleenex and twisted it between her fingers. "Tom was able to joke about it. 'I've got stomach cancer? Gee, I guess I shouldn't have eaten so much cancer.' If he knew that I was still crying and dwelling on the bad times, he'd be devastated. That's all I have to say, I guess. I'm glad to be here."

The other people in the circle nodded sympathetically. The

leader, a middle-aged man, looked at Toby and gave him a kind smile. "Your turn."

"Oh, I pass."

"At least tell us your name."

"Toby."

"And, Toby, how long were you married?"

"I wasn't. I—I'm in the wrong room. I came for the artists' meeting."

"That's in 301."

"Yeah, I think my flier had the wrong number. I just thought it would be kind of—you know, terrible to walk out on people sharing cancer stories. I'm sorry. Please skip me."

The leader gave him a very strange look. "Uh, you don't have to stay."

"I'm fine." The only way Toby thought he could feel more awkward was to get up and have all of these people watch him sheepishly slink toward the door. He'd actually figured out that he was in the wrong room before the group had started speaking, but he'd been transfixed by Sarah, who'd seemed to be silently trying to talk herself out of bolting for the exit.

When he got called on, he momentarily considered making up a story about how his wife died of cancer, just to avoid admitting that he was in the wrong room. But if he was found out then they'd think he was the kind of sicko who got his cheap thrills by attending meetings of people whose spouses succumbed to cancer and pretending to be one of them, which was a pretty bizarre thing to do.

The leader mercifully moved on to the next person. Toby sat there for the rest of the meeting, trying not to fidget and trying not to stare.

He thought maybe he was in love with her.

He wouldn't share this information with her, of course. There weren't many better ways to terminate a potential romance than by walking up to her and saying "I think I'm in love with you." Just feeling that way probably made him kind of creepy.

Still, he'd never seen anybody who captivated him in quite that way. Was it her sadness? He didn't think so. He could walk into any bar and see a lot of sad women.

Toby sat there for the rest of the meeting, trying to listen in a caring manner to the other participants. The stories were even more depressing than he would have expected, given the subject matter, and more than once he had to wipe away an embarrassed tear.

"Okay, we'll see you next week," said the leader. "Thank you all for coming."

Everybody stood up. Toby had to go over and talk to her. He just had to. This was unquestionably one of those "do this, or regret it for the rest of your life" moments. As she slung her purse over her shoulder, he walked across the room and offered up a feeble smile.

"Hi," he said.

Sarah looked wary. "Hi."

"I just wanted to say I'm sorry. You know, about what happened to your husband."

"Oh. Thank you. I appreciate that."

"I'm not trying to hit on you," he clarified. "This would be the most inappropriate place ever for that kind of thing."

"I appreciate that, too." She smiled, just a bit. "The funeral would probably be worse, though."

"Yeah."

Say something better than "Yeah," moron! Be witty! Be charming! Be clever!

Toby said nothing else.

"So you're an artist?"

"Yeah. I apologize for being a dumb-ass and disrupting your meeting. I'm a dumb-ass a lot, but not usually at quite this level."

Don't talk about being a dumb-ass!

"It's okay."

"Good."

"I need to get going. Best of luck with your art."

"Thanks."

There was no possible way to justify continuing the conversation further, and so Toby let her go.

"Philosophical question," said Toby, reclining in the beanbag he'd dragged out to Owen's shack. Owen had made a big slit down the side, but it was still usable for now. "What do you think is a worse way to die? Cancer, or being devoured by somebody like you?"

He broke his Slim Jim in half and tossed a piece to Owen, who caught it in his mouth.

"I'm going to go with cancer. In fact, I would say any kind of cancer. No offense, I'm sure your jaws hurt like hell, but it can't possibly compare to a slow, lingering death."

Owen did not seem to have taken offense.

"It's hard for me to even conceive of what she went through. I mean, I haven't seen pictures of the guy, I never got to meet him, I don't even know what color his hair is, but it just seems like an unimaginably awful way to go. How do you deal with somebody you love dying that way? With you, it's just gobble, gobble, gobble and it's over."

He nibbled the Slim Jim and then tossed the rest of it to Owen.

"And it's not the whole 'her husband died of cancer' thing that fascinates me about her. The whole room was filled with people whose husbands and wives died like that. I dunno, I just looked at her and...it's hard to explain, but you know what I mean, right? Are you getting tired of hearing me talk about her?"

The next Saturday at 1:00 PM, Toby sat at home in his living room, extremely aware that the meeting had just started. The support meeting was weekly. The artists' meeting was monthly. He had no legitimate reason to be in that building.

Showing up there made him the creepy stalker guy.

He didn't want to be the creepy stalker guy.

There was no rule saying that he couldn't be at that meeting just to offer moral support for their personal tragedies, but he didn't want to come off like a—actually, maybe there *was* a rule about that. It would make sense. You wouldn't want a bunch of people like him causing disruptions. So if he showed up, the leader would most likely look a bit uncomfortable for a moment, clear his throat, and politely but firmly inform Toby that this was really meant to be a support group for people who'd lost loved ones to cancer, and that while he appreciated Toby's presence, he was going to have to ask him to leave.

And as he wandered out of the room, Sarah would think: *Creepy stalker guy* and ask somebody to walk her to her car after the meeting ended.

So he stayed home.

He worked on a new cartoon, sort of, while checking his watch every few minutes. At least he tried to pretend that it was only every few minutes. He hadn't even finished drawing the rabbit he was working on when he noted that the meeting was down to its last five minutes.

They'd be wrapping things up at this point, and then Sarah might be gathering her purse. Would she have even showed up? She didn't much look like she wanted to be there the first time. Maybe last week was the only time she'd ever attend this particular support group, or any support group. Maybe it had helped. Maybe she'd cry less.

He checked his watch. The meeting was over.

Good. Now he could finally focus on this cartoon.

He'd heard a rule that if you *thought* you had Alzheimer's disease, you didn't really have it, because those suffering from it were never aware. Was the same true of being a creepy stalker guy? If he was sitting on his living room couch, thinking "Wow, I'm being kind of obsessive here," then that by definition meant that he wasn't a stalker. A genuinely creepy stalker would be unaware of the impact he was having on others. He would walk up to her with a bouquet of flowers and say "Here, I got these for you. They match your soul."

And, most importantly, he'd successfully kept himself from actually hanging around the support group meeting. So even if he *was* a stalker, he was a stalker with restraint.

She was so beautiful, though.

———

THE NEXT SATURDAY was quite a bit easier. He was still very much aware that he knew (probably) where she was at that moment, but he didn't obsess over it. At least he didn't think he did. When asked, Owen answered "no" to the question of whether all of this talk about Sarah was making him want to rip Toby's head right off his shoulders and gargle the geyser of blood, so Toby figured that he wasn't overdoing it.

———

AT THE MEETING of local artists, Toby was the celebrity cartoonist superstar. He didn't consider this a good thing, since the sum total of his professional accomplishments was that one cartoon he sold to *The Blender*, for which he had not yet received his five dollars.

He was about twenty years older than the average person in the room. Most of them had yet to send their work out to a single market. Granted, Toby was forty and he hadn't really done crap with his drawing "career" until he was in his thirties, but he'd hoped to use this group to acquire knowledge and make valuable industry contacts, not have kids say "Wow! The old guy sold something!"

Most of the meeting was spent listening to them bitch about how much art sucked these days.

Finally, the torment ended, and they cleared out of the room. Toby wasn't going to seek out Sarah. Absolutely not. He wasn't going to do it. No way.

Instead, she found him.

"Hi!" she said, tapping him on the shoulder just as he opened the door to walk out of the building and making him flinch in surprise. "Oh, sorry, I didn't mean to scare you."

"No, no, it's okay, you don't scare me. I mean *didn't* scare me. I mean you just startled me. How are you?"

"It's me, from the support meeting last month."

"Yep, I remember you," said Toby. "I was the dumb-ass."

"Did you find your artists' group this time?"

"Yep, I sure did."

"Was it worthwhile?"

"Well, have you heard that Groucho Marx quote about how he wouldn't want to belong to any club that would have him for a member? It was kind of like that. I'm all in favor of people appreciating my accomplishments, but they pretty much suck."

Great job, Toby! Sell yourself! Refer to yourself as a dumb-ass again! Impress her!

"What do you draw?"

"Cartoons."

"You mean like Bugs Bunny?"

"No, not animated. Comic strips. Like Garfield."

"Oh, that's great! Are you in newspapers?"

"Not yet."

"Well, you'll get there someday. Are you on your mom's refrigerator?"

"Uhhhh, no. She died. She killed herself."

Way to keep the mood light, dumb-ass.

"Oh my God, I'm so sorry. I shouldn't have said anything. That was really thoughtless."

Toby shook his head. "No, no, that's totally fine. It's not like you asked me that while we were in a support group for orphans whose parents killed themselves. That would've been bad. I would've judged you for that."

"Well, I'm sorry anyway. It must've been hard."

"Yeah...it had its downside."

"Is your father still alive?"

"Uh, no, actually he died right before she did. Stroke. So you can sort of see the foundation for my mom's suicide."

"Wow, I'm really digging myself in deep here, aren't I?"

"You're fine. We'll just say that the awkward dead parents thing evens out the dumb-ass wrong-room thing, and now we've both got perfect records."

Sarah ran her fingers through her hair. "Well, my perfect record is going to last for maybe another thirty seconds. I'm such a spaz. I barely have any foot left from always having it in my mouth."

"Hey, some people are into that."

Seriously? You're going to make a foot fetish joke this early in the conversation? Are you trying *to make her slowly back away from you? Why don't you just punch yourself in the brain, huh?*

Sarah laughed. "Yeah, I guess so. So what do you do when you're not drawing the next Garfield?"

I hang out with a monster in the woods. His name is Owen. He's eaten the corpses of a couple of bullies I murdered, and he also killed my first and only girlfriend, but I forgave him because I'm one seriously screwed up individual. Hey, we should date!

"I work for the Orange Leaf Times. Some layout, some proofreading. I've been getting into doing some local ad design, which is a lot of fun."

"Graphic design's a good career to be in."

"Yeah. I wish I'd known that twenty years ago."

She shrugged. "It's never too late. I'm going back to school part-time."

"Really? To study what?"

"Music."

"That's great! You mean playing music or teaching it or what?"

"This sounds so lame, but I'm not sure yet. I can't sing—if you believe nothing else I tell you, believe me when I say that I can't sing. And I can sort of play the saxophone."

"Saxophone? Seriously?"

"Yeah. I'm not professional level by any means, but it's fun. And I just—I wanted to learn more about it. My regular job is a waitress, and that's fine, I'm not miserable, but I never really did anything creative. I wanted to change direction. I haven't decided on the direction yet, but I want to change it. That sounds really stupid, doesn't it?"

"No. Not at all."

"It sounds a little stupid. You can say it."

"No, it doesn't, really." They stood there for a moment. Sarah giggled at the awkward silence. "How old are you?" Toby asked.

"Are you trying to start the *faux pas* count again?"

"You're right. That was dumb. Sorry."

"No, I'm kidding. I'm thirty-six."

"I'm forty."

"Damn, you're old."

"And decrepit. And I talk about my medical problems all the time. The ache in my knee means it's getting ready to rain."

"You're a very goofy man, Toby."

"Thank you." Holy shit! She remembered his name! "Usually I'm awful at carrying on conversations."

"Me too. I just babble and forget words and stuff."

"Did you already have lunch?"

"I did. But I didn't have a hot fudge sundae."

"Do you want to get a hot fudge sundae?"

"Yes, I think I do."

22

It occurred to Toby that if he talked and behaved this way in all of his social interactions, he might not have a life where his best friend had fur. Oh, sure, he wasn't a brilliant conversationalist or a sparkling wit or a charismatic force of nature, but he was comfortable, reasonably charming, and Sarah seemed to genuinely like him.

Toby told her that he didn't have children. She explained that she and Tom had never had kids, either—they'd wanted to, but the time never seemed right. Tom had one daughter from a previous marriage who had never really warmed up to Sarah and who she hadn't seen since the funeral.

He talked about the deaths of his parents. He did not talk about the death of Melissa.

She talked about the death of her husband. And then the death of her cat, Rexford, who got hit by a car. Then they joked about the fact that they were eating hot fudge sundaes and talking about death, and decided to move on to more lighthearted subjects.

They were both always the "weird kids" in school.

Her grades were usually C's and D's, because it took until the tenth grade to discover that she was dyslexic. Now she loved to read, but she was slow and had to really concentrate—no distractions. So school was taking up almost all of her free time, but it would be worth it in the end. If she figured out what she wanted to do by the time she graduated, of course.

Toby told her about how much he loved to spend time in the woods. He did not tell her about Owen.

They continued talking for over an hour after the sundaes were reduced to a thin layer of melted goo in the bottom of their bowls.

"I should get this out of the way," Sarah said, twisting her napkin. "I'm not looking to see anybody right now. But I could sure use a friend."

"So could I."

"Anyway, you don't want to date somebody as messed up as me. I'm a wreck. I figure you'll probably be even looking for a way out of the friendship in a couple of weeks, so here." She took a pen out of her purse, wrote on the back of the receipt for the sundaes, and gave the receipt to Toby: "*Get Out Of Friendship Free.*"

"That's really dark," Toby noted.

"Yet considerate."

"I'm sure I won't need it. We've only just scratched the surface of my own issues. I guarantee you, if we made a list of reasons why the other one of us should run as fast as they possibly can, mine would be longer and scarier."

"I'll take your word on that. I don't think we should actually make the list, though. This dessert was going so well."

"I agree."

"I should get going. I promised my next-door neighbor that I'd watch her yard sale while she took the kids to baseball practice. Call me sometime, okay?"

"I will."

They walked out of the ice cream parlor, and Sarah extended her hand. "Very nice to meet you, Toby."

"And very nice to meet you, Sarah."

"Talk to you soon."

"Absolutely."

———

TOBY THREW AWAY THE RECEIPT.

———

"I DIDN'T SCREW IT UP!" Toby cheerfully proclaimed. "Can you believe it? I wasn't creepy, I wasn't a babbling idiot, I didn't spill hot fudge all over my shirt—okay, one small spot, but I don't think she even noticed. It was amazing. She says she's not looking to actually date right now, but that's totally fine with me. She's still getting over her husband. But I had such a good time. It's so great to finally have a friend like that."

I'm friend.

"I know you are, Owen, you're my best friend. That's not what I meant."

Only friend.

"You are my only friend. I mean, were my only friend. I mean —you know what I mean. Don't get jealous on me. What the hell? I'm telling you about the beautiful woman who likes me. I'm middle-aged now, and I didn't exactly have women swarming me when I was young and virile. Just chill."

Owen turned away from him and sat down on the beanbag.

"Oh, what, you're going to pout now? You're going to give me crap because I suddenly have a *human* friend? You need to grow up, Owen."

Without looking back, Owen waved for him to leave.

"No, I'm not going anywhere. Which, I would like to emphasize, is my whole point. Did I abandon you when I was with Melissa? Did I?"

No response.

"No, I didn't. And you know what, she was insatiable. There were lots of times when I came out here to spend time with you when I could be getting laid like a porn star! Did you see me getting jealous when you ditched me for *two years* to be with your other monster buddies? Two years! If you're so goddamn jealous of me having a relationship with my own species, why don't you go visit them, huh?"

Toby's shoulders fell. "Aw, shit, Owen, I'm sorry. There's no excuse for that. It was just mean."

He stepped toward Owen. Owen didn't look back, but let out a menacing growl.

"Don't do that, Owen. I'm serious."

The growling got louder. Owen looked back at Toby, teeth bared.

"I'm going to leave while you get yourself sorted out," Toby said, "but if you think that I haven't made sacrifices for our friendship, *huge* ones, then you can fuck off and die."

He stormed out of the shack. What a horrible, ungrateful friend. Owen should be happy for him, *thrilled* for him, not all pissy. How dare he show his teeth like that? Toby wanted to walk back in there and kick them out, like he had Brutus'. Watch Owen spit fangs out onto the floor. He wouldn't be so inclined to throw a jealous fit after that, would he?

Toby really shouldn't have made the comment about visiting the other monsters. That was an awful thing to say. Cruel.

But, still, he wasn't going to beat himself up over it. Owen was the one being unreasonable. Owen was the selfish one who didn't want to see his friend happy if it meant getting in a few minutes less playtime.

Screw him.

Screw that stupid, selfish, murdering monster.

Toby didn't need him. What value did he bring to Toby's life? Some growling and some fucking hand signals? Wow, how could he ever live without *that*? He might not get to hear Owen's one-word vocabulary anymore. "*Toby*." What a loss.

Toby got madder and madder as he walked away from the shack —the shack that Toby had done most of the work on, thank you very much. It wasn't an architectural marvel, but it was a shitload better than the filthy cave he was lurking in for two decades, and if Owen didn't appreciate his efforts, then Toby would just leave him out in the woods to rot. He could sit there and tear apart his beanbag some more and grow old and die and decay right into the wood.

And screw walking away. He was going to march back there and tell that asshole that he was on his own from now on. If he wanted to be a great big jealous baby, he could find himself another best friend, somebody with absolutely no life who had nothing better to do all day long than sit in a shack with an animal.

He went back and pushed open the door. "You know what, Owen, I just want to say—"

Owen rushed towards him.

Then threw his arms around him and gave him a hug.

Toby was still pretty pissed, but he patted the monster's back as they hugged. "It's okay. It's okay, buddy."

Owen pulled away. *I'm sorry*, he signed.

"You should be."

Owen looked so sad that Toby couldn't help but feel his anger fade away. He tried to keep it—Owen deserved to have Toby furious at him—but he couldn't.

"Everything's going to be okay," Toby assured him. "I'm not going to let a woman come between us. Nobody, no matter who it is, will ever come between us. We're friends forever."

Promise?

"Cross my heart. Hope to die. Stick a pitchfork in my eye."

Stay?

"Of course. I'm not going anywhere, Owen."

213

As he walked home, it occurred to him that he hadn't even considered the idea that Owen might try to rip a big chunk out of his chest. They'd been friends for a long time, but...wow, that could have gone terribly wrong.

And Owen had gone on a rampage before.

Toby needed to remember what he was dealing with here: an animal. Maybe one that was closer to a human than any other creature on the planet, but still, an animal that liked the taste of human flesh.

Perhaps he needed to consider moving Owen back to the cave.

Nah. If anything, he wanted his friend to be closer, now that he'd have less free time to spend walking through the forest.

There was no magical moment.

Toby would've expected one. He and Sarah would be sitting on the couch, watching a movie. He'd reach into the popcorn bowl, she'd reach into the popcorn bowl, their buttery fingers would touch, there'd be a jolt of pure romantic electricity, and suddenly they'd be passionately kissing, spilling popcorn everywhere.

Or, after months of angst, Toby would confess all, tearfully explain that he loved her, that he couldn't live without her, and that if she wasn't ready that was okay, he'd wait for her. And she'd tearfully say that she was ready, that she'd been ready for a while now, and they'd kiss and cry together and then make love.

It wasn't like that. For a few months, they just hung out like friends. Not dating—Sarah always paid her own way—and nothing more physical than pats on the arm and goodbye hugs.

And then they were holding hands while walking downtown, window-shopping. They didn't mention it, didn't acknowledge any kind of change this might mean in their relationship—it just felt natural to hold hands, and they did it without comment.

Then quick goodbye kisses.

Then quick hello kisses.

But it still felt like friends who just happened to be affectionate. No big deal.

She studied a lot, and during that time Toby hung out with Owen. Sarah and Toby shared secrets—she told him how she'd felt watching her husband die, and he'd told her about the freakish night when some sort of escaped animal slaughtered his girlfriend—but of course he could never tell her the whole truth.

More kisses.

Snuggling on the couch during a movie.

She told him that she wasn't crying over Tom as much these days, but didn't directly relate it to what may or may not have been a blossoming romance.

She asked him what he did in the woods, and he lied. He just walked through the trees, enjoying the fresh air and solitude, getting exercise, being one with nature.

He took her with him, several times. It was a big forest. Plenty of places to go. She pretended to have a good time, but he called her out on it, and she admitted that she was much more of an indoor person, or at least preferred the outdoors without so many bugs. They laughed and happily found other things to do besides hiking in the forest.

She comforted him every time he got a rejection, which meant that she did a lot of comforting. They joked about killing comic strip editors.

When she wanted to go to an all-weekend bluegrass music festival, they went together. They sang during the drive, as loudly as they could—they loved enduring each other's vocals, as long as they didn't torment innocent bystanders.

Neither of them said anything, but it was understood that they would share a hotel room, and a bed.

They lay together, kissing gently, Sarah down to her bra and panties. Then the look of sadness from the support group appeared, and she pulled away from him.

"I'm sorry, I...you understand, right?"

"Of course I do."

They held each other all night.

The music festival got rained out, so they spent the day singing in the hotel room. They kissed some more after darkness fell, and she said that she was ready.

Then she warned him that she was ending a dry spell of several years and that he might be in very serious danger.

Somehow, he survived.

1986

"What if we got married?" Sarah asked.

"Um, are you proposing to me?"

"No, I'm not trying to steal your thunder. I'm just throwing the idea out there. I love you, you love me, we want babies someday, so let's make them legitimate before they're accidentally conceived."

"Wow." Toby kissed her. "That's the most flowery, poetic—"

"I know, I know. But I'm serious."

"—heartfelt, romantic—"

She punched him playfully on the arm. "Enough! You know what I mean. Let's do it. We're not getting any younger."

"So, what, do I just drop to one knee?"

"No. You should get a ring first."

"How do you know I don't already have it?"

"Do you?"

"Yes. It's back at my place. If you'd been considerate enough to start this conversation *there*, I could've run into my bedroom, brought it out, and it would've been this great big romantic deal. But instead, we have to drive eight miles."

"You're joking, right? Do you really have a ring?"

"Yes."

"Seriously, Toby, don't kid around. You really truly bought an engagement ring?"

"Let's go get it."

He'd decided to buy a ring the weekend after they made love for the first time. He knew it was too soon, way too soon, and that he might never get to give it to her, but he wanted to have the ring.

Owen had helped him pick it out. Toby had brought pictures of the top three possibilities, and Owen had tapped his talon against the princess cut diamond, which was Toby's first choice, too. If he asked again with the same three pictures, Owen would probably point to something different, but that was okay.

He also had his mother's engagement ring in his top drawer. It was a beautiful ring—much more expensive than the one he bought for Sarah. But he couldn't give his future wife a ring that came from the finger of a woman who slit her wrists. He just couldn't.

As they drove toward his home, Toby wondered about the impact of his marriage on Owen. They'd have to move into a new home—his house was okay for himself, *maybe* for the two of them, but definitely too small for an expanding family.

She knew he loved the forest. He'd just have to insist that they get a home in the same general area. He'd start researching possibilities.

He made Sarah wait in the living room, then went into his bedroom and got the ring box. He walked back to her, got down on one knee, and took her hand.

"Sarah Habley, will you marry me?"

"Oh my God! You had the ring!"

"I wouldn't lie about something like that. So will you?"

"Yes!"

They kissed.

It was going to be wonderful. They'd get a new house, stay near the forest, and nothing would change. Maybe he'd have to visit Owen less often, but that was fine—Owen would just have to understand. He wouldn't abandon his friend. Not ever. Nothing would change.

Nothing changed after the wedding. They bought a wonderful little house at a great price, not as close to his old place as Toby would have liked, but still acceptable. While Sarah went to classes at night, Toby spent time with Owen. He and the monster weren't too old to make up new games, even if there was much less running around involved these days.

They'd planned to wait a couple of years before having kids. Not too long—they didn't want to be parenting from a nursing home—but long enough to give themselves time to travel the world and for Sarah to get her degree.

One positive pregnancy test and some quick calculations showed that she'd gotten knocked up during their honeymoon.

Things did change after that. Toby didn't go out to visit Owen on weekends—well, not every weekend. Owen understood. There were no more jealous rages.

Love her?

"I do. Who would've thought that a loser like me would ever get married, huh?"

As her belly swelled, Toby grew less comfortable leaving her alone. He still visited Owen, just not as often. He brought him extra treats to make up for it. Life was good. They were still best buddies.

The night Garrett Andrew Floren was born, weighing six pounds, three ounces, Toby held his son and vowed that nobody would ever harm his child.

Nobody.

For all these years, he'd allowed a monster to live in the woods outside of his house.

Not anymore.

23

1987. 42 years old.

"He doesn't have either of our eyes," Sarah said, taking Garrett back from Toby. Toby and Sarah both had brown eyes, but Garrett's were a beautiful shade of blue. "Recessive traits."

"He does have your nose, though."

Toby scrunched up his nose. "I don't think so."

"Yes, he does." She gently stroked the newborn's forehead. "He's so precious. Can you believe I'm sitting here saying things like 'He's so precious?' That's not like me. Do you think we're going to become those parents who show pictures of their baby to strangers and tell everybody that he's the most beautiful baby boy in the entire world?"

Toby gave her a kiss. "I hope so."

HE WALKED through the woods with a clarity of vision. He'd lived a confused life—a mixed-up, crazy, confused life, but he wasn't confused now.

Sarah had been nervous about having a gun in their house, even an unloaded one, so she'd insisted that he keep it in the attic. He'd pointed out that an intruder would be unlikely to let him climb into the attic to retrieve his weapon for the purposes of self-defense, and she'd argued that the idea of guns in their bedroom scared her more than the idea of intruders, so he'd conceded.

That was fine. He didn't need to defend his wife and son in their home. He was going to get rid of the threat before it came to that.

Owen was his best friend. For most of Toby's life, he was his *only* friend. And that, ladies and gentlemen of the jury, was one fucked up concept. Best buddies with a snarling, flesh-eating monster? He'd have to be insane.

Owen would not be coming to his house in the middle of the night. Owen would not be looking in Garrett's crib. Owen would not be reaching out with a single talon, perhaps to lovingly stroke the infant, perhaps to slit his throat. Owen would not be doing to Garrett what he'd done to those other two people.

Or what you *did.*

No. Toby's secret was long-buried, something that could never happen again. Owen was a monster. If Toby allowed Garrett to come to harm because he let that creature lurk out there, hungry, then Toby might as well kill himself.

Up the arms, not across the wrists.

He had to do it tonight, while Sarah was still in the hospital. Tomorrow, she'd bring home the baby.

Owen stood outside the shack when Toby approached. Toby stopped about twenty feet away and shone the flashlight on the monster's face.

Owen made a rocking gesture with both hands: *Baby?*

"Yes. Sarah had the baby."

Picture?

"No. I took a bunch but I haven't got them developed yet. Maybe tomorrow."

He raised the gun and pointed it at Owen, ready to squeeze the trigger instantly if Owen attacked. Owen didn't attack or even cry out—he just looked sadly at Toby.

"I'm sorry," said Toby. "I really am. You've always been there for me, but I have a son now. You don't know what it's like, and I can't even explain it right—it's this feeling where I'd rather die than have something happen to him. I can't let that happen. I'm sorry."

"*Toby...*"

"I can't let you live, Owen. I can't put my baby at risk."

Owen signed: *No.*

"You could hurt him."

Not hurt baby.

"You killed Melissa. She was everything I had and you killed her. I'm not going to let you take Garrett away from me. I hate that it has to be this way, but it does, and I'm sorry, I hate myself for this..."

Shoot him, Toby screamed inside his mind. *Stop talking and shoot him, goddamn it!*

Owen signed: *Ice cream.*

"What?"

Ice cream.

"Are you asking for a last meal?"

Yes.

For a moment, Toby wanted to do it. Go home and make Owen the biggest, sloppiest, most chocolate-drenched banana split ever constructed. He deserved a last moment of happiness before Toby executed him.

But then he shook his head in disbelief. "You know I can't do that. Please don't make this hard for me." Jesus, what a dumb thing to say. As if Toby was getting the short end of the stick here.

There was nothing else to say. He needed to pull the trigger and begin a normal life.

His finger wouldn't move.

Attack me, he thought. *Rush at me with those claws. Make me do it. Give me no choice.*

Owen just watched him.

At least look scared! At least freak out! Do something to create a moment of frenzy that I have to end with a bullet!

Nothing. No mercy.

"We'll always be friends," Toby said. It was another stupid thing to say. They wouldn't still be friends when Owen lay dead on the ground because Toby shot him in the fucking head, now would they?

Owen signed: *Please.*

"Don't."

Not hurt baby.

"I can't put Garrett in danger."

Not hurt baby.

"You killed Melissa."

Not hurt baby.

Toby lowered the gun.

"God, we just keep having horrible moments, don't we?" he asked. "We've known each other almost our whole lives and I keep pulling guns on you."

He couldn't kill his best friend. Who gave him the most comfort when he was bruised, bloody, and humiliated from the beating by Larry? Who did he confide all of his secrets to? He loved Sarah, loved her deeply, but did they share the same bond that he shared with Owen?

Owen understood him.

Owen knew what he'd done. If Sarah ever found out that he stabbed two kids to death, would she stay with him? Even if he explained that they were awful, mean bullies who made his life a living hell, would she stay with him if he described his moment of blind rage, mimicked the sound of the blade as it plunged into Larry's chest?

Not a chance in hell.

But Owen did.

He'd have to be insane to give up a friendship like that. Certifiably insane to lose his confidant. Completely bonkers to murder the one friend with whom the grisly past was shared.

He didn't have to lie to Owen about the prostitutes, the way he did to Sarah. "Sex for money? God, no. Do you see any green splotches on my penis?"

If you thought about it, really dug deep, got to the core of the matter, with Sarah he had to lie about his own best friend. He couldn't tell her about Owen! Even without the gore-drenched aspects, he couldn't tell her. What would she say? "Gosh, Toby, it's so sweet that your best friend is covered with fur and has flesh-piercing jaws. Why not invite him over for brunch?"

She'd never understand.

He had secrets he could never tell her. What if he killed Owen, and then she found out about the murders? Or even the friendship? He'd be alone again.

Alone forever, this time. Who the hell else was he going to find?

Hurt Owen, his only friend for so long?

Madness.

Toby cried, apologized, begged for forgiveness. He hugged the beast, promising that it would never happen again, insisting that all of the emotional turmoil had messed with his head, but that he would never do anything to hurt Owen, not ever, and that no matter what, he swore that the two of them would be friends.

Not hurt baby.

"I know you wouldn't. God, I'm so sorry."

Ice cream.

Toby chuckled and wiped his eyes. "Yeah, Owen, I'll get you some ice cream."

24

GLIMPSES
1988

"Aw, c'mon, Garrett! Why would you do that to me?"

"What's wrong?" asked Sarah, peeking into the bathroom.

"He pooped on the new diaper while I was changing it! That had to be on purpose. There's no way he just happened to be about to go when I changed the diaper."

"You don't think so? He poops eighty-five thousand times a day. Why wouldn't one of them be while you're changing the diaper?"

Toby recoiled. "Have you ever smelled anything so foul? Maybe he has some sort of digestive problem or something. That can't be natural."

"You're acting like your own feces have a flowery aroma."

"I'm not sayin' my poop don't stink. I'm saying that his poop smells worse. Just come in. Come closer."

"No, I'm fine out here."

"It's like, I'm worried it's going to dissolve through the sink. It's that nasty. I think it's a specially formulated kind of baby food designed by the government to keep people from having more kids."

"It's not working. I'm pregnant."

Toby froze. "What?"

"Kidding."

"I'll fling some of this at you."

"Then I'll be leaving. I'm proud of you. You're a good daddy for facing the stinky poo menace."

"Do you remember that time in our life, long ago, when we talked about other things? I don't recall the subjects, exactly, but I have this vague recollection that there actually existed conversations that weren't related to diaper contents."

"No idea what you're talking about. Sorry."

"OKAY, this is going to be a challenging concept for you to grasp, but I need you to work with me." Toby held up the jumbo-sized bag of beef jerky. Owen sniffed the air and reached for it.

"No, no, not yet. What we're going to discuss today is 'rationing treats.' There's no way I'll be back here for at least a week, and I want you to have some tasty snacks while I'm gone, so you need to learn how to not eat this entire bag in one gulp. What I'm going to do is set the pieces of jerky in different places, and when you feel like a treat, you'll pick a single piece and enjoy it. If you gobble it all down, there won't be any treats for a few days. Do you think you can handle that idea?"

The lesson in rationing treats was a failure.

1989

"Toby! I can't believe it!"

"Mr. Zack! Hi! How are you enjoying retirement?"

"Never worked so hard in my life. Janet has me remodeling the entire house, now that I'm a lazy bum and not working for a living." Mr. Zack cooed at Garrett in Sarah's arms. "Wow, he's a handsome little lad, isn't he?"

"You say that like you're surprised," Sarah said with a grin.

"Nothing surprises me less! So, Toby, I keep checking the newspapers for you!"

"Yeah, I'm still working on it."

"What was that one you were in? *The Cocktail?*"

"*The Blender.* It ended up going under."

"Did you get your ten bucks?"

"Five bucks. No."

"You keep working at it. Those successful youngsters, they have meltdowns. When you make it big, it is going to be the sweetest fruit you've ever tasted, and you'll be able to give your lovely wife and your lovely son a life of luxury."

"We do okay," said Sarah with a smile. "He's doing great at the newspaper, and I've started selling songs."

"Songs? You sing?"

"I write them."

"That's great! Anything I would've heard?"

"Do you listen to folk music?"

"No, I sure don't, but I'll start. Hey, I think your son is about to spit up, so I'm going to bid you *adieu*, but it was great talking to you."

Garrett puked all over Sarah's shirt.

LARRY AND NICK STAYED AWAY. Toby thought about them a lot, but in the past tense.

"LIKE THAT—JUST LIKE THAT!" Sarah urged as Toby thrust into her. "Oh, yeah, that's perfect—right there—oh, yeah, right there—don't stop—oh, God, I'm gonna come—if the baby doesn't cry I'm gonna come—!"

"*DEAR MR. FLORREN...*"

Toby crumpled up the rejection letter and threw it against the wall. "It's one R, asshole!"

1990

Owen lay on the floor. His fur was moist and his eyes were glassy.

"Do you think it's...I don't know, the flu or something?" Toby asked. "Do you get the flu? I don't know what to do here, Owen. It's not like I can call a vet. Do you feel really bad?"

Yes.

"Have you thrown up?"

No.

"I'm going to make some calls and find out what I should do. I won't say who I'm calling for. I'll just, I don't know, find out what they would do for a gorilla with your symptoms."

Stay.

"I'll stay, but I can't stay for very long. You know I have to get back. You're not dying, right? If you're seriously ill, I'll stay and see what I can do, but I don't think you look that bad."

Though he tried to hide it, Toby felt queasy. How long did forest monsters live? Owen had a lot of white and grey hair now, but so did Toby, and he planned to be around for at least another half-century. Owen couldn't be dying, could he?

"On a scale of 1 to 10, how bad do you feel?"

Sick.

"I know that. Give me a number."

Sick.

Toby sighed. "Okay. I'll stay with you."

"Where were you?"

"I lost track of time."

"How do you lose track of time when you're outside? It's dark out!"

"I walked further than I realized, and I turned back when it got dark. What's the big deal?"

"I was *worried*, that's the big deal! I don't like you wandering around the forest in the daytime, much less at night. What if you got hurt?"

"I didn't."

"I know you didn't. But what would happen to Garrett if you did?"

"You'd write a hit single about your loss and make him rich."

"Did you really just say that? You really just made that joke?"

"No—I mean, I did, but it was thoughtless. You're absolutely right. I got lost in thought and wasn't paying attention. I promise it won't happen again."

"I just got scared, you know?"

"I know."

"You got me in all kinds of trouble," Toby told Owen. "I hope you're feeling better."

Yes.

1991

"Guess what time of the month it is, and guess what I missed...?"

"Okay, how about Toby for a boy, Sarah for a girl?"

"Nah," said Sarah. "I don't like having two people in the same household with the same name. It's okay for a boy, I guess, because you could call him 'junior,' but what do you call a girl who's named after her mother?"

"She could go by her middle name."

"Then why not just make her middle name her first name?"

"You're right. How about Owen for a boy?"

"No."

"Why not?"

"Other kids will make fun of him. They'll say 'You're Owen us money!'"

"I bet they won't."

"Sorry. Veto on Owen."

"Michael?"

"Maybe."

"Hannah for a girl?"

"Do you know anybody named Hannah?"

"No, I just like the name."

"Me too. We'll keep it in mind."

"You see, Garrett, when a mommy has a baby in her tummy, sometimes she acts all weird, and it's best to give her anything she wants. This helps daddies stay alive."

1992

"It was a girl!" Toby announced.

Owen smiled.

"I HOPE everyone in this house is ready, mommies and sons included, because it's time for... *Tickle War*! *Rrrraaarrrr*!"

"CAN I GET ONE?" Garrett asked, eyeing the puppies in the cages at the pet store.

"Maybe when you're six," Toby said.

"That's forever!"

"You say that now. It goes fast."

1993

"Look what came in the mail today!" said Sarah, waving the envelope.

Toby took it from her. "Wow. I didn't think there were any still circulating. It's even my old address."

"Open it."

"What is it, Daddy?" Garrett set down his tentacled alien action figure and hurried over to join the excitement.

"Nothing. It's just Daddy's dreams being crushed."

"Don't talk that way around him," Sarah said.

"I'm just kidding."

"He doesn't know that."

Toby tore open the envelope and handed the letter to Garrett. "Do you want to read it?"

Garrett enthusiastically grabbed the letter. He looked at the words and frowned.

"Sound it out," Sarah said.

"*We re...reg-ret...*"

Toby sighed. "Let's give him some Dr. Seuss."

"GUESS WHO GOT A GOLD STAR TODAY?" Toby asked Owen.

Owen reached for the drawing, but Toby put it behind his back. "Sarah will kill me if you rip it. I just wanted you to see it. Look at that. He's pretty good, don't you think?"

Yes.

"You're not just saying that, are you? I'm biased and all, but let me tell you, I was at the open house and I saw what the other kids had up on the wall, and there was some *shit*. Look at that hand. How many six-year-olds do you know who draw knuckles? I didn't have any talent chromosomes to pass on, so I don't know where he got it, but this kid's a freakin' Rembrandt. Gold star. Right there, baby."

He held the paper behind his back again. "No, seriously, Owen, you can't touch it. But it's impressive, right? It's not just me? I need you to provide a neutral opinion because Sarah and I are flipping out over it. Of course, he did also wet his pants during recess, but when you have immense talent you can't always focus on bladder control."

1994

"Oh."

"You have more to say than 'oh,' right?"

"It just took me by surprise, that's all. The way you said it. No build-up."

"Like they say in the newspaper business, don't bury the lead, right?" Sarah was practically bouncing with excitement.

It was, to be fair, outstanding news. A children's television show wanted her to join the staff and write new songs each week. An incredible opportunity. She could go from being a waitress with a few songs that occasionally got radio play on local stations to a full-time songwriter.

"But it's in Chicago."

"Well, yeah."

"I'd have to quit my job."

"Yes, you would. You don't have any great love for that job. You never have."

"We'd have to pull Garrett out of school."

"Yeah, and he'd go to school in Chicago."

"He'd have to make new friends."

"He's six. He hasn't formed lifelong friendships yet." Sarah stared at him in disbelief. "Why are you giving me crap about this?"

"I just don't want to move."

"Why? What ties do you have to Orange Leaf?"

"I've lived here my whole life."

"And...?"

"That's not enough?"

"Of course it's not enough! This is a dream come true. I realize it doesn't pay that much, but I'd get to write songs for a living. That's what I'd do instead of bringing people ketchup and extra napkins. I thought that you'd want to grab the suitcases out of the garage and start packing."

"Well, I don't."

She looked at him with such hurt that Toby wanted to fall to the floor, clawing his eyes out in a fit of self-loathing.

"Are you jealous?" she quietly asked.

"No."

"Then why?"

"I don't have a job there."

"You'd find one. That's not an answer. It's not like we're moving to Antarctica—it's Chicago. It's two states away."

"I can't leave Orange Leaf. It's my home."

"Your home is with Garrett, Hannah, and me, wherever we are."

"We can't leave."

They didn't speak for a few moments, as her shoulders began to quiver and tears streamed down her face. "You're really going to take this away from me?"

Toby couldn't answer her.

She called and declined the offer.

25

1995. Age 50.

Everything hurt.

His feet hurt, his back hurt, his *brain* hurt...the people who'd said that getting old was a bitch knew of what they spoke. Forty was "over the hill," mid-life crisis time, but regardless of his family history, Toby had plans to live well past eighty. Past one hundred? That was pushing it. It could happen, but more likely than not, Toby had passed the halfway mark. More years behind him than ahead of him.

What did he have to show for a half-century?

It wasn't too bad, he supposed. Two great kids. A beautiful wife whom he loved dearly, even if she resented him. And the friendship of a monster whose talons had turned from ivory to yellow without him really noticing the transition, and whose teeth were starting to fall out. Owen had held up the tooth in dismay, as if asking "What the hell is happening to my body?"

Pretty soon, the flesh-eater might be on a liquid diet.

Mr. Zack had died a couple of weeks ago. "Natural causes."

That's where Toby was headed. Natural causes: "Yeah, he died, but that's what was *supposed* to happen."

The big five-oh had not been a happy birthday, even though Garrett got him a copy of *Close Encounters of the Third Kind* on VHS (which he'd already had, but which Garrett had painted all over with nail polish a couple of years earlier) and Hannah made a portrait of him out of jelly beans glued to construction paper. Fifty was just too old. He wanted a rewind button.

No, not rewind. Reset.

Jesus. What a whiny baby he was being. He might clean up some past messes, given the chance, but he certainly wouldn't wish away the path of his life. He was best friends with a monster. Who else in the world got to say that? Probably nobody. His life was *cool*.

He wished Garrett was with him right now. They took lots of walks in the forest together and had a great time, but of course when he went to visit Owen his son had to stay at home.

A pity. Garrett would love Owen.

Owen would love Garrett.

Toby had been eight years old when he first saw Owen. Admittedly, his reaction had been to scream and run home crying to Mom, but there hadn't been anybody there to reassure him, to show him that Owen was nice. If Dad had been there to hold his hand, Toby would have been filled with awe, not terror.

Not that Toby was considering bringing Garrett to meet the monster. Not a chance.

Owen wasn't there when Toby arrived at the shack, but he showed up soon after, a half-eaten dead rabbit in his claw. He took a great big nasty bite out of it, then held out the dangling remains, offering them to Toby.

It was polite of him to do so, though Toby had never once accepted his offer. Toby waved it away and Owen resumed dining.

"So do you think I've been obsessing about turning fifty?" Toby asked. "Sarah thinks I have. I don't know, I probably have, but I guess my real question is, do you think there's anything *wrong* with obsessing about turning fifty? It's what I'd expect other people to do. And Sarah wasn't exactly bouncing with joy when she turned forty—you know that, I told you about it. Hey, chew with your mouth closed. Nobody wants to see that."

As always, Owen continued to chew with his mouth open. Toby hated being here right after a fresh kill. "Do you really have to do that in front of me?"

Yes.

"Okay, then. That answers my question. I can't stay long today, anyway. I promised Garrett we'd get started on that treehouse."

Bring him.

"You say that every time. Not going to happen, buddy. Not if I want to stay out of divorce court."

Owen looked disappointed. But, let's face it, life was full of disappointments.

"There's one behind the tree!" Garrett shouted.

"Holy cow! Shoot it! Shoot it!"

Garrett pointed his fingers at the tree and zapped the imaginary space invader. Then he made a sound effect to indicate that the alien had blown into a million pieces, the bits scattering across several acres.

"Good job," Toby said. "The woods are safe."

They stood in the backyard. The tallest of the three trees in their yard had been declared the site of the new treehouse, which meant that they'd have to saw off a few branches and displace a squirrel.

Toby looked over the plans that Garrett had carefully drawn up. They depicted a two-level structure with a fireman's pole connecting them. There was a secret passage, a guest bedroom, a room with a fully functional alligator pit where enemies could be deposited, a pizza parlor, and a cannon. Garrett was aware that the project had to be scaled back, though Toby promised to respect his creative vision.

"All right," Toby said, brandishing the hacksaw like a knight's sword, "neither one of us has a clue what we're doing, so we'll make a good team. Your job is to hold the stepladder, while Mom watches us through the window and gets really nervous. Can you handle that?"

"I want to cut down the branches."

"Okay, here, have a dangerous saw—no. I'll do the cutting. You can haul away. That's a lot more fun."

"Watch out, Daddy!" Garrett shouted, pointing at the same tree as before. "It's another one!"

Toby turned and shot at the alien with the hacksaw, which didn't make logistical sense but seemed effective. "Okay, we need to drop the alien stuff," he said. "We've got hard work ahead."

Garrett saluted. "Yes, sir!"

Toby scooted the stepladder closer to the trunk of the tree and then climbed up a couple of steps. "Make sure it's sturdy," he said. "Hold it with both hands."

"I've got it."

Toby sawed away at the excess branches, carefully tossing them aside as he cut each one from the tree. This was going to be a fantastic treehouse. Garrett was going to be the envy of the neighborhood kids. This would make him some friends.

"Do you think it's going to be safe?" Sarah asked.

"Yep. I've already given him the lecture about not going near it until it's finished, and I won't let him up there alone until I've done jumping jacks inside."

"How's your back?"

"It's fine," Toby lied. It wasn't anything a few aspirin couldn't fix.

She kissed him. They still kissed, and laughed, and made love, but it really wasn't the same. The jokes felt more forced, the Sunday morning cuddling less intimate. She didn't seem to have missed him as much when he came back from the long walks in the forest by himself.

Still, he had a lot of joy in his life. Garrett, Hannah, and Owen.

"CAN I COME?" Garrett asked, looking away from his video game. Toby figured he had to be doing pretty good as a father—it was a place of high honor to pull Garrett's attention from his Nintendo. Toby had played games with him on a few occasions, and found himself getting embarrassingly addicted, so he tried to avoid them when at all possible.

"This is Daddy-alone time," Sarah explained. She sat on the couch, holding Hannah on her lap.

"Please?"

"Not this time," said Toby. "Next one's yours."

Garrett returned to his video game. Toby and Sarah had gotten lucky—he rarely got whiny about anything. Having kids forced them to socialize with other parents, and some of those other children were tantrum-throwing demons.

He hadn't seen Owen in three days. It just wasn't easy to get out of the house alone, except to go to work. He really wished there was another Owen-creature, maybe Esmerelda, that lived nearby to keep him company. It would help ease his guilt about not being able to visit more often.

He had a brand-new picture of Garrett and Hannah, covered with pancake batter, to show Owen. Owen loved seeing the pictures. He'd only accidentally ripped two.

Toby hated not being able to bring his son along.

Hated it.

Sarah would never understand, but Garrett would. Garrett

would think it was the greatest thing ever. Toby could picture his expression of wonder. Some fear at first, yeah, but it would transform into pure joy at the discovery his father had shared with him.

They could come out and visit Owen every day.

Just Garrett and him. Father and son.

But it could never happen. Not a chance. This was always going to be Toby's secret, hidden from the world forever. Maybe even after he died. Some kid would be wandering through the woods fifty years from now, and he'd find the remains of a quaint old shack, and thoughts of what might have lived there would capture his imagination. Maybe he'd envision something with even bigger talons, bigger teeth, and scarier eyes.

Or maybe Owen would still be alive, and he'd find a new friend.

Goddamn he hated not being able to share this with his son. What a cruel joke, that something that gave him this much joy had to remain hidden, a dark, dirty secret. In what kind of universe was it fair that he couldn't tell his own son about the greatest discovery of his life?

Granted, there were murders involved...

Still...

Owen looked particularly happy to see him this time, and Toby didn't even come bearing treats. As Owen hugged him, Toby wondered why he *couldn't* bring Garrett out there to meet him.

Garrett was old enough to keep a secret. Toby had kept his own secret at age eight. No, wait, he hadn't—he'd told his parents everything, but when they hadn't believed him, he'd kept it a secret from everybody else.

Until Melissa.

Forget the past. No, don't forget the past, learn from it. Garrett would keep Owen a secret. Toby knew he would. And if he didn't, well, Toby's parents hadn't believed him, so why would Sarah believe Garrett now?

"Yep, that's one crazy kid we've got," Toby would say with a laugh. "What an imagination! Reminds me of me when I was his age. I thought I saw a monster out there, too. Garrett's lucky, though—I got a spanking, and we don't believe in physical punishment."

Melissa had accidentally scratched Owen's eyeball. The monster had been peaceful until then. Owen would never hurt Toby's son on purpose, and if Toby took every possible precaution...

No. Terrible idea.

Or, life-changing brilliant idea.

He'd have to think about this some more. Brainstorm from every angle.

Good Lord, was he excited.

"OWEN, I may bring you another friend," Toby said, one week later.

Owen looked positively delighted at this prospect.

"But there are parts of this that you're not going to like, and if you don't agree to them it's not going to happen. So, how do you feel about being in a cage?"

No.

"Okay, see, if you're already unwilling to compromise then this whole idea is over. You remember what happened last time. There is no way in hell I'm going to let anything happen to my son. Not one scratch. So you can work with me, or I'll be your only company for the rest of your life. Your choice. So what about the cage? You think that might be all right?"

Owen hung his head a bit. *Yes.*

"It may not have to be a cage. I'm going to look at chains. Chains can be stylish. They make you look tough. But I need to make it very clear that you *will* be restrained, and if you're going to fight me on that, it's no deal. I don't want to spend the money for a cage or chains until I'm positive that you're all right with the idea. Are you?"

Yes.

OWEN DIDN'T LOOK cool in the chains. He actually looked kind of pathetic. But still, the plan was coming together.

"Tug," Toby said.

Owen wore a thick leather strap around his neck, which was connected to a chain that was wrapped around a tree. Owen was pretty damn strong, but he didn't have the strength to rip trees out by the roots, and according to the guy at the hardware store, this chain "could withstand a half-dozen elephants pulling on it at once." Toby doubted that this claim had been tested in the field, but it was definitely a solid chain.

Toby signed: *Heavy.* This was made more difficult for him because he was also chained by the wrists.

"I know it's heavy. But you can handle it for a while, right?"

Yes.

"So tug."

Owen yanked on the chains.

"No, really tug. I'll know if you're faking, so give it everything that you've got."

Owen pulled against his restraints, teeth clenched together, muscles bulging. Those chains, and those trees, weren't going anywhere.

"Good job," said Toby. He walked over to the cooler, opened it, and took out a surprise. "If you can break free, I'll give you this banana split. Otherwise, I'm eating it myself." He spooned up a bite and slowly slid it into his mouth. "Mmmmmm."

Yeah, it was a mean thing to do, but he really had to make sure that Owen couldn't break free. And Owen strained to get the ice cream, strained so hard that he thought the monster might start popping blood vessels. But the chains and the trees held.

"Perfect. I was only kidding—of course you can have the ice cream." Toby walked over, unlocked Owen's right wrist, and gave him the bowl. Owen raised it to his face and licked up the banana split within seconds.

It was set. Tomorrow he'd bring Garrett.

"How good are you at keeping secrets?"

"Good."

Toby shook his head. "That's not enough. I need you to be the biggest secret keeper in the entire world. Even better than the president. Do you know how many secrets the president keeps?"

"No," Garrett admitted.

"He keeps thousands of secrets. He knows things that could destroy the entire United States if he let them get out. That's how serious I am."

Garrett looked doubtful. "You're going to tell me something that could destroy the entire United States?"

"No, not that extreme, but I would like to show you something that you can never tell. You can't tell Mommy, you can't tell Hannah, you can't tell Mrs. Kingston, you can't tell anybody in your class...nobody. No matter how much you want to tell, you can't tell this secret to anybody, no matter who asks."

"What about the president?"

Toby pointed to the ground. "If the president were standing

right here, right now, I wouldn't tell him. He might say 'Darn it, Toby, I demand that you tell me this secret or I'll have the entire Secret Service punch you for hours!' and I would say 'No, I refuse to tell my secret.' But if you can keep it to yourself, I'll tell you."

Eyes wide, Garrett nodded. "I won't tell."

"Do you swear?"

"Uh-huh."

"Do you *blood* swear?"

"What's that?"

"It's where we cut our hands and press them together, and swear in blood that we won't tell."

Garrett looked a bit tentative, but nodded.

"I won't really make you blood swear. Mommy wouldn't like that. But I think you're old enough, so we're going for a walk in the woods..."

"IF YOU GET SCARED, it's okay," Toby assured him. "I'm not going to make you do anything you don't want to do. Just know that you'll be safe, I promise. I'll take care of you. Are you scared now?"

"No."

"Good."

They weren't far from the shack—maybe another two minutes of walking. What if this was a really, really, really bad idea?

It wasn't. He'd taken almost absurd safety measures. There was no possible way Owen could escape. Even if he somehow developed supernatural strength and broke free from one of the chains, there'd be two more holding him, each fastened to a different tree so even if the tree itself ripped in half he couldn't get loose. And if a chain broke, Garrett wouldn't be anywhere near close enough to get hurt by a swinging claw.

It was completely safe.

Maybe not safe from weeks of nightmares, but Toby just knew that Garrett would understand. He'd be delighted.

The three of them, friends forever.

The shack came into view. "Remember your promise," Toby said. "It's a blood swear."

"I know."

"We're almost there, then. It's behind that little house."

Owen looked extremely unhappy in his chains, but that changed as soon as he saw Toby and Garrett. His face lit up and he stood up straight.

Garrett stopped walking. He gasped and clenched Toby's hand tight.

"It's okay," said Toby. "He can't get loose."

"Daddy I want to go home."

"He won't—"

"*Daddy I want to go home!*"

"Okay, okay, we can go." Toby led him back through the trees, away from Owen, who let out a whine of disappointment. "I should've told you what we were going to see, it was my mistake, I'm sorry."

"What is it?"

"It's my friend."

Garrett scowled as he tried to process that. "Is it—is it a guy in a costume?"

"No. He's real. He won't hurt you, I promise. He lives in the forest. I've known him since I was a kid."

"You have not."

"I have! I blood swear that I have. I wouldn't play a joke like this on you. He's my best friend. His name is Owen."

"Owen?"

"Yep."

"Is he always locked up?"

"No. I did that for you. He won't hurt you, but I didn't want you to be scared of him. He'd like to say hi to you."

"He talks?"

"Not like you and I talk, but he can do hand signals. I'm going to leave it up to you. We can go home, and maybe come back some other day, or we can go over now and see him. Just remember that you promised not to tell anybody."

"I won't."

"Do you want to see him?"

Garrett considered that for a long moment. "Yeah."

They walked back around the shack. Twenty feet away, Owen's chains rattled as he signaled: *Hello.*

"Say hello," Toby urged.

"Hello, Owen."

Hello, Owen repeated.

"Is he a Bigfoot?" Garrett asked.

"I don't think so. He might be a Bigfoot's cousin. I don't know what he is, for sure. Nobody else knows about him, though. Just you and me."

Well, nobody else alive...

"Can I go closer?"

"No."

"Does he like the chains?"

"He hates the chains. Don't you, Owen? You hate those things."

Yes.

"See? He can do thumbs-up to mean yes. Ask him a question. He doesn't always understand, but he can get it a lot of the time."

Garrett seemed hesitant, but Toby nudged him. "Go ahead."

"Owen, are you going to eat me?"

No.

"Owen," said Toby, "are we best friends?"

Yes.

"And are you and Garrett going to be friends?"

Yes.

"And would you ever do anything to hurt Garrett?"

No.

"See, Garrett. He understands. Ask him something else."

"Owen, is one plus one two?"

Owen didn't respond.

"Smartass," said Toby. "I didn't teach him addition. Ask him a real question."

"That *was* a real question!" Garrett insisted. "Owen, could you get loose if you wanted?"

No.

"Ask him his favorite food," Toby urged.

"Owen, what's your favorite food?"

Owen mimed scooping a spoon into a bowl.

"That means ice cream."

"I like ice cream, too," Garrett said. "What's your favorite flavor?"

"He likes strawberry," Toby said. "But I don't think he much cares one way or another, as long as it's ice cream. Sort of like your mom with pie."

"I like mint chocolate chip," Garrett told Owen. "There was one kind of mint chocolate chip that Daddy brought home one time that I didn't like, but usually it's my favorite."

"Isn't he cool?" Toby asked.

"He's super cool. Does Mommy know?"

"No."

"Why not?"

"She'd be scared."

"But he wouldn't hurt her."

"I know, but you can be scared of things that wouldn't hurt you. You have to admit, it's kind of *weird* to have a best friend who's a monster in the woods, isn't it?"

"Yeah."

"We're a couple of weirdos!"

"Yeah! Big weirdos!"

"Big weirdo dorks! But that's okay. There's nothing wrong with being weird. Do you know anybody else who has a monster friend?"

"No way!"

"You think the kids at school would be jealous?"

"Yeah! I bet nobody would pick on me if they knew."

"They sure wouldn't. But you can't tell them."

Garrett rolled his eyes. "I know. You've already told me a bazillion times."

"So I'm telling you a bazillion and one times."

"Can I touch him?"

"No."

"Next time?"

"Maybe."

"You're going to bring me back again, right?"

"I sure am." Toby gave his son a hug. "You'd better believe it."

GARRETT TALKED non-stop about his new monster friend as they walked home. Toby was absolutely elated—giddy, even. In fact, it was a good thing that he had to immediately turn back around to unfasten Owen's chains, or Sarah might question his emotional state.

"You can go in and play Nintendo, or read a book," Toby said.

"I'll play Nintendo."

"Or draw."

"Nintendo."

"Fine. Have fun."

"THAT WASN'T SO BAD, was it?" Toby asked, unfastening the collar around Owen's neck.

Hurts.

"Yeah, it looks like it chafed a bit. I'm sorry, buddy. There's nothing else I can do. You liked seeing Garrett, though, right?"

Loved it.

"Well, he loved you, too. When I'm dead and buried, you and he can hang out just like we do. If you didn't have those damn hooks for fingernails we could bring out his handheld video game and you guys could play together."

He unfastened the strap around Owen's right wrist. The monster immediately began to lick the area.

"I know, I know, it hurts. Was it worth it?"

Yes.

"Good."

Again?

"Yes. All the time now."

"SO WHAT DID you two do today?" asked Sarah, plopping a large spoonful of mashed potatoes onto Garrett's dinner plate.

"Cool stuff."

"Well, I know that! What kind of cool stuff?"

"It's a secret."

"A secret from your own Mom? That's not allowed!"

Garrett put a hand over his mouth and giggled.

Sarah gave him a mock-stern glare. "This is no He-Man Women Hater's club, bucko. What trouble did you two get into?"

"Ummmmm. Dad showed me naked boobies."

"*What?*"

"He's kidding," Toby said.

"Naked booooooobies in a magazine!"

"You'd better not have shown him anything like that," Sarah told Toby.

"I would never expose our child to breasts. I don't know what that little bozo is talking about. What are you talking about, bozo?"

"At school, Jimmy Wilson said that his dad had a stack of

magazines with naked boobies, and he left them right in the bathroom."

"Well, Jimmy Wilson's dad is a *pervert*," Toby said. "Naked boobies are *evil*. They should be *banned*."

"What's a pervert?"

"This is not appropriate dinner table conversation," said Sarah. "And naked boobs are not evil, they just shouldn't be shown to an eight-year-old boy."

"I didn't show him any!"

"I know, but don't talk about it."

"The bozo brought it up!"

"I was just kidding," said Garrett. "We went to look at some stupid moss."

"Oh, well, I'm sorry that the moss wasn't as exciting as your video games, your highness."

"It sure wasn't."

Toby kicked him under the table.

"I'm glad you were able to keep a secret," said Toby as he tucked Garrett into bed. "But you really need to work on a better cover story."

"Will Owen be okay out there by himself?"

"Yeah. Owen will be fine. He's been out there for a long, long time."

27

V isiting Owen had always been inconvenient because of
the distance. It became much worse when Toby had to
walk out there, chain him up (Owen never fought against
the process but made his displeasure quite clear), go back home and
get Garrett, walk to Owen's place for the visit, walk Garrett back,
return to the shack, unchain Owen, and walk back home. It was
ridiculous.

By the fourth visit, he just made Toby wait for him a short but
safe distance back. He'd been friends with the monster since the
1960's—Owen wasn't going to suddenly jump out of nowhere, grab
Garrett and run off.

"Can I pet him?" Garrett asked, as he'd asked on every previous
visit.

"No."

"Why not?"

"Why do you think?"

"But he wouldn't do anything to me. You wouldn't do anything
bad, would you, Owen?"

No.

Toby chuckled. "Still not gonna happen."

―――――――

"Okay, we're going to walk up to him very slowly. Don't make any sudden moves. Think of him like a lion in a cage."

"He could kill any lion."

"Yes, he could. And he could rip a little boy's head off as easy as snapping his fingers."

Garrett grinned and snapped his fingers.

"We're done. You're not taking this seriously."

"But Dad―!"

"I said we're done."

―――――――

"He's probably the most talented in the class," said Mrs. Kingston. "Look at the detail on that. A lot of kids his age haven't progressed beyond stick figures."

"He's always loved to draw," said Sarah, beaming with pride.

Toby nodded. It was a wonderful, accurate drawing, and there was a little boy who was going to get a very stern lecture tonight.

―――――――

"Part of keeping a secret involves *not* drawing pictures of Owen to turn in for a class project," Toby explained.

"I didn't tell anybody he was real."

"I realize that, but it looks just like him. What if somebody asks you how you drew it so well?"

"They already did. I said I made him up. He's a monster."

"Right, but...do you think the president draws pictures of secret nuclear weapon stockpiles?" Toby could feel the logic of his argument slipping away. "Just don't draw Owen any more, okay?"

"Okay."

"But we'll show him this picture. He'll love it."

"Careful. Be *very* careful."

One month and ten visits later, they walked toward Owen again. Owen stood in his chains, arms at his sides, head lowered slightly as if to say "I'm a humble, harmless creature."

While Garrett stayed back a few feet, Toby moved right up to Owen and stroked his fur. "Yeah, you're a good boy, right? The best buddy ever. It's going to be a pleasant experience for everybody. No gore at all. Is everybody calm and happy?"

Yes.

"One more time: you're a good boy, right?"

"You're treating him like a dog," Garrett said.

"I'm being cautious."

"He doesn't like that, though. He's smarter than a dog."

"Yeah, and he's also got way bigger claws and teeth than a dog, and as your father I'm allowed to be overprotective. Put your mask on."

"This is stupid."

"Mask."

"Yes, sir." Garrett put on the mask, which completed his baseball catcher's uniform. It wasn't as good as a suit of armor, but if Owen did lash out unexpectedly, this would help protect him from scratches. Toby would much rather have his son look like a fool than risk having this encounter end with bloodshed.

"Gloves too."

Garrett put on the thick padded gloves without protest.

"All right. Come on up."

Garrett stood there for a moment, as if working up his courage.

"You can take as long as you need."

It took Garrett another couple of minutes. Then he stepped

forward, reached out, and gently touched Owen with his index finger.

"Easy," Toby warned Owen, even though Owen hadn't moved.

Garrett moved a bit closer, then began to pet Owen's arm. The monster remained docile.

"Isn't that cool?" Toby asked.

"Not with the gloves."

"Okay, you can take the gloves off. But that's it."

Garrett pulled off the gloves and shoved them back into his pocket. He ran his fingers through Owen's fur. "He's got bugs on him."

"Yeah, I know."

"You should give him a bath."

"Do you want a monster or a poodle?"

"A monster."

"He's got lots of knots in his hair, too. I haven't been combing him as much as I used to."

"Can I do it?"

"Not today. But you can someday."

"I like him."

"Me too. Okay, that's enough for now."

As Garrett stepped away, Owen signed: *Friend.*

"He says you're his friend," said Toby.

Garrett smiled and made the friend sign back.

"W͟ʜʏ ᴄᴀɴ'ᴛ we go see him?" Garrett asked.

"Do you know what 'arousing suspicion' means?"

Garrett considered that. "It means people think you're doing something bad?"

"Pretty much. If we go out there too often, then your mother will question what we're up to, and then there's a bigger chance that she'll find out about Owen. Does that make sense?"

"Yeah." Garrett looked disappointed.

"I'd be out there with Owen all day, every day if I could be. Heck, I'd have him move in with us, give him his own bedroom. But since we can't, we have to be careful."

"Okay."

Toby had to admit to himself that it probably wasn't a very good parenting technique to give his child advice on how to avoid arousing suspicion in his parent when breaking the rules, but this wasn't a normal situation. There was nothing better than the excitement in Garrett's eyes when they went off to see Owen, and he couldn't risk Sarah finding out.

"We'll go tomorrow, though. I promise."

———

"CAN HANNAH COME WITH US SOMETIME?"

"Not until she's eight."

———

As THEY APPROACHED THE SHACK, Toby realized that it had been over three months since he'd visited Owen by himself for any reason except to fasten the chains. It was a wonderful realization.

"Oooh, yeah, you're getting a welt there," Toby said, inspecting Owen's right wrist. "Maybe we can pad it somehow. Do you think they sell fuzzy handcuffs in your size?"

Owen either didn't get the joke, or didn't find it amusing. Toby suspected the latter.

"We'll leave one of them off, just for today. Will that make you happy?"

Yes.

OWEN KEPT his arm at his side the entire time, just as Toby knew he'd do.

It was cruel to keep his best friend chained up like this. Sure, Owen loved getting to interact with somebody besides Toby (excluding the unfortunate animals he killed for food) but these conditions were becoming tiring. It was sadistic, as if he was bringing his son to gape at the sideshow freak every three or four days.

Regardless, it was several more months before Toby felt comfortable enough to let Garrett see him without the chains.

1996

There was no danger.

None at all.

Owen was gentle, even when Garrett started roughhousing with him a bit. Yes, Toby had to call for them to stop a couple of times —okay, a few times—when the game of tag got too feisty, but his son was far rowdier than his monster. Owen played with him like a grandfather might—having fun, but always aware that he was the adult and Garrett was the child and that it was his responsibility to make sure Garrett didn't get hurt.

Garrett loved feeding him. He'd toss popcorn and beef jerky and jelly beans into his mouth, and Owen would show off his impressive catching abilities with far more glee than he'd ever shown with Toby. It was as if having a kid around made the monster feel young again.

"We should build a roller coaster out here for him," said Garrett.

"No way. How much do you think a big guy like him pukes? We can't be cleaning that up all day." He playfully tapped Garrett on the head. "Use your brain, boy."

"What about a merry-go-round?"

"No offense to Owen, but if I build a merry-go-round, it's going to be for your sister."

"She could use it, too."

"How about we build him a chair? A rocking chair. You exhaust the hell out of the poor guy, and he needs something to relax in after you're gone."

Yes.

Garrett was fascinated by Owen's love for ice cream, but not a fan of the process of lugging an ice-filled cooler out there in order to provide his friend with a non-melted treat. However, once the first snow fell, the three of them scooped snow into bowls, added syrup, and had homemade slushies.

"Are you sure I can't bring him to school?"

"You will never, ever be allowed to take him to school. He's not a Show and Tell project."

"What about his tooth?"

"No." Owen had lost another tooth, and Garrett had volunteered to keep it under his pillow and split the unquestionably huge Tooth Fairy payout with Owen. Toby explained that the Tooth Fairy's payment process was not based on tooth size, and that, no, he could not put the tooth under his pillow, and no, he could not bring it home, and actually, he shouldn't even be touching it because, no offense to Owen, it was a nasty smelly tooth.

"Will I ever be allowed to come out here by myself?" Garrett asked.

"Sure."

"When?"

"When I'm dead."

"But that's going to be a long time!"

"And don't sound so disappointed about that! What you mean is 'Gosh, Daddy, I hope you live forever and ever, even if it means that I never get to see Owen all by my lonesome.'"

"'Gosh, Daddy, I hope I get to see Owen by myself tomorrow!'"

"Garrett!"

"I was joking!"

"Did you think it was a funny joke? Do you think it makes me feel good to hear you say things like that? Both you and Owen will be really sad if I die."

"I said I was only kidding! Jeez!"

"I don't care if you were kidding or not. There are some things you don't joke about. I think it's time to go home."

Garrett folded his arms over his chest. "I'm staying."

"No, you're not. And if you keep up that attitude, I won't bring you back."

"Then I'll tell everyone."

Toby simultaneously wanted to throttle his son, and double over and throw up. "What did you say?"

"I'll tell."

"You'll tell, huh? You'll break your promise to me? Your blood promise?"

"There wasn't any blood."

"You know what I mean. I know that you're just kidding, that you wouldn't really tell anybody, but it's really horrible of you to say something like that, even when you're mad. What do you think they'll do to Owen if they find him?"

"I don't know."

"They'll kill him. They'll cut him apart and study him. Is that what you want to happen to your best friend?"

Garrett looked mortified. "No."

"Then you need to apologize to him."

"I'm sorry, Owen," Garrett said in a very soft voice.

"And apologize to me."

"I'm sorry."

"You're not coming back for two weeks. And no Nintendo."

2 8

1997. Age 52.

"Has Owen ever eaten anybody? Hey, Owen, have you ever eaten anybody?"

No.

"Would you ever eat anybody? I mean people."

"Of course he wouldn't," Toby said. "Why would you even ask something like that?"

"If I were Owen, I'd eat people."

"Well, that's because you're one disturbed little boy. Why would you eat people? Just people who were mean to you?"

Garrett shook his head. "I'd start with them, I guess. If I were a big monster like that, I wouldn't just eat rabbits and squirrels and stuff."

"He also eats deer."

"Yeah, but I'd go for more challenging prey."

"More challenging prey? What books have you been reading?"

"It's this game I borrowed where you have to hunt humans because they're the ultimate prey."

"I'm so very happy to see that you're basing your sense of morality on video games. Don't talk to Owen about eating people. Ten-year-old boys aren't supposed to be that sick. And you're only talking to get out of work. C'mon, stop being a slacker."

They were doing some desperately needed repairs on Owen's shack, which they'd avoided during snowy season but which they could no longer justify postponing now that spring was here. Some of the wood had started to rot, and Toby had decided that even a creature in the forest deserved better accommodations than this.

The job basically involved ripping apart the far wall, a board at a time, and replacing each of the decaying boards with new wood. They'd started at the bottom and were about halfway up. Garrett's enthusiasm for the project had waned after he pulled off a board and ants swarmed all over his hand, though fortunately none of them had stung him.

Garrett held up the new board, and Toby nailed it into place. Owen, who did not possess a skill set that would come in handy for this particular project, watched intently, as if playing supervisor.

Toby gave a gentle tug on the board. "Think it needs any more?"

Garrett pointed to a spot near the top center. "One more right there."

"Yes, sir." Toby hammered in one more nail. "You thirsty?"

"Yeah."

"Coke or 7-Up?"

"7-Up." Garrett leaned against the wall, bracing himself with his right arm.

"You'll get ants on your hand again."

"There aren't any here."

"Don't cry when you get stung." Toby walked around to the front of the shack and removed the lid from the cooler. He fished through the ice for a moment. "Did you already drink all the 7-Up?" he called out.

"No."

"What did you have before?"

"7-Up."

"Then you drank it all."

Toby took out two Cokes. Garrett shrieked.

Immediately dropping the cans, Toby rushed back around the shack. Garrett's arm had broken right through the wood. Still screaming, Garrett pulled his arm free from the jagged hole. It glistened with blood and a huge deep gash ran from wrist to elbow.

Owen scooped him up into his arms.

"Owen!" shouted Toby, hurrying forward. "Put him down!"

Garrett thrashed and screamed, but Owen held him tight.

He's not gonna hurt him, Toby promised himself. *He just wants to get him help.* "Owen, give him to me, now."

Owen looked down at the struggling boy, his eyes wide with concern.

Then he leaned down and ran his tongue over the wound.

Toby's vision went blurry for a split second, then returned to sharp focus. "*Owen!*"

The monster held Toby's son out to him. Toby grabbed him, and a sharp pain went through his back. He cursed and tried to adjust Garrett's position so he could hold him better, then shook his head.

"I'm not going to be able to carry you," he said, setting Garrett down onto his feet. He took his hand. "Come on, I'm going to get you to the hospital."

They ran from the forest.

"What happened?" Sarah asked, hurrying outside as Toby led the sobbing boy across their backyard.

"He gouged up his arm pretty bad—he'll be okay."

Sarah ran over to them and crouched down in front of Garrett to inspect his arm. "Oh my God! Look how deep it is!"

"I know, I know, it's bad. I'll get him in the car. You go get Hannah."

Toby led Garrett over to their car, opened the back door, and helped Garrett into the back seat. "You'll be okay," Toby promised. "It looks worse than it is."

Garrett nodded silently. His face was frighteningly pale, and his breathing was rapid and uneven. Sarah came out of the house with towels and the first-aid kit. Toby got Hannah strapped into her child seat as Sarah squeezed into the back as well and pressed one of the towels tightly against Garrett's arm.

"How did this happen?" Sarah asked, as they sped down the road.

"He was leaning against a piece of rotted wood, and it broke."

"Why was he leaning against rotted wood?"

"We found this old shack out in the forest. Abandoned. It was my fault, we should have been more careful."

Sarah pulled the bloody towel away and winced. "This is really bad, Toby. Drive faster."

"I'm already doing eighty." His heart hammered with panic. Garrett couldn't possibly bleed to death before they got to the hospital, could he? No. The cut wasn't *that* bad. He'd require a huge number of stitches, but this wasn't a life-or-death situation. Kids got hurt. It happened.

"Garrett, talk to me, honey," said Sarah. "Does it hurt a lot?"

"Yeah."

"The doctor will make it all better."

"Owen licked the blood."

"What?"

"Owen, when he picked me up, he licked the blood."

"Who's Owen?"

"Our friend in the woods."

Toby could barely focus on the road, but he tried to keep himself calm, even as he screamed *Fuck!* in his mind over and over.

"Toby, what's he talking about?" Sarah demanded.

"Nothing—he's delirious. It'll all be okay, I promise."

Garrett's eyes closed.

GARRETT SAID nothing about the monster in the forest as the doctor stitched up his wound. With the blood cleaned off, the gash didn't look as...well, it still looked *bad*, but Toby's mind had flashed through scenarios involving amputation.

Toby noted with grim humor that Garrett had been brave throughout the ghastly stitching process, but still cried when he had to get a tetanus shot "just in case."

He'd have a nasty scar, but he could move his fingers fine and there was no permanent damage beyond the cosmetic. He'd be fine.

The drive home was long and quiet.

It was still early afternoon, but Garrett was exhausted and wanted a nap. Sarah called her friend Becky and asked if she could come over and watch Garrett and Hannah for a bit.

"Why'd you do that?" Toby asked, as Sarah hung up the phone. "Who's Owen?"

"Nobody. An imaginary friend. We play around with him."

"When Becky gets here, I want you to take me to where he got hurt."

"It's an old shack we found. I never should have let him near it —the blame for this is entirely on me. I promise you, first thing tomorrow I'm going to tear the place down, make sure no other kids get hurt. Bad judgment on my part. I'm sorry."

"No, Toby. I want to see it today. I want to know what the hell you two are doing out there."

"We're goofing around! Playing make-believe! There's nothing wrong with that. We're not hanging out with some crazy old blood-licking man named Owen—we like to pretend that we're fighting monsters."

"Becky will be here in ten minutes."

"Call her back. I'm not leaving my son after he just got hurt. Look, how many times do I have to apologize for this? Don't you think I feel terrible?"

"I don't want an apology. I want to know exactly how our son's arm got ripped up."

"I told you, he was leaning against some wood—"

"Stop it, okay? If that's the real story, then fine, I'll yell at you for being an irresponsible dad and we'll be done with it. But you're going to show me that fucking shack."

"Don't curse around Hannah. I can't believe you don't trust me."

"You're right, I don't."

TOBY PACED around the living room, frantic. What was he supposed to do? Refuse to take her out there? She wouldn't give up. If she knew they were hiding something, she'd be absolutely relentless.

He wished he hadn't said it was a shack. If he'd said that Garrett injured himself on a branch, he could've just taken Sarah anywhere. But he'd thought about that during the drive to the emergency room, and he wanted to keep his story as close to the truth as possible. If he said a branch and Garrett said a shack, they'd be screwed.

What could he do? What could he do?

What the hell was Sarah going to do when she found out about Owen?

Okay. Calm down. It's going to be...

A disaster. A total nightmare of a catastrophe of an Armageddon.

Way to think positive.

No. Maybe there was a solution. Well, not a solution, but a way this could work out. Owen didn't spend all day and all night in the shack. In fact, daytime was when he did most of his hunting. Toby had shown up countless times when Owen wasn't there. So it was entirely possible that he could get lucky and Owen wouldn't be home.

"See, sweetie? Here's the shack. Yeah, I see the boards and tools. We were just trying to fix the place up. Yeah, I should have told you about it. No, I don't think it was responsible to let him play out here—but to be fair, I was with him the whole time. Well, yeah, that includes when he hurt his arm, but it's not like he was running around rusty nails without parental supervision. I agree, I'm a total dumb-ass and bad Dad. It'll never happen again."

Why shouldn't it work out that way?

Or, he could leave right now, run into the woods, tell Owen to get the hell out and not come back until tomorrow, and then return, apologize to Sarah for running off, and—

No. He'd stick with the plan that did not involve him rushing out into the woods like a complete lunatic, and just pray for good luck. He'd had enough bad luck in his life that it wouldn't be out of the question for this particular instance to work out in his favor, right?

He wished he and Owen shared some sort of psychic bond, so he could send a telepathic message for Owen to leave.

Maybe they did share a bond, and Toby just didn't know it. *Leave,* he thought. *Owen, you need to leave. Leave now. Stay away.*

Oh, Jesus, he was cracking up. Which was not unexpected at a time like this, but he needed to keep his mental focus. This could still turn out okay. There was no reason to let an accident—a stupid, careless accident—ruin his life.

When this day was over, he'd still have Owen and his family. Absolutely. No question about it.

He continued to pace until he heard Becky's car pull into the driveway.

BECKY MADE a big fuss over Garrett's bandaged arm, though not loudly enough to wake him up. She sat Hannah on her lap and promised to take good care of her. Sarah explained that they were going into the forest to retrieve the broken board for the doctor, just so they could run some tests on it and make sure there wasn't anything dangerous that might have entered Garrett's bloodstream.

It was a pretty good cover story. Toby wondered if she was hiding her own monster.

They walked into the forest.

"I'm sorry I made a big deal about going out here," Toby said. "I just don't like leaving Garrett alone when he's hurt like that."

"He's not alone."

"You know what I mean."

"Just take me to the shack."

As they walked, moving at a brisk pace, Toby prayed that Owen wouldn't be there when they arrived. He mentally pleaded for it. He continued trying to send telepathic messages to his friend, no matter how insane that was. It wasn't that much to ask, for him to be out on a stroll, perhaps grabbing a bite to eat.

Please, Owen, please, please don't be there when we get to the shack. Go hunting, go back to find Esmerelda, go swimming... hell, go into town and rip the guts out of another old man, I don't care, just please don't be there.

When they arrived at the shack, Owen was waiting for them.

2 9

One of the most perceptive observations Toby had heard about the aging process was that time sped up as you got older. At eight years old, summer lasted forever, and it seemed as if Christmas would *never* come. In your fifties, you said things like "Is it August already?" and wondered how it was possible that you were ready to celebrate the New Year when you'd just celebrated the last one.

But this moment, the moment with Sarah staring at the monster in shock, with Owen staring back at her—that moment lasted as long as Toby's previous fifty-two years, and yet somehow he didn't have time to fantasize about the possible ways the moment could end.

Owen looked confused, yet happy. Sarah looked terrified.

"Don't run," Toby said. "He won't hurt you."

Sarah didn't speak. He could see how tense her body was, see that she was ready to run, just like she'd wanted to run from that support group meeting but a thousand times worse. But he couldn't let her. Owen would chase her if she ran.

"He won't hurt you," Toby repeated.

Owen signed: *Who?*

"This is Sarah. You know Sarah. You've seen pictures."

Owen spoke. "*Toby.*"

The horror that crossed Sarah's face brought a pain to Toby that was worse than a monster talon plunging into his heart and wrenching it out of his chest in a bloody spray. She covered her mouth with her hands and began to hyperventilate.

Owen signed: *Friend?*

"Yes, friend," said Toby, using every bit of energy he could summon to keep his voice steady. "Tell her that you'd never hurt your friend."

Not hurt friend.

"Toby, get me out of here," Sarah said. "Get me away from that thing."

She was losing it. Toby put his arm on her shoulder, trying to calm her, but she shook him off. "I said, get me the fuck out of here!"

Owen frowned, obviously hurt by her reaction.

"It's okay, it's okay, we're going. Owen, don't follow us. Garrett's fine, he's okay, so you don't have to worry about him, everyone's fine."

He led Sarah away, checking over his shoulder every couple of seconds to make sure Owen wasn't following them. He wasn't. Owen just stood there, disappointed and lonely.

When they were out of sight of the shack, they ran.

———

THEY EMERGED from the forest into the backyard, and Sarah spun toward him, the horror in her face now gone, replaced with pure anger. "*What the fuck was that?*"

"His name is Owen, he's—"

"*What the fuck are you doing with our son?*"

"Just let me explain."

270

Sarah slapped him, so hard that Toby felt his eyes well up with tears. "Your ex-girlfriend got eaten by a giant animal—you think I can't put the pieces together? You think I'm a fucking idiot?"

The door opened, and Becky stepped out onto the back porch, holding Hannah.

"It's not like that. Give me a chance and I'll help you understand."

"What am I supposed to understand, Toby? What exactly do you think in that fucked-up head of yours that you're going to convince me of? I cannot even describe how sick this is, you son of a bitch!"

"Becky, you should go inside," said Toby.

"Maybe you guys should do this later."

"*Becky, go inside!*" Toby shouted.

Becky hesitated, then went back inside, shutting the door behind her.

Sarah took several long, deep breaths. "Okay. Explain."

"Owen would never hurt Garrett."

"You *named* it? You named that thing?"

"Yes! Because he's not some wild animal! I know it sounds deranged—"

"You have no idea how deranged it sounds."

"Let me talk, okay? I swear to you, I'd never put our child in danger. Owen had nothing to do with this. It was an accident that could have happened anywhere."

"Garrett told us that thing licked his blood."

That part of today's events was hard to overlook, and Toby had planned to address it, perhaps never bring Garrett back to the forest again, no matter how much the boy begged to see his friend.

"That never happened," Toby said. "I don't know where it came from. You saw Garrett—he'd lost a lot of blood and barely knew where he was."

"How long have you been taking him out there?"

"I'm not sure. A while."

"How long?"

"It doesn't matter, okay!"

"*Why did that goddamn thing say your name?*" Sarah wailed.

"Because he's my friend. I've been friends with him since high school. I didn't know you, I didn't know Mr. Lynch, I didn't know Becky, but I knew Owen! He's been with me through everything! Do you know when I found him in his cave? 1960! That's how I knew he wasn't going to hurt Garrett! That's how I knew he wasn't going to hurt you! Because he's my best friend!"

Sarah stared at him, her eyes cold with hatred. "He hurt Melissa."

"You don't know what happened."

"If this is the way you want to live your life, that's fine." Sarah was no longer shouting, and the even tone of her voice was far more disturbing. "You can hang out in the woods with your magical creature friend and just have yourselves a ball. Do whatever the hell you want. But you're not going to risk the lives of our children."

"I didn't—"

"I'm leaving. Garrett and Hannah are coming with me. I don't want your mental illness anywhere around us. You're not going to visit us, you're not going to call us, you're not going to fucking *exist* for us, do you understand?"

"You can't take my kids away."

"When you took Garrett out there and let him go near that *thing*, you gave up all rights as a parent. You're out of the picture. I love you, but there's something hideous in your brain, and I'm taking our children far away from it."

Toby shook his head. "No. There's no way I'm letting you do that. You want a divorce? Fine. Bring me the papers. I'll sign whatever you want. Just don't take Garrett and Hannah away from me."

"This isn't your choice anymore."

"I'll fight it."

"The hell you will. You do one thing to stop me and I'll tell everybody about your dearest, most darling friend. I'll hold a goddamn press conference. They'll tear those woods apart looking for that freak, and they'll blow him away. I'm not bluffing." There was a cruel edge to her voice now, almost sadistic.

"Please don't take them," he said in a soft voice.

"You're lucky I'm not calling the police right now. What you need to do is go out into the woods, put a bullet into that thing, and straighten your life out. Is that where you were all those times, those hundreds of times? What's wrong with you? How can you not see the insanity of this?"

"I do see it."

"Then why the hell are you bringing our son out there?"

"Because he's our friend!"

"Not anymore. We'll work the money and property out like civilized people, and you can say good-bye, but if you ever try to contact our kids, it's over."

"If you spent time with him, you'd understand."

"Get help, Toby. Go to a hotel. I'll call you when we're ready to leave."

"YOU SHOULD KILL HER," said Larry. "Orgy of violence!"

"I'm not going to kill anyone."

"Change of heart? You killed *me*. What'd I do, beat you up a couple of times? This bitch is stealing your kids."

"I deserve it."

"Nobody deserves that! Did you see how smug she looked? Go get the gun and shoot her in the back while she's packing. How long has it been since Owen's had a nice taste of juicy human flesh?"

"Go away."

"So you're going to let her win? What a loser. Loser in high school, loser now. Think how good it would feel to pull that trigger and watch the back of her head explode."

"It would feel horrible."

"You're not using your imagination. Picture it with me. The bullet slamming into her skull, shattering it, grey matter splattering against the wall. Let's see her steal Garrett from you when she's a bloody corpse. I'll cheer when Owen starts ripping tendons away from bone with his teeth."

"You can just go to hell," Toby said. "I'll never hurt her."

"No more sneaking around. Remember how great it was when you moved out of your parents' place? You could see Owen whenever you wanted. Why'd you get married? All that freedom, gone. For what?"

"I love her."

"And she loves you right back, huh? Is that why she's taking everything away from you? Did she even *try* to understand? She thinks that she's so much better than you that she can just kidnap your kids without letting you tell your side?"

"My side is fucked up."

"It is. I won't argue with you there. It's fucked up in a way you don't see very often. But you know what? When you're twelve years into a relationship, the other person should be willing to deal with the occasional fucked up situation."

"I put Garrett's life in danger."

"How long did you keep the chains on Owen? How many precautions did you take? And Owen didn't do anything!"

"He might have."

"Had you not been there, Owen would've carried him to safety. The newspapers would all have a front-page cover story on the hero monster who saved the life of an innocent little boy. Kill that bitch."

"No."

"Shoot her."

"No."

"Make all of your problems go away."

"I'm not going to hurt her. This was all my fault. Maybe...maybe she'll get over it and she'll let me see them sometimes. It doesn't have to be a lot. Just sometimes."

"Yeah, all right, way to stand up for yourself. If you change your mind, you know where to find me."

SARAH WAS KIND AT the end. She let him give Garrett a kiss. He whispered that everything would be all right, that he'd take good care of Owen.

He brushed Hannah's hair one last time. She was too little to understand what was going on, but when she gave him that last hug, she seemed to acknowledge the finality of it.

Toby didn't cry when they left. He just sat there in the living room, numb. He stared at nothing.

He should have never brought Garrett out there.

But that was obvious from the beginning, wasn't it?

Then, when he could bring himself to stand, he went out into the forest to see Owen, and then he did cry.

"I WAS RIGHT," Toby said. "No matter what happens in my life, no matter what I go through, you're my only real friend."

Yes.

30

GLIMPSES
1998

The second beer went down even smoother than the first. He had quite a few more to go, but he'd gotten an early start and he'd be nice and unconscious before sundown. It was funny, really. He'd suffered through all this misery, and the solution was right here in a couple of six-packs of cheap beer.

He drank until he was comfortably buzzed, and then he drank some more.

"I UNDERSTAND that there are extenuating circumstances, but this is the newspaper business. No-shows are just not acceptable."

Toby shrugged. "Am I fired?"

"You should take a leave of absence, until you get things sorted out."

"Paid leave?"

"I can't do that."

"Then take this job, and twist it right up your ass. Just right up in there, all the way."

"I think you should leave now."

"Yeah, that's probably not such a bad idea."

"HEY, KIDDO, HOW'S IT GOING?"

"I miss you, Daddy."

"I miss you too, Hannah. Are you taking care of your brother?"

"He's stupid."

"Well, so are lots of people. You're speaking to one of them right now. Did you do anything fun today?"

"Toby?" It was Sarah.

"I wasn't done talking to her."

"She has to get ready for bed."

"Come on, Sarah, it's not like I can feed her to a fucking monster over the telephone. I don't even know where you guys are."

"We'll try to call you next week."

Dial tone.

Toby wanted to throw the telephone to the floor and stomp on it until it was reduced to plastic powder, but he really couldn't afford to buy a new one.

"OH, YEAH, I'M ROCKIN' now," Toby told Owen. "I'm working at the fac-to-ry. Monkey work. You wouldn't believe the crap that a grown man will do for eight hours a day. Hour two, I want to put a bullet in my head. Hour three, I want to put a bullet in everyone else's head. Hour four, I just sort of space out. I can still do the job, though. I don't know why they don't have a robot do it. Probably because even a robot would go crazy doing that for eight hours a day—it would take out a gun and blow its microchips out of its head. I did draw a cartoon today, though. Started to draw one, at least. It was a piece of shit so I threw it away. Christ, my head hurts."

1999

"Happy, happy birthday to me!" said Toby, alone in his bedroom. "You know what would be nice? A *phone call* from my *family*! Is that such a big request? Am I asking for a fuckin' unicorn? I don't need a cake and candles, but maybe a thirty-second phone call would keep my life out of the sewer! Pretty good revenge, ex-wife of mine! Leave me alone on my birthday! Yeaaaahh, good one, Sarah! You win!"

"You know, Sarah, I understand that I did something terrible, but seriously, why wouldn't you let me talk to my own kids on my birthday? Are you taking pleasure from this? Is this fun for you? The newest game sensation to sweep the nation, Torture Toby?"

"You did talk to Garrett," Sarah informed him. "You scared him and he hung up the phone crying."

"I..." Toby had no response to that, so he trailed off without completing his thought. "Oh."

"And your birthday is tomorrow."

"Owen, Owen, Owen. We should get out of this dumpy town. Go on the road. Have adventures. See shit. What do you think?"

Owen said nothing. Actually, though it was a hard trick to pull off, Owen looked kind of disgusted with him.

"What's the matter? Am I scaring you?"

Yes.

"Ooooh, the big bad monster is scared of the skinny drunk guy! Sorry to make you uncomfortable, sir. Want me to leave? I'd hate to think of you spending the last year of the millennium with a drunken dick like me. Unless you're one of those whiners who doesn't think the millennium ends until 2001. Either way, hopefully the 21st century will bring better things to your life. Let's drink to that."

2000

"Oh my God, is it Christmas time already...?"

2001

Garrett had quit asking how Owen was doing, no doubt upon strict orders from Sarah, which made sense since she'd forbidden Toby to discuss the subject during their increasingly rare phone calls.

When he'd brought up the subject of an actual in-person visit, she'd gently suggested that it wasn't a good idea. When he'd pushed the issue, she'd hung up on him.

———

THE DOCTOR's expression was unreadable as he walked into the examination room, studying his clipboard. Why was he looking at the clipboard? Surely he knew what news he was delivering. Was he just avoiding eye contact?

"We're going to run some more tests just to be sure, but it appears to be benign, so that's good news. I don't anticipate that news changing, but we like to cover all of our bases. Now, as I'd warned, you are going to need surgery to have the tumor removed, which is a relatively simple procedure."

"Slicing me open and cutting something out is simple?"

"That's why I used the word 'relatively,' Mr. Floren. Compared to a quadruple bypass surgery, yes, this is simple."

"You're right, I apologize. I'm just nervous. I should consider myself lucky. Fifty-six years old and this is my first surgery."

"That *is* a pretty good run. Don't worry. We'll take great care of you. You'll be off your feet for a few weeks, but this is far better than the alternative, trust me."

TOBY LAY AT HOME, watching television. He was going absolutely stir-crazy. He really hoped that Owen had understood him when he described the procedure and explained that he wouldn't be able to visit for a couple of months. It sickened him to think that his friend might be wandering around, lonely and frightened and thinking that something horrible had happened.

Well, technically, a surgeon had sliced open Toby's body. That was pretty horrible. He was certainly feeling the effects of the scalpel. The way he felt now, he might not be up for a trip to the woods ever again.

Of course, that wasn't true. As soon as he could walk a couple of miles without his stomach popping open, he'd be out there to see Owen. Maybe sooner.

"YOU WOULDN'T BELIEVE IT," Toby said. "I don't think I've ever shown you pictures of the World Trade Center, but they're these huge twin towers in New York City. There was this plane sticking right out of it—terrorists flew a plane right into the building! Can you imagine that? And we were all watching this in the lunchroom, totally freaked out, and then right on live TV the towers collapsed! People were gasping and crying and getting mad—it was one of the most messed-up things I've ever seen. And another frickin' plane bashed into the Pentagon. The *Pentagon.* I'm surprised they didn't go for the White House. Trust me, Owen, you're much better off living out here in your bubble. The world has gone berserk."

2002

"I need to repair my life. You've gotta help me out, Owen. I can't do it by myself."

"I JUST DON'T EVEN CARE ANYMORE. Maybe someday I won't wake up. That'll be nice. You could take care of all of my funeral arrangements. You get the house, you know. Everything else is going to my kids, who might be dead for all I know, but you get the house. It's like some crazy old lady leaving her worldly possessions to her cats. I don't know what you're gonna do with it, but it's there if you want it."

"HE SAYS this one might be malignant. Can you believe that shit?"

2003

"Hello, my name is Toby, and I'm an alcoholic. I had my last drink in the hallway before I came in here."

"SO SHE SAYS, 'Sorry, if you can't get it up, that's not my fault.' And I said 'I'm the one paying for this, so it's your job. If you can't do it right, I'll take my business someplace else.' That's exactly what

I told her. And then she tries to leave without giving me my money back! I said, 'Hey, you can't do that! I know what I paid for!' and she says she's going to call her boyfriend. And so I said fine, you know, if that's the kind of service she wants to provide, she'll learn that this is a word of mouth type of business."

"DODGED ANOTHER BULLET. These things keep growing inside me, and the doctors keep cutting them out. I had this dream where it was guilt manifesting itself. It might not have even been a dream. I probably do have guilt tumors floating around in my stomach acid, waiting to take hold and start growing like tomatoes."

"CHECK THIS OUT. It's a cell phone. Everybody's got them these days. I can call anybody I want. Not very good reception out here in the woods, though. Wish I had somebody to talk to."

2004

"Well, they finally figured out that a robot can do my job. It was always just a matter of time. I'd better learn to flip burgers, or you might have yourself a roommate."

"A REAL FRIEND wouldn't let me keep doing all this self-destructive stuff. I'm just sayin'."

TOBY WONDERED how much sympathy he'd have for himself if he

could watch his life from the outside. Probably not a lot. He'd probably just give himself a disgusted look, shake his head sadly, then call for a janitor to sweep it all away. Get the repulsive bum out of the way so decent people didn't have the eyesore.

He really had to fix this mess. Even Owen didn't seem to enjoy his company all that much anymore.

And he would, after a couple more beers.

31

2005. 60 years old.

The best thing about being a drunken babbling idiot was that nobody believed you when you blurted out secrets about your monster friend. Toby was a laughingstock in the small bar, whatever it was called, and he rarely ventured there more than once a month, and only when he was already half-plastered.

He'd never said anything about the murders, at least as far as he knew, but he'd told the bartender all about Owen. The bartender hadn't cut his drinks off. It wasn't that kind of place.

Toby sat alone in a booth surrounded by empty bottles, although many of those were left over from the last patron. He wondered if he should try to walk home, take a cab, or let the bartender sort it out after he passed out.

A man slid into the seat across from him.

"You're the monster guy, right?"

The man was probably a few years older than Toby, smelled truly vile, and had wild hair and an unkempt grey beard. Even by

Toby's drastically reduced standards, the guy looked like a complete bum.

"No."

"Yeah, you are! You don't have to pretend anything with me, man." The bum had a lazy eye and sounded like a hippie. Toby was embarrassed to admit to himself that despite the odor he was happy to have somebody to talk to.

"There's no monster," Toby said. "I make stuff up."

"Man, lower your defenses. I know all of these. Loch Ness Monster, Jersey Devil, aliens in Area 51 and Hangar 18...you go online and know where to look, you can find the truth on anything."

"Fine. So I'm friends with Bigfoot."

"Nah, man. What you described to Jimmy isn't a Bigfoot."

"The bartender's name is Jimmy?"

"I dunno. Might be." The man picked up one of the discarded bottles, shook it, and finished off the drops that remained. "You don't know the story?"

"I didn't know there was a story."

"1946. These American soldiers are back from World War II, and they take their girlfriends out camping, right? Maybe a hundred miles from where we are right now. Nice and peaceful, everybody's having a good time, probably gettin' it on because you don't get laid much when you're out fighting Nazis, and then these things attack them. They've got these scary-ass teeth and claws, and they just rip those people *up*. It's like a war, man. One of our heroes gets away. A girl. Yep, three trained soldiers and it's one of the girls who escapes. So she makes it out of the woods and she's going nuts and she tells somebody what happened, and the next thing you know this team goes in there with rifles and they just mow those things down!"

"Sounds kind of far-fetched."

"I know! It's crazy! So you've got this government operation and a bunch of dead creatures, and they think 'Well, shit, we can't have

Americans panicking over soldier-killing monsters after we just got over the whole Nazi thing!' and they cover it all up. The lady who survived goes into an asylum. Rips her own eyes out. Dies a few years later."

"What did they do with the bodies?"

"Underground bunker. They studied them for a while but couldn't figure out what the hell they were, so they froze the bodies until the technology could improve. They're still there."

Toby laughed. "You're a numbfuck. You're telling me that in 2005 we can't do an autopsy on a dead animal and figure out what it is? Your whole story is crap."

The man shrugged. "Hell, for all I know, they've already cloned thousands of 'em and they're gonna take over the planet. Not all information on the World Wide Web is reliable. But I'm just saying, it's a big forest. One of those creatures could have escaped and hid out all this time."

"Yeah."

"I'd love to see one."

"I bet you would."

"Come on, man, you can't hold out. You've gotta share the wealth. I wanna see Aaron."

"It's not Aaron, it's Owen."

"You got a picture?"

Toby took another drink of beer, swished it around in his mouth, then swallowed. "How do I know you're not from that government unit?"

"Man, if I were from a government unit like that, I'd be gettin' some pussy right now, not talking monsters in a crap-smelling pit like this, that's for damn sure."

"Sorry. I don't know where you'd find any soldier-killing super-monster. Good luck on the pussy, though."

"Man, I will blow every whistle I've got if you keep being selfish like this. I'll have the Men in Black scouring those woods for your friend. Next time you see me, I'll be on the front page of a *Cryptozoology Today*, grinning like a son of a bitch."

"I'm a drunken moron. Why would you believe me even if I said I did have a monster buddy?"

"Because you're still drunk, and now you're denying it. And I'm drunk, too."

"Fuck it. Buy me a beer for the road and we'll go."

THE MAN never offered his name during the drive to Toby's house, and Toby didn't ask. Better that Toby didn't know—it would make it easier to deal with the guilt when the man disappeared forever. Everything but his bones.

Toby had done a lot of irresponsible things, but before now he'd managed to avoid driving while intoxicated. One more to add to the list, he supposed.

What did the man think, he could threaten to expose Owen's presence to the world and not die tonight? The vagrant probably wouldn't make good on his threat; if anything, he'd spend the evening passed out in a gutter and forget he'd ever seen Toby by sunrise. But Toby wasn't taking that chance. He had too much invested in his friendship to let this pathetic hippie scumbag mess with it.

The man decided to start singing as they walked through the woods, which made his upcoming death even more essential.

"You need to shut up," said Toby.

"Sing with me!"

"You'll scare him away."

"Yeah, I suppose I might." The man stopped singing. "Did I tell you about when I went to Scotland?"

"No."

"Went to Scotland just to go to Loch Ness. Well, that wasn't the whole reason, I had relatives, but that was the selling point. Spent a week out there, staring at the water. Just wanted to see Nessie."

"Did you?"

The man shook his head. "They say it's fake. A lot of scientists and other people say it's a hoax, and even the guy who shot that one movie said it wasn't real. Why would you say that? Even if you could prove it was a fake, why would you take it away from people like that?"

"I don't know."

"I spent seven days sitting there, watching the water. Never saw any hint of the Loch Ness Monster. But I bet he was down there the whole time, watching me. Best vacation of my life."

He resumed singing as they walked through the woods.

THEY STOOD OUTSIDE THE SHACK. Toby shone the flashlight on the door.

"Is he in there?" the man asked.

"He might be. Hey, Owen, I've got somebody for you to meet!"

The door opened, and Owen emerged. The monster rubbed his eyes sleepily, then frowned as he noticed the man standing next to Toby.

The man stared at Owen in pure wonder, lips trembling. "*He's real*," he whispered.

"Yeah."

"I can't believe I'm standing here seeing this."

Owen stepped out of the shack. *Friend?*

"No," said Toby. "He's not."

"He's not what?" asked the man.

Toby ignored the question. "Do you want to touch him?"

Twenty years seemed to vanish from the man's face. "Yes!"

The man apparently had no fear as they walked over to Owen.

Maybe he wanted this to be his last moment. Or maybe he was just too drunk to realize the danger.

Owen stood there, motionless, as the man ran his fingers down his chest, a tear trickling down his cheek.

Toby grabbed the man by the back of his shirt collar and shoved him to the ground. Then he kicked him in the spine. "Kill him, Owen! Hurry!"

Owen continued to stand there. The monster looked surprised and upset.

"Do it, Owen! He'll tell everybody! Rip him apart!"

The man cried out and tried to get back up, but Toby tackled him and held him down. He grabbed a handful of hair and slammed his face against the dirt.

"Owen, come *on*!"

No.

"This is food! I'm giving you food! For fuck's sake, Owen, do something before he gets away!"

"I didn't do anything!" the man wailed.

Toby slammed his face into the dirt again. "Eat him, goddamn it! He's gonna tell the world!"

"I'm not! I swear!"

Toby twisted the man's arm behind his back until something snapped. The man screamed in pain. He deserved it. He was going to destroy everything.

"Owen, *please*!"

The monster let out a roar and lashed out with his right claw. A large piece of the man's bloody scalp remained stuck to one of his talons as he did it again. The man's scream became much higher pitched.

Toby moved away from the man as Owen pounced upon him, raking his talons across the man's back. He opened his jaws wide and took the first bite, ripping off a large chunk of meat from the man's side.

"Make him stop screaming!" Toby shouted.

Owen rolled the man over and bit off his jaw.

Toby sat against a tree, shivering, and watched Owen devour the man. He wasn't sure when he actually died. He guessed that it didn't much matter.

"Had to be done," Toby whispered. "Right? You threaten my friend, you die. That's the way things work around here. Right, Owen?"

Owen ignored the question and continued eating.

Toby had some blood on his shirt. Head wounds definitely did their share of bleeding. He touched each spot.

"We probably shouldn't have done this," he noted with a slight giggle. "Not a wise idea at all. Nope. But that's you and me, Owen, a couple of kids always getting into mischief..."

3 2

Toby's hands, arms, and face were covered with lacerations, but he didn't care. It was completely worth it.

He'd placed every single bottle of beer in his refrigerator—at least twenty of them—into the kitchen sink, stacking them in a nice neat pile. Then he'd taken a claw hammer and smashed them to bits, bashing over and over until he had a sink full of glass shards.

It felt *good* when pieces flew up and cut him.

When he was done, he wasn't quite far gone enough to just reach in there and scoop up the glass with his bare hands, so he got a towel and carefully moved the pieces from the sink to a cardboard box. He'd drive it to the dump and safely dispose of it there.

He should be a spokesperson. Travel to schools: *Hey, kids, you should never drink alcohol. I did, and I woke up next to a mutilated corpse! It goes without saying that when the first thing you see in the morning is a hollow bloody eye socket, you'll realize that your life is moving in the wrong direction.*

He'd thrown up the entire contents of his stomach (including, it felt like, the lining) and crawled away from the sight of Owen leisurely chewing on the man's still-glistening intestines. When he felt that he could finally speak, he'd shouted at Owen, cursed him for what he'd done. Then he'd sobbed and begged his friend to forgive him.

Owen had growled at him when he tried to take his food away, so Toby decided to leave it alone for the time being. "I'll be back," Toby had promised. "Eat as much as you can now, because I'm burying the leftovers."

When he returned that evening, there wasn't much left on the bones. It was amazing how much Owen could eat. Toby dug a hole, now wishing that he'd saved the symbolic bottle-breaking act for after he needed to use his hands for manual labor, and hid the bones and scraps of the poor old man who just wanted to see a monster.

No, the old man who wanted to ruin everything.

The rest of 2005 was spent trying to cope with guilt while sober, and frantically trying to predict when the police would burst into his home.

Nobody even questioned him. Toby knew that it was probably because the man had no job, no relatives, and nobody would ever miss him, but he secretly liked the idea that the man might have been part of some top-secret government agency, working undercover, and that his disappearance would be discovered after the deadline arrived for him to file his report on the bizarre Owen-Creature that had befriended a human.

2006

Toby's cell phone rang while he leaned against a tree, sharing a bag of gummi worms with Owen. Wow. The phone company had promised outstanding reception, but it had never worked out here before. He glanced at the display and didn't recognize the number. Probably a telemarketer—naturally, they'd have the technology to boost the signal to try to sell him a magazine subscription out in the woods.

"Yeah?"

"Is this Toby Floren?" The voice sounded young, like a college kid.

"Who is this?"

"I'm Steve Crown. You probably have no idea who I am, but I run the website Three Window Giggle Fits."

"I don't know it."

"We've been around for about a year, and our hits are going up every single month. It's all original content. Right off the bat I want to say that we can't pay, yet, but it's great exposure and Kirk Hart who does our strip *Wheelies* just got a major syndication deal."

"Why are you calling me?"

"It's the weirdest thing you've ever heard. I supplement my income by reading slush, and I was clearing out boxes of stuff from years and years and years ago that they were going to throw away. My job was just to make sure that they didn't have some old strip by Gary Larson or something that could be valuable. So I was looking through some of it, and I found *Rusty & Pugg*, and there's this weirdness to it that I really tapped into. It's not laugh-out-loud funny, and I don't even get all of the punchlines, but it's got this odd, enchanting charm."

"You want to publish *Rusty & Pugg*?"

"Yes. Online."

"Every day?"

"It doesn't have to be every day, but some sort of regular schedule. *Fleece* is weekly, and *Crush Manhattan* is three times a week, but *Wheelies* and most of our other strips are daily, although *Wheelies* is the only one that does a Sunday strip."

"I'm in."

"May I ask how old you are?"

"Sixty-one."

"See, no offense, but you'll never get a major syndicate to pick you up. Me, I think that's awesome. I'm going to use that as a selling point."

When the conversation ended, Toby slipped the phone back into his pocket and turned to Owen. "Three Window Giggle Fits. What a shitty name."

Yes.

"But people are going to read my strip!"

Toby went out that afternoon and bought a computer. The salesperson, a girl in her early twenties, thought that it was unbearably cute that such an old man wanted to learn how to use a computer. He was pretty sure she sold him features that he didn't need, but the whole thing was gibberish and he pretty much just handed over his credit card.

The next week, he began taking classes.

2007

Kirk told him that *Rusty & Pugg* was getting seven hundred hits a day.

"Is that a lot?"

"Third highest-rated strip on the site."

2008

Toby had yet to receive a single check, but quite honestly he didn't care.

Kirk sent him links to some online discussions about the strip, and Toby didn't care much about those, either. He'd started to register for the first site, decided they wanted too much personal information, and didn't bother completing the process.

He was happy just to write and draw the strip and know that it was out there.

Owen was happy for him, too. Toby had the software to draw the strip directly onto his computer, but he stuck with paper and ink and a scanner, and mostly drew the comic while spending time with the monster.

2009

Kirk called him to let him know that he was shutting down the website, effective immediately. It wasn't a decision that came easily, but advertising had never really picked up the way he'd expected, and the site was one big time sink for him.

However, he had a friend who was looking for original content for his own website, and he'd already expressed interest in *Rusty & Pugg*.

Toby was fine with the switch. One month in, he was told that the hit count for the strip's new home was "through the roof," though the actual number meant nothing to him.

Still no check, but he didn't care.

His hands hurt, all the time, and he didn't care.

He could feel that something was wrong inside of him, but he didn't go to the doctor. He knew what it was. They'd give him chemotherapy or radiation treatment and he'd be too sick to draw. He couldn't allow that to happen. He had an audience to make happy. A faceless audience, but still an audience.

He introduced a hairy monster into the cast, and apparently it was a big hit with readers, especially when it ate a couple of bullies named Larry and Nick.

A CAR PULLED up in front of his house after dark.

Toby cursed. He was soaking his hands in warm water to ease

the pain, and didn't feel like being bothered so that some inconsiderate jerk could ask him if he believed that he would be ascending to the Kingdom of Heaven.

He looked through the peephole, and then opened the door. A twenty-two-year-old boy stood there and gave him a nervous smile.

"Hi, Dad."

33

2010. 65 years old.

"I wish you'd called first," said Toby. "When someone's reunited with their son for the first time in twelve or thirteen years, it's nice to be able to shave and clean up the house."

"I thought about it, but I don't know, I thought it would be weird. I'm not a phone person, I guess."

"You look good." Toby was telling the truth. Garrett had grown into a handsome, healthy young man. Opposite of his dad, that was for sure. He wore a nice watch and a wedding ring.

"Thanks."

"How's Hannah?"

"She's fine. Got into some trouble but worked through it."

"And your mom?"

"She's fine, too. You know she got remarried, right?"

"Haven't heard a word from her. But that would make sense. It's been a long time."

"Yeah. She's actually been married for quite a while now, but, you know, it's not important."

Toby nodded. "So why'd you decide to pay me a visit?"

"I hate the way things ended. The way we left you alone like that."

"It wasn't your fault. You were just a kid."

"I'm not a kid now, though. Marianne and me...here, let me show you a picture." Garrett handed Toby his cell phone, which had a photograph of a lovely brunette girl. "We've been married three years already—"

"Wow."

"I know."

"Was she pregnant?"

"Nope. We just 'got' each other, I guess, and didn't see any reason to keep shopping around. But we had a really long talk last weekend, and we decided to start trying to have a kid."

"Congratulations."

"Thanks. I mean, we haven't succeeded yet, as far as I know, but we want to do this. The fringe benefits are definitely nice. But a decision like this is the kind of thing that makes you evaluate your whole life, and I look back at the day I got hurt and think 'I can't leave things like that.'" He pulled up his sleeve and showed Toby his arm. "Look at that scar. That's how I met Marianne. I told her I was in a knife fight."

"You ever tell her the truth?"

"Oh, yeah, she called me on my bullshit in about three seconds. That's when I knew I wanted to marry her. I mean, I just told her that I broke through some wood, not about, you know..."

"Owen."

"Is he still alive?"

Toby grinned. "Sure is. Chatty as ever."

"Still in the same shack?"

"Yep."

"Can we..." Garrett looked as if he were going to cry. "Can we go out there and...fix the place up? I know it sounds like a stupid reason for me to make a six-hour drive, but..."

"It doesn't sound stupid at all." Toby got up off the couch. "We should go now. He'll love to see you."

"Well, we don't have to go *right* now. It's dark out."

"But we should. Don't worry about the dark—I've got a great new lantern. He'll be thrilled. There aren't any repairs to do, but I've meant to paint it for a long time."

"I wanted to talk about your comic strip first."

"Oh, you heard about that?"

"I've been following it. Marianne found it, actually."

"I still have all of the originals except for a couple that Owen ruined. I'm going to give them all to you before you leave. You can keep them or sell them or do whatever you want with them, but I'd like you to have them."

Garrett stood up. "That would be awesome. Thank you, Dad."

"Let's go! Let's go! A wonderful monster in the woods awaits our arrival!"

TOBY KNEW he was babbling like an incoherent old man, but he couldn't help himself as they made the trek through the woods, their way illuminated by a lantern Owen had gotten him for Christmas, in much the same way that Toby's favorite shoes ever were "from" Garrett when he was only two. He told Garrett all about how he'd finally gotten *Rusty & Pugg* published, and all about his miserable job that he couldn't afford to retire from, and his arthritis. He didn't talk about the other medical issues.

He also didn't talk about the man he'd murdered. Technically Owen had delivered the killing blow, but Toby had murdered him. That wasn't information with which to burden his son. He'd have to take that to his own grave.

Mostly he talked about Owen. That's where he could sense he was blathering on the most, but Garrett didn't interrupt, he barely spoke at all, apparently quite happy to let his father talk and talk and talk. That's what old people did, he supposed.

Owen wasn't there when they arrived at the shack, so Toby subjected his poor son to another half hour of talk while they added a coat of dark brown paint to the outside of the structure.

Movement to the side.

"That's him," said Toby. "Hey, Owen!"

Owen growled a greeting.

"I've got somebody who wants to see you!"

Garrett tensed up as Owen came into view. Toby wasn't sure if it was fear—which was only to be expected at first—or shock at Owen's appearance. His fur had turned almost completely grey, and small patches of it were missing all over his body. The monster looked...well, *old*.

Owen walked over to them, slowly, gazing at Garrett as if trying to remember where he'd seen him before.

"Does he recognize me?"

"Owen, do you remember Garrett? My son? Your friend?"

Owen stepped into the clearing around the shack, still obviously trying to place Garrett. He ran his talons along the side of the shack, a gesture that Toby found vaguely threatening—not something Owen had ever done before.

"It's Garrett. I know you remember Garrett."

And then Owen's face beamed with pure joy that went beyond anything Toby had ever seen from the monster. Yeah, his smile was rather grotesque with his missing teeth, but you simply could not deny the emotion behind it.

Toby was so overcome with his own happiness that he didn't immediately realize that Garrett had taken out a gun.

Owen howled with fright and put his hands over his face.

Toby grabbed for the weapon. He struck Garrett's arm just as he pulled the trigger. The gun fired.

Owen roared and clutched at his side, blood spurting between his fingers.

Garrett tried to shove Toby out of the way, but Toby didn't care if he *was* a sixty-five-year-old arthritic mess, there was no way in hell he was going to let anything happen to Owen. He threw a punch that connected solidly with Garrett's jaw, knocking him to the ground.

Think how much different your life could have been, if you'd done that to Larry forty-five years ago.

Garrett pointed the gun back at Owen and squeezed off another shot. The bullet tore across Owen's left arm.

Owen was a close target, but a target in motion.

The monster pushed Toby aside and dove at Garrett, attacking him in a flurry of teeth and claws. Toby's son screamed in agony, and Toby screamed for Owen to stop.

There was blood everywhere.

Including on Toby's chest. Owen had gouged him deep with his claws when he pushed him away.

"*Owen, stop it!*" Toby screamed.

Owen tore off a particularly meaty strip of Garrett's flesh.

"*Stop it, goddamn it!*" Bleeding and hurting and terrified, Toby moved over to the carnage and kicked Owen as hard as he could. Owen yelped, then stood up and backed away.

"*Owen, that's my son, you fucking beast!*"

Owen looked at Toby, absolutely devastated, then ran off through the trees.

It wasn't his usual direction. He was headed toward Toby's home.

Toby dropped to his knees next to his son, who was coughing up blood and clutching helplessly at his shredded chest. Toby pulled out his cell phone to call for help.

No reception out in the forest. There almost never was.

"Why did you hurt him?" Toby asked, sobbing. He knew the answer, but felt the need to say *something* instead of just silently watching Garrett die.

Gotta kill the monster before you bring a kid into the world.

Toby couldn't run for help. It wasn't worth pretending, not even to say that he'd done everything he possibly could. He couldn't even say anything reassuring, tell his son that everything would be fine, that he'd called 911 and a helicopter had been dispatched.

When your body was torn up like that, you weren't going to survive.

"What should I tell Marianne?" Toby asked.

Garrett opened his mouth and blood ran down the sides of his face. He stared at the sky and died.

Toby stood up, picked up the gun, staggered away from his son's body, and walked away from the shack, going after Owen.

THE GASHES on his chest from Owen's talons hurt like crazy, which Toby took as a good sign. When the pain started to seep from his body it was time to get worried.

This would be his last time walking through these woods. He wished his final journey could've been a peaceful stroll, like hundreds of others had been, and not what he was doing now, stumbling through the night, barely able to keep his flashlight steady, shirt covered with blood.

But this was typical of life, wasn't it? You tended to quit doing things after the bad times, and not the good times.

Dear God, what kind of cynical bullshit was that? Regardless of how this turned out, Toby was going to make one more trek out to Owen's home, even if he did it in a goddamn wheelchair, just to prove himself wrong.

The pain was starting to fade a bit.

HE EMERGED FROM THE WOODS, half expecting to see Owen in his backyard, cowering next to the back of the house, scared and wanting his friend to tell him that everything was going to be all right.

The backyard was empty.

What would Owen do? Was he just running around the forest? Was he lying somewhere, bleeding to death? He wouldn't have left the woods, would he? He would have stayed where he felt the safest.

Toby went inside. He couldn't hide this. Not the death of his own son.

He turned on the television as he peeled off his shirt to examine his wounds, praying not to see a newscaster telling the local viewing audience about reports of a wild animal on the loose, much like one that had gone on a rampage thirty-five years ago.

"...at least two confirmed dead, in a story that's almost too bizarre to believe..."

34

Somebody had captured video images of Owen with their digital camera. The footage of the mauling was online before the police even arrived at the scene.

It was a middle-aged couple, just walking down the sidewalk. Probably in their own neighborhood, though it was too early to say, since the bodies hadn't yet been identified. It was almost comical the way the man spun around, sort of like a dancer doing a pirouette when Owen's claw got him in the face.

Toby drove toward where the murders had occurred—not too far from where he lived, maybe four miles. Quite a bit further than he would've expected Owen to be, at least after being shot twice. Rage and fear must have kept him moving quickly.

He had no idea how to go about accomplishing his task, but Toby knew that he had to kill Owen. He couldn't let him hurt —massacre—anybody else. Decades of friendship or not, he had to destroy the monster.

How was he supposed to find him, though? Keep his car window rolled down and listen for screams?

"Nothing has been confirmed by authorities yet," said the voice on

the radio, "*but there may be a third victim tonight, apparently a sixteen year-old girl...*"

Christ...

Blue and red flashing lights up ahead. Toby had considered calling the police and telling them what he knew, but what useful information could he convey? That the creature's name was Owen? That it had killed his son?

Why hadn't he shot him all those years ago. Blown him away with the shotgun when he had the chance.

Stop it. This wasn't the time to wallow in regret.

"*...strongly recommend that you remain indoors until this situation has been resolved...*"

"Excellent advice," Toby told the radio.

He turned right, away from the parked police cars, then slowed down as he drove down the suburb street. "Owen!" he shouted out the window. "Come out, Owen! It's Toby!" If the police stopped him and asked, he'd say he was calling for his grandson.

"Owen!"

He drove slowly around the entire four-block neighborhood, constantly shouting Owen's name, but there was no sign of his friend. It looked like the police were starting to cordon off the area, and a young police officer waved him through as he drove past.

What now?

Where would Owen go?

What a stupid question. There was no logical place a wild animal would go during a killing spree. He just had to follow the trail of bodies until he got lucky, or until the police took Owen down first.

"Owen!"

He turned into the next subdivision. It was a much wealthier neighborhood than the first, one that Toby occasionally liked to drive through at Christmas time because of their rather spectacular display of lights.

He continued to shout Owen's name.

"What's wrong?" asked a man walking along the sidewalk. "You lose a dog?"

"No. And you need to get inside."

"Why? What's going on?"

"Just get inside. It's not safe." Toby turned the corner. Was this a complete waste of time? Maybe he *would* be better off just turning himself in to the police and telling them everything?

"Owen!"

And then Owen was there.

He stood between two homes, his whole body slick with blood. Toby slammed on the brakes, put the car into park, and got out, taking the gun with him as he left the running vehicle in the street.

"God, Owen, what have you done?" asked Toby, stepping onto the lawn. "Why do things always get so screwed up with us?"

Owen signed: *Scared.*

"Me too."

Toby wanted to apologize, to beg for forgiveness from his friend before he did what needed to be done, but instead he silently raised the gun and pointed it at Owen.

Owen turned and ran.

Toby fired.

Missed. He was pretty sure he'd done it on purpose, and cursed himself as he hurried between the houses after Owen. He felt like he might die of a heart attack if he didn't bleed to death first, but forced himself to move as quickly as his pain-wracked body could handle.

Another row of homes shared the backyard space with the homes Toby was between now. As he reached the backyard, he saw a woman standing in an open doorway on her back porch, most likely peering outside to see where the gunshot had come from.

Didn't she know that there was a wild animal on the loose? Didn't she know that when you heard bullets fired you stayed the hell inside your home?

Toby's heart took another big step toward a coronary as Owen got her, pouncing like a lion. The two of them disappeared inside the house.

Toby screamed. He could feel his body trying to shut down around him. Couldn't Owen see that there was no happy ending to this madness?

He walked over to the house and staggered through the doorway. The woman lay flat on her back, covered with blood, insides exposed as her body twitched. Owen hadn't even tried to eat this one. He was just killing.

Yet another death on Toby's conscience. How many was that, now? It was hard to even keep count.

A trail of blood led through the living room into the kitchen, but the scream of terror would have alerted Toby to where Owen was even without the visual cue. He stepped over the woman's body and ran forward.

He got into the kitchen just as Owen bit the throat out of a teenaged boy. The boy was in front of Owen, blocking his shot. Toby knew it was absurd—the boy was dying if not already dead—but he couldn't risk hitting him.

"Owen, *please!*" Toby shouted.

The boy's body dropped to the tile floor.

Owen pounced at Toby.

He hadn't expected this, and he wasn't able to fire off a shot before Owen knocked him to the floor, jaws open wide. The gun popped out of his hand and slid along the wet tile, out of reach.

Owen gnashed his teeth. A large blob of bloody foam fell onto Toby's face. The monster raised his claw, then hesitated.

Toby tried to say the kind of thing you were supposed to say in this situation, something like "Owen, it's me, Toby, your best friend!" but he was paralyzed with fear.

Would he be Owen's final victim, or just one more corpse in the series of deaths in what the press might dub the Night of the Beast?

Owen looked down at him, lowered his claw, then leapt up and ran from the kitchen, back into the living room.

Toby remained motionless for a few seconds, trying to catch his breath. Then he retrieved the gun and started to race out of the kitchen, but his foot shot out from underneath him as he slipped on some blood. He landed on his side, hard, knocking the wind out of him.

He lay there in a daze.

He wondered if Sarah would curse him to his face, or to his tombstone?

Would he have to speak to Marianne?

Hannah?

Maybe he was better off dead.

No. That was cowardly. Pathetic. The thoughts of a loser. He couldn't leave this unfinished.

He got up, shook off the dizzy spell, and ran out of the house. There was no sign of Owen outside.

He walked around the entire shared yard, calling out for Owen and listening for sounds of distress.

Nothing.

Finally he got back in his car and resumed the search in his vehicle. Owen could be hiding, licking his wounds, or he could still be on the move, seeking more prey. Toby had to assume the latter.

The next news report, two minutes later, was about the deaths Toby had just witnessed. There were also reports of a gun-wielding man in his seventies running around the area, so citizens should be concerned about an armed maniac as well as a wild animal.

Seventies. Jesus.

For fifteen minutes, there were no new deaths—at least no reported ones. Toby passed countless police cars as he drove, but none of them stopped him. Obviously, no witnesses had described the maniac's car.

Then a report of a possible sighting in a park. Toby had been there a few times with Garrett and Hannah, a nice place with a few shops and restaurants around it. He could just imagine Owen running loose amidst dozens of shoppers and diners.

Where was he? Where would he go?

Then, suddenly, Toby thought he knew the answer.

THE ICE CREAM shop wasn't particularly good, although Garrett had always wanted to stop there after a hard day playing on the slides and swing sets. But it was shaped like a giant ice cream cone, complete with a swirl on the top.

Toby parked next to it, got out of the car, and waited, calling Owen's name every few moments.

Lots of sirens in the background.

He didn't even see where Owen came from. He just looked over and Owen was there, staring longingly at the ice cream cone.

Owen signed: *Ice cream.*

"Yeah, ice cream. I'd buy you some if they were open."

Bad.

"Very bad. Both of us. Neither one of us deserves ice cream tonight, buddy."

Toby pointed the gun at him. Owen didn't move.

Maybe it didn't have to be this way. He could coax Owen into his car, and just drive away. Get as far out of this town as they possibly could. Nobody would be watching for an old man with a monster in his car, right?

They could start over. It was a huge forest. And there were other forests.

No.

It was time to end this. He couldn't undo his mistakes, but he could stop more innocent people from dying.

And the sirens were too close. In fact, Toby could already see the flashing lights.

He'd be seen as a hero, briefly. A few minutes of being the old guy who killed the monster, before the truth came out, and he became the scary old man with the carnivorous pet.

That's how the story would always be told: Owen was his pet. Nobody would ever believe that Owen was his best friend.

Toby wasn't sure how many bullets he had left. He walked closer. He couldn't miss this time, and he felt that he should look his friend in the eye when he pulled the trigger.

Voices behind him. Commotion.

Owen didn't run as Toby walked right up to him, close enough to give him a hug.

What did you say to a lifetime friend?

He settled for "I'm sorry, Owen," and then shot him.

Chaos behind him. A voice shouting for him to get away from the creature.

Toby glanced back. Three cops, all pointing their guns in his direction. Owen hadn't fallen yet.

He wanted to tell them to go away, that it was already done, that the monster was dying, but his body was wracked with sobs and he couldn't speak.

Owen didn't have an expression of pain, or betrayal, or sadness. He looked...concerned.

He thinks they're going to shoot me!

As blood gushed from his chest, Owen pushed past Toby, trying to get in front of him.

The police fired. Two more bullets slammed into Owen's chest.

Toby found his voice and screamed for them to stop. That's not how his friend was supposed to die. Not shot by a bunch of strangers.

He pushed himself back between his monster friend and the panicked cops, and felt surprisingly little pain as the bullets hit.

35

GLIMPSES

Toby lay on the ground, bleeding and dying.
It could have been so much different...

"I'll take you right to where I saw him!" Toby told Dad, before he could begin the spanking. "I'll prove it!"

Though Dad was skeptical, Toby led him right to the place where he'd seen the monster. Though the monster wasn't there anymore, there were clear tracks in the dirt. Dad couldn't deny that something had been out here, just like Toby said.

"Don't tell anybody about this until we have solid proof," Dad said, "but I'm sorry I doubted you."

Years of searching had paid off. "Can we name it Owen?" Toby asked.

"We can name it anything you want," Dad said. "You're the one who found it."

"Don't go near Toby Floren," Larry told the other kids at school. "I hear he's got a monster friend who lives out in the woods, and if you mess with him, the monster will be *furious*."

Finally, the time was right. You didn't want to rush these things. Mom and Dad watched proudly as Toby introduced Owen to the world.

"*Toby*," Owen said to an astonished and delighted crowd, as hundreds of camera flashes went off.

Toby and Owen, man and monster, best of friends and one of the most popular television and movie acts in the world. How could the fictional likes of Frankenstein, Dracula, and even aliens from Mars compete with a real-life monster?

"I've never met a real celebrity," said Sarah.

"Are you talking about me or him?" asked Toby, jokingly pointing to Owen.

JUST WHEN YOU thought they were old news, Toby and Owen shocked the world yet again. Toby and Sarah announced the birth of their son Garrett, while Owen and Esmerelda announced the birth of their own son, Scruffer.

"WELL, YOU SEE," Toby told the talk show host, "I've always felt that a boy should remain close to his mother and father."

"Does it count as living with your parents if it's in a fifty-room mansion?" the host asked. The audience laughed.

"YES, both Owen and I will be retiring. We're still young, but it's time to enjoy life. Garrett, Hannah, and Scruffer will continue performing, but expect lots of exciting changes to their act for the 21st century."

"SO, Owen, aren't you glad I rescued you from that miserable cave?"

Yes.

"Who would've ever thought this could happen to a couple of ugly guys like us?"

Not me.

"Not me, either. Not in a million years."

Time goes so fast.

"Nah. We've got all the time in the world."

GOD, there was a lot of blood.

The cops stood over him, looking horrified at what they'd done. Toby wondered if they'd try to lie about it, say that he'd rushed at them with his gun. *Did you see that psychopath? He came right at us! You saw it, didn't you? We all saw it.*

It didn't matter.

Owen lay next to him, making no sound. It was probably a matter of seconds as to who would die first.

We should race, Toby thought. *Make a game out of it.*

Or maybe not. Maybe there were more games to come.

Toby could barely feel anything. Before he completely lost sensation in his arm, he twisted his body, flopping his arm over and putting his hand into Owen's claw.

Owen's claw tightened around his fingers. Toby closed his eyes and they began their next adventure together.

— The End —

ACKNOWLEDGMENTS

First of all, monster-sized thanks to Michael McBride, who was subjected to this thing chapter-by-chapter as it was written. Thanks are also due to my volunteer test-readers Tod Clark, Adrienne Jones, Rhonda Wilson, Joe Konrath, Jonathan Piccinini, and Elizabeth White for their vicious typo-hunting and feedback. And I need to fling additional thanks in the direction of Don D'Auria, Stephanie Rostan, Monika Verma, Norm Rubenstein, Joe Morey, Greg Lamberson, and my wife Lynne.

There are about forty-eight tons' worth of other people who deserve to be thanked (I weighed them) for countless reasons, but then I'd forget somebody, and then that person would scream "Why was _____ thanked and not me?" and then they'd start a smear campaign that would create a lot of hurt feelings and eventually result in the tragedy of six or seven lost lives. So I'm taking the "complete wimp" route and ending these acknowledgments here. Can't be too safe.

BOOKS BY JEFF STRAND

Wolf Hunt 3. George, Lou, Ally, and Eugene are back in another werewolf-laden adventure.

Clowns Vs. Spiders. Choose your side!

My Pretties. A serial kidnapper may have met his match in the two young ladies who walk the city streets at night, using themselves as bait...

Five Novellas. A compilation of *Stalking You Now, An Apocalypse of Our Own, Faint of Heart, Kutter,* and *Facial.*

Ferocious. The creatures of the forest are dead...and hungry!

Bring Her Back. A tale of revenge and madness.

Sick House. A home invasion from beyond the grave.

Bang Up. A filthy comedic thriller. "You want to pay me to sleep with your wife?" is just the start of the story.

Cold Dead Hands. Ten people are trapped in a freezer during a terrorist attack on a grocery store.

How You Ruined My Life (Young Adult). Sixteen-year-old Rod has a pretty cool life until his cousin Blake moves in and slowly destroys everything he holds dear.

Everything Has Teeth. A third collection of short tales of horror and macabre comedy.

An Apocalypse of Our Own. Can the Friend Zone survive the end of the world?

Stranger Things Have Happened (Young Adult). Teenager Marcus Millian III is determined to be one of the greatest magicians who ever lived. Can he make a live shark disappear from a tank?

Cyclops Road. When newly widowed Evan Portin gives a woman named Harriett a ride out of town, she says she's on a cross-country journey to slay a Cyclops. Is she crazy, or...?

Blister. While on vacation, cartoonist Jason Tray meets the town legend, a hideously disfigured woman who lives in a shed.

The Greatest Zombie Movie Ever (Young Adult). Three best friends with more passion than talent try to make the ultimate zombie epic.

Kumquat. A road trip comedy about TV, hot dogs, death, and obscure fruit.

I Have a Bad Feeling About This (Young Adult). Geeky, non-athletic Henry Lambert is sent to survival camp, which is bad enough *before* the trio of murderous thugs show up.

Pressure. What if your best friend was a killer...and he wanted you to be just like him? Bram Stoker Award nominee for Best Novel.

Dweller. The lifetime story of a boy and his monster. Bram Stoker Award nominee for Best Novel.

A Bad Day For Voodoo. A young adult horror/comedy about why sticking pins in a voodoo doll of your history teacher isn't always the best idea. Bram Stoker Award nominee for Best Young Adult Novel.

Dead Clown Barbecue. A collection of demented stories about severed noses, ventriloquist dummies, giant-sized vampires, sibling stabbings, and lots of other messed-up stuff.

Dead Clown Barbecue Expansion Pack. A few more stories for those who couldn't get enough.

Wolf Hunt. Two thugs for hire. One beautiful woman. And one vicious frickin' werewolf.

Wolf Hunt 2. New wolf. Same George and Lou.

The Sinister Mr. Corpse. The feel-good zombie novel of the year.

Benjamin's Parasite. A rather disgusting action/horror/comedy about why getting infected with a ghastly parasite is unpleasant.

Fangboy. A dark and demented fairy tale for adults.

Facial. Greg has just killed the man he hired to kill one of his wife's many lovers. Greg's brother desperately needs a dead body. It's kind of related to the lion corpse that he found in his basement. This is the normal part of the story.

Kutter. A serial killer finds a Boston terrier, and it might just make him into a better person.

Faint of Heart. To get her kidnapped husband back, Melody has to relive her husband's nightmarish weekend, step-by-step...and survive.

Mandibles. Giant killer ants wreaking havoc in the big city!

Stalking You Now. A twisty-turny thriller soon to be the feature film *Mindy Has To Die.*

Graverobbers Wanted (No Experience Necessary). First in the Andrew Mayhem series.

Single White Psychopath Seeks Same. Second in the Andrew Mayhem series.

Casket For Sale (Only Used Once). Third in the Andrew Mayhem series.

Lost Homicidal Maniac (Answers to "Shirley"). Fourth in the Andrew Mayhem series.

Suckers (with JA Konrath). Andrew Mayhem meets Harry McGlade. Which one will prove to be more incompetent?

Gleefully Macabre Tales. A collection of thirty-two demented tales. Bram Stoker Award nominee for Best Collection.

Elrod McBugle on the Loose. A comedy for kids (and adults who were warped as kids).

The Haunted Forest Tour (with Jim Moore). The greatest theme park attraction in the world! Take a completely safe ride through an actual haunted forest! Just hope that your tram doesn't break down, because this forest is PACKED with monsters...

Draculas (with JA Konrath, Blake Crouch, and F. Paul Wilson). An outbreak of feral vampires in a secluded hospital. This one isn't much like *Twilight.*

For information on all of these books, visit Jeff Strand's more-or-less official website at JeffStrand.com

Subscribe to Jeff Strand's free monthly newsletter (which includes a brand-new original short story in every issue) at http://eepurl.com/bpv5br

And remember:

Readers who leave reviews deserve great big hugs!

Printed in Great Britain
by Amazon

38958367R00189